HILL FOXES

The Hunt

B.J. Mayo

This is a work of fiction. The events and characters described herein are imaginary and are not intended to refer to specific places or living persons. The opinions expressed in this manuscript are solely the opinions of the author and do not represent the opinions or thoughts of the publisher. The author has represented and warranted full ownership and/or legal right to publish all the materials in this book.

Hill Foxes
The Hunt
All Rights Reserved.
Copyright © 2012 B.J. Mayo
v3.0

This book may not be reproduced, transmitted, or stored in whole or in part by any means, including graphic, electronic, or mechanical without the express written consent of the publisher except in the case of brief quotations embodied in critical articles and reviews.

Outskirts Press, Inc.
http://www.outskirtspress.com

ISBN: 978-1-4327-8891-9

Outskirts Press and the "OP" logo are trademarks belonging to Outskirts Press, Inc.

PRINTED IN THE UNITED STATES OF AMERICA

Also by B. J. Mayo
All Prayed Up

*This is for my son
Garry Walker Mayo*

ACKNOWLEDGEMENTS

Sharon Norman Lindsay has given me so much encouragement and support, thanks Sharon.

Thanks also to Reggie W. for being a real cheerleader—your support has been amazing!

PROLOGUE

THE HILL FOX

Generally shy but always curious, a fox on the hunt has a keen sense of hearing and a remarkable sense of smell.

The grey and the red fox indigenous to North America, are not only found in the density of our forests, but have been found in the city streets of urban America.

Sometime during the late 60's to early 70's, men began using the *slang* term—*Fox*, for a beautiful attractive woman.

The six close girlfriends in this story were all considered in slang term—*Bona-fide Foxes*.

They were young career women in their early to mid-thirty's and were known as **Hill Foxes**; they lived and worked in proximity to Capitol Hill in their hometown, Washington, D.C.

Go with them on their journey of thrilling, thought-provoking, startling dilemmas, and watch them tactfully maneuver—much like the Carnivore species of fox, the passion of the hunt, the thrill of the chase, and the pure joy of the capture.

INTRODUCTION OF THE HILL FOXES

JILL DRAKE

Jill's Anthem...
> *"Hit and run just for fun,*
> *Girl you played your game so well,*
> *You really made it hard to tell,*
> *That all you were was a one night stand*
> *Hit and run just for fun…….."*
>
> *The Bar-Kays*

Jill nervously closed her eyes and said a quiet prayer as the plane started its descent over the Potomac River to Washington's National Airport runway. D.C.'s National airport was one of the most frightening landings she personally experienced—bump the fact she was aware that pilots had to have a special license to land there. As quiet as it was kept it terrified her, especially after that Flight 90 accident on the 14th Street Bridge.

Jill was a flight attendant, and had worked for Eastern Airlines since she finished the training program after high school. Jill was 5'9, with a flawless Mocha Chocolate complexion, long thick naturally curly hair, and a knock-out body. Jill Drake was a *Fox*!

She had grown up in a large apartment complex called Wheeler Gardens in Southeast D.C. Noel Ross and Brea Jones lived there too. They were together from kindergarten through high school. Wendy Haines had been part of their little circle until her parents moved out of Wheeler Gardens to Northwest D.C., but they kept in touch over the years.

Jill was single but had been dating Julius Collins since meeting him on a flight from Atlanta to D.C., they exchanged phone numbers. After the first date, their relationship developed almost immediately. Jill was sure she'd finally met her soul mate, the one she'd give her heart to.

Since Jill flew in and out of D.C. most of the week, her time with Julius was limited. She juggled her schedule to spend as much quality time with him as possible.

She was scheduled for a late flight and overnight layover in West Palm Beach, she spent all day at his house and said her goodbyes to Julius; he had taken her to the airport. As soon as she checked in, they told her she'd been rescheduled for that flight later in the week, and that they had tried to reach her. *"Damn"*, she said, under her breath, *"let me try to catch Julius before he gets too far."* Jill beeped him and couldn't get a response. After several attempts, she took the Metro train home and tried to get him when she got in, again with no luck. Jill was excited to tell him the good news. She had a couple of extra days. She jumped in her Saab and drove to his place, knocked a few times but he didn't answer the door. *That was strange she thought.*

The night was quiet, as Jill began walking away from the porch, she noticed from Julius' front bedroom window, the soft flicker of candlelight against the blinds and the sounds of jazz playing. *What?*

NOEL ROSS

Noel's Anthem…
    "I'm gonn'a make you my wife,
    'Cause you're my everything,
    All my hopes and dreams come true,
    I'm gonn'a buy you some rings……."
                                The Whispers

All she needed to do was stroll through the courtyard of Wheeler Gardens back in the day, and everything stopped! All basketball, kickball or touch football games stopped! Noel was 5'4, with caramel-colored skin, shoulder length hair, big brown eyes, and when she walked you could just hear the Commodores singing "Brick House"—*In stereo*! Noel Ross was a *Fox*! She liked hanging out with her girls Brea, Jill and Wendy, that is before Wendy moved away.

After graduating from high school, Noel enrolled at The University of DC into a two year Associate Degree program, for court reporting. She graduated and became a CCR-Professional Certified and Licensed Court Reporter, took the Civil Service exam, and landed a job as a Court Reporter on Capitol Hill at the District Court.

Noel was engaged to be married to a lawyer, Attorney Marcus Holbrook. Noel and Marcus met in the courthouse cafeteria one day during a snow storm too nasty for anybody to go out in. She was sitting at a table that had a vacant seat which was almost impossible to find that day. He asked if he could sit there. That would be the beginning of the whirlwind love relationship between Noel Ross and Marcus Holbrook.

Marcus was a serious, serious man determined to reach the goals he had set for himself. First, to become a partner in his law firm, and second, to become a Judge. Most of his time was spent quietly campaigning and politicking in an attempt to accomplish this. Noel's only complaint—he was always busy!

Noel spent most of their "*relationship*" alone or with the *Foxes*, while he met with this one, participated with that one, and networked with everyone. Marcus was as they say, "crazy about him some Noel". She was excited and could hardly wait for him to keep his promise—to make her his wife…..

BREA SHAREE JONES

Brea's Anthem…
*   "Oh………..I, Oh…..……I Miss you, miss you,*
miss you, miss you, miss you…..»
*   …….Harold Melvin and the Blue Notes*

Brea Sharee Jones, a professional model, was known nationally and internationally in the world of high fashion as *Brea Sharee*. She was unmistakably, a Bona fide *Fox*!

She grew up in Wheeler Gardens with Jill, Noel, and Wendy. Brea survived a rough childhood in Wheeler, but through it all, she emerged victorious despite the adversities she'd endured. She earned her celebrity modeling for the famous Adams-Thorne Agency based in Chicago.

Not only was Brea beautiful, she possessed one of the most magnificent voices you'd ever want to hear. Midway Brea's modeling career, she pursued her lifelong dream and signed a recording contract with the famous Natural Element label. As luck would have it, her first two albums topped the charts and she received a gold record for her title cut. After the release of her second album however, she broke her contract with Natural Element Recording Studios, and the romantic involvement with its CEO and owner, Melik Iverson. He broke her heart. She packed up her belongings, packed up her dignity, and moved back home to Washington.

She plans to return to her recording career at some point but right now, she'll only make local appearances until she's healed... her public anxiously waits.

LAUREN LINDSAY

Lauren's Anthem......
> *"I'm getting' tired of your shit, You don't ever give me nothin',*
> *See every time you come around you gott'a bring Jim, James, Paul and Tyrone,*
> *See why can't we be by ourselves sometimes,*
> *See I been having this on my mind for a long time,*
> *I just want it to be you and me, like it used to be...."*
>
> *........... Eyrkah Badu*

Lauren, a tall beautiful woman, was a *Fox*! She had slanted hazel eyes, long gorgeous legs, and natural premature mixed grey locs that hung almost to her waist.

Lauren met Wendy, Noel, Jill, and Jade, through Brea. Lauren was a fashion photographer. She had often worked on photo shoots and in shows Brea had modeled in. She had done a portfolio for Brea early in Brea's career when she modeled for "Woodies"—Woodward & Lothrop. They had remained good friends. Lauren was graciously welcomed into the circle of Hill Foxes.

Lauren was single now, but had once been married to who she proclaims was the Spawn of Satin!

Lauren liked to party when she could get away from her agency Banks & Shane, and from her freelance work for The Washington Post's Style section.

Lauren had done well, and was on the "look-out" for a decent man, an honest caring man, if one actually existed.

WENDY HAINES

Wendy's Anthem……..
"I want A …………………..Sunday
Kind of Love,
A love that last past Saturday night,
I'd like to know it's more than love at first sight,
I want a Sunday Kind of Love…..
…..Etta James

Wendy stood six feet tall, was simply breathtaking, and often mistaken for a runway model. Her golden complexion was flawless, and her "boy-bob" haircut accentuated her keen features and high cheek bones. Wendy was without question, a *Fox*!

Wendy had lived with her family in Wheeler Gardens in Southeast, until her tenth grade in high school. Her parents moved away from Wheeler to a new home in Northwest D.C. She sadly left her childhood friends Jill, Noel, and Brea, behind.

After Wendy graduated high school with honors, she continued her education, with the help of a scholarship, at Georgetown University. After graduating from Georgetown, she was accepted to the Georgetown School of Law. Wendy worked as an attorney in the Law Offices of Whitted & Whitted before she opened her own law practice on Bladensburg Road.

She dreamed of helping people in the community who otherwise, couldn't afford good legal counsel. Eighty-two percent of her cases were Pro-Bono cases but God had blessed her financially, she could afford to do that!

JADE ALISHA ZELLMER—"JAZZ"

Jade's Anthem……..
"My love, I'll never find the words my love,
To tell you how I feel my love,
Mere words—could not—explain,
God Bless you,
You Make Me Feel Brand New……………"
………………….. The Stylistics

Jade was a *Fox*! She was petite, with a light complexion, sandy hair and depending on what she wore, had eyes that seemed to change between green and blue. She had often been mistaken to her chagrin, for Vanessa Williams and she hated that sh**!

Jade, or "Jazz" to some of her friends, attended school with Wendy Haines after Wendy moved to Northwest. Jade was an out-of-boundary student and they became best friends until they graduated. Her introduction into the circle of "*Hill Foxes*" had been through Wendy.

Jade was a reporter for local Fox 5 Television's Sports Department. She was single, but dated when she could find the time. The nature of her career allowed her to meet the most interesting men, but she wasn't serious about anyone in particular. She had never been able to find that right someone, the kind of someone like her first and only love, Keith Lassiter. Jade went to college in North Carolina. Keith attended the university in Virginia. They eventually lost touch as their lives began to go in different directions. He was drafted into the NFL, and married a rich co-ed from his university. He played pro-ball, lived in upper state New York, so that was the end of them, or so she thought!

ONE

THE SWEET SMELL of honey suckles danced on the summer breeze as Jade slowly glided on the porch swing. Only the hypnotic hum of crickets invaded the quietness. Jade had learned to love that place, it was so peaceful and it held so many memories. She'd spent every summer there at Westbury Farm with her Aunt Judith and Uncle Ron growing up, and she had hated every moment of it back then. Her mother would pack her up, shove her into the car, and drive her down to that Virginia farmland just to get her out of the city for the summer. All she wanted to do was stay home in D.C. with her girlfriends.

Judith Westbury's Black Lab "Buddy", stood at the edge of the porch and looked toward the road, he sensed someone coming. People were beginning to arrive from Aunt Judith's interment. It was customary in the country to go to the house after a funeral, for the big feast. Jade had waited at the farmhouse, she couldn't bring herself to go to the burial, just couldn't.

Neighboring farm women were arriving with food enough to feed the US Navy, and a few good Marines on the side, they set up tables buffet style. There were hams, cakes, pies, greens, string beans, biscuits, potato salad, turkey, chicken, *plus* there was a whole pig being roasted out back.

Her first love, Keith Lassiter, walked up behind her while she was being seriously warned by a neighbor named Flo. The heavy-set woman was warning Jade not to eat anybody's potato salad but hers! She pointed out *her* blue bowl on the table, and didn't want Jade to possibly eat someone else's by mistake and die.

"Why don't you sit down and let me make you a plate Jazz," Keith whispered, softly, "I know you're tired."

"Thanks, but I'm not very hungry. Go ahead and fix yourself something."

"Seriously, let me fix your plate, you haven't eaten much since you've been here."

"Alright Keith, I'll fix a plate if you eat with me. Mama and Daddy have already eaten, and I could use your company." Jade whispered, "Rev. Brooks has been on my tail-literally, all day. Do you know he was standing behind me looking at my butt and actually shouted "Hallelu-yer!" What's wrong with that man of the cloth?" Keith started laughing so loud people turned around to look.

"I wouldn't put it pass Rev. Brooks, he's always been a lady chaser. Around here, he's the man-Dapper Dan! Don't pay him any attention, and to make you feel better, I'll watch your butt for you." Keith said, laughing, and looked behind Jade. "Come on, let's eat."

Jade watched Keith admiring how handsome he was. He had grown to be a magnificent man, he had always been fine when they were younger, but now, he was fine *and* sexy. His sculptured body unmistakably confirmed daily workouts, and he still had that drop-dead smile. He was six-three, about 210 pounds, and his voice was deep and sexy like Barry White's. When Keith finally sat down at the table to eat, he took off the jacket of his Armani suit. His carved arms were screaming for release from the Versace shirt. He wore A.Testoni shoes and yes Lord, *Black* socks. Amen to the former country farm boy!

Jade fixed a garden salad, a few pieces of cheese, crackers, and poured a cup of punch. She had just noticed that Keith had two plates.

"Okay, Keith, you still eat like that?" She teased him.

"I don't eat rabbit food like some people, but the church sis'tah's get insulted if you don't eat their food. They insist you taste theirs, then you end up with two or three plates, and I don't want to be rude."

"Keith, I've been thinking," she said, changing the subject. "I have some serious decisions to make in a hurry about this house and property. I have to get back to D.C. as soon as I can, there's no way I can get everything in order before I leave. I'm not sure what to do." She whispered.

"Jazz, you need to concentrate on just getting through today. There's too much going on right now for you to focus. After everyone has gone tomorrow, sit down and come up with a plan and of course, I'll help you as best I can. Since school is out right now, I have some free time."

"You're right," Jade said, agreeing with him.

The past few days had almost been a blur. The family was thankful Aunt Judith had the foresight to leave written instructions in case of her death, and she had simply slept away. She had gone on to join her beloved Ron, who preceded her two years earlier. Her little church had been packed with neighbors, faculty from her school, and lots of former students. Some had flown in from far-away places. The Right Reverend R.L. Brooks hummed and shouted and prayed all over the little church, amen. Indeed, Judith

HILL FOXES

Westbury had been loved. Keith was right there taking care of everything and everybody. He was a Godsend, the son Aunt Judith never had. He had taken care of her every need after his return to Brathwell County.

Jade's mother was Judith's only sibling, and she was taking it hard. Her adoring big sister "Jew" was gone.

After the crowd finally left that night, Jade got to bed but found she was too tired to fall asleep. She lay there in the dark listening to the songs of the tree crickets. She noticed that Aunt Judith hadn't changed much in the little room that had always been hers when she visited. Jade's teddy bears and stuffed animals were still on their shelves, along with her pink record player. She needed to think, but she also needed rest. Aunt Judith left Westbury Farm, according to the will, to her along with acres of land throughout the county, money, and several expensive pieces of art that needed to be appraised. *Oh hell, I can't do all of this before I leave, she thought.*

Jade awoke the next morning to the smell of bacon, eggs and coffee. She felt like she had a major hangover. The clock on the nightstand said Ten-fifteen! She jumped up and grabbed her robe, running downstairs. Her mother was in the kitchen fixing breakfast, and her daddy was on the porch swing reading the newspaper with Buddy sleeping under his feet.

"Good morning baby girl, glad you decided to get up, I was getting worried." Her daddy said, peeping over his bifocals.

"Morning Daddy, I didn't know it was so late, why didn't somebody wake me? We've got a lot to do today." She was stretching and yawning.

"Not too much you can do on a Sunday around here," he said. "Why don't we just take today to rest? We can start taking care of business tomorrow."

"That's right, it's Sunday", she said, recalling what day it was. "Have you had your coffee yet Daddy?"

"I was about to get some, but your mother asked me to walk damn near to Baltimore to get the Sunday paper. When I got back, I was too tired to go to the kitchen and get it," he said, laughing.

"Oh Daddy, it was only down to the road. I'll get coffee for you."

Jade went into the kitchen to get her father's coffee. "Daddy's out there complaining about having to walk to the road for the paper Mama. He needs his coffee!" She was laughing. "Did I hear the phone?"

"Yes, you did baby, it was Keith. He said not to wake you and left his number for you to call. He offered to take us all to breakfast but I told him I had already started cooking, I invited him to join us. He should be here in any minute."

"MA!" When were you going to tell me, after he got here and saw me standing here in my pajamas?"

"What's wrong with your pajamas baby?" Her mother looked at what Jade had on expecting to see tattered or torn pajamas.

"Ma!" Jade started running upstairs to start the shower. *Oh hell, I forgot about poor Daddy's coffee.*

"Ma, take Daddy a cup of coffee outside please, I forgot," she yelled downstairs.

Jade stepped into the warm shower and it felt good. Her nerves were frazzled, and she was still tired. She closed her eyes while the stream of water cascaded around her shoulders. She was secretly excited at the thought of seeing Keith again. He had met them at the house when they arrived from D.C. after receiving news about Aunt Judith. When he opened the door for them, Jade's heart almost stopped beating. Seeing him for the first time in almost sixteen years was like time had stood still. Jade's thoughts suddenly turned toward Mitchell. She was positive if it hadn't been for training camp, Mitchell would have been there to support her the last few days. He may have had a problem getting away from camp. Aunt Judith wasn't his relative and if he came, he might have had to pay a fine. Carlisle was a good six or seven hours away, which would have required his staying overnight. He couldn't afford to do that.

Mitchell Dawson had been traded to the Washington Buckskins by the Broncos. He had fallen in love with Washington. He loved the power of that city. Jade smiled, she thought about how they first met.

She had been assigned to interview new players to the Buckskins team that year, and she found out—the hard way—that a woman in the locker room got no mercy. She had just finished her assigned interview with "Stormin' Norman" Harris, and looked up to see Mitchell Dawson standing in front of her in nothing but a towel.

"Hey Reds, you wann'a interview me too?" He asked her, grinning.

"Sure," she said, not letting his attempt to intimidate her work. The players could have cared less that she was in the locker room. It almost smacked of disrespect, and like it or not, that was her assignment. Jade's interview with Mitchell—*Mitch,* went well. "Since I was nice enough to give you this interview, why don't you be nice and give up your digits baby?" Mitch said, grinning.

"First of all, I'm not allowed to do that. Second, I was here to interview "Stormin' Norman" and if I remember correctly, *you asked me* if I'd interview you."

"Well, at least you can give me your name Reds," he asked, licking his lips and looking her up and down.

"My name is Jade, not Reds, but thanks for the interview anyway." Jade and her cameraman Anthony left to head back to the studio.

"You handled that quite well Jade," Anthony said. "Personally, I'm having hot flashes as we speak. Honey, did you see Joe McCay walk by in his jock strap? I thought I was going to d-rop the camera oh Jesus in heaven!"

"Yes girlfriend, I saw him," Jade said, laughing at Anthony.

"You could have given Mitch your number Miss Thang, you know I won't tell", Anthony said. "You do realize he's after them panties don't you?"

"I'm sure I won't ever see him again, so I won't have to worry about that," Jade told Anthony.

Jade and Anthony drove down the highway headed for the studio. They were coming off of the BW Parkway when they got a radio call from the station asking them to head immediately to the D.C. Armory Starplex. There was a mob of people protesting the black-out of the Cowboys game. By the time Jade and Anthony pulled up, things had gotten a little out of hand and a fight had broken out. D.C. police were screaming by on their way to the scene. They jumped out of the truck, and Anthony started rolling. "Where the hell is the news crew?" Jade asked, in a panic.

"Damn if I know, I just work here." Anthony answered confused, "let's just do this." Jade grabbed a comb from her bag and freshened up her lipstick, as Anthony began the countdown…. "In three, in two, go!"

"This is Jade Zellmer, live at the D. C. Armory Starplex….."

Their live cut-in was placed on breaking news. Jade and Anthony had been asked to do it, because they were the closest crew to the area and the other stations were already there. When they got back to the studio, Jade and Anthony were greeted by Bob Norris the news director, as they got off the elevator. They were also greeted with loud applause from the newsroom staff.

"Fabulous guys, thanks for getting that story for us." Bob said, grinning.

"Where was your news crew?" Jade asked him. "You know news is *not* my forte, Bob."

"I know, I know." He said, apologetically. "I guess you haven't heard our crew was involved in an accident on South Capitol, the truck antenna hit a power line…."

"Oh, my God!" Jade said, holding her hand over her mouth. "Is everybody okay?"

"I'm afraid we had a casualty, we've been dealing with that all morning. We just couldn't get anybody else out to the Starplex fast enough. Let me try to finish getting this situation cleared up, and I'd like to talk with you in my office tomorrow Jade, say around ten-thirty?" Bob asked her.

"Sure Bob and I'm so sorry." Jade and Anthony went down the hall toward her office.

"Oh daaaamn", Anthony whispered. "Electrocuted."

"That's awful." Jade said, opening the door of her office. "What the hell is this?"

"Oooh! Miss Thang! Who all them flowers from?" Jade could hardly get into her office for the flowers, they were everywhere. They were on the desk, the floor, the window seals, the bookcases just everywhere, dozens and dozens of red roses. Jade opened one of the cards and it read...*When can I get those digits? Mitch XXX.*

"Whooooo?" Anthony screamed. She handed him the card. "No he di-dent!" Anthony said, with his hands on his hips. "Told you he was after them panties."

"What am I going to do with all these flowers?" Jade asked, looking around the office. "It smells like a funeral polar in here, but they are beautiful aren't they?" She said, smiling.

"Uh-uh-uh! That's all I have to say," Anthony said, and snapped his finger.

"Back to the real world," Jade said. "Let's get that film to editing and call it a day, Anthony. I'm going to see you tomorrow, kisses."

The next day when Jade got into her office, her phone rang. "Good morning Jade, you have a call on line three," the receptionist told her.

"Who is it Michelle, I just got here, damn."

"He won't give me his name, sorry. Do you want me to take a message?"

Jade took a deep breath. "I'll take it Michelle, hello?"

"Hey Reds, what's hap'nin baby?"

"Who is this please?" Jade asked, as if she didn't already know.

"This is Mitch Dawson. Did you get my little present?"

Jade smiled, "Yes I did Mitchell, and thanks. They are all beautiful and don't forget, my name is Jade."

"What time do you take lunch Jaaaaaad?"

"If I get one, it's usually around one o'clock, why?"

"I thought you might let me take you to lunch today. I know a nice little place over in Georgetown, and the food is the bomb!"

"I'm up to my eyebrows in work Mitchell and I have a meeting, maybe I could get a rain check." She lied as she was looking in the mirror at what she had on. She had scheduled interviews with the Eastern and Anacostia head coaches and she had on Jeans and a sweat shirt.

"Awh, come on baby, can't I drag you out of there for just a little while?"

"Gosh, I'm really sorry Mitchell. How did you know where to find me anyway?"

"It won't too hard reading Fox 5 on the camera, and guessing you worked for the sports department baby. "Look, all I want is for us to get together. You're the best thing I've seen since I got to D.C."

"I can't give you a definite date Mitchell. My schedule for next week isn't available until Friday, but I know this week is definitely out. Why don't you give me your number, I'll give you a call and let you know when."

"Uh, I'm embarrassed to even admit this, but I just moved out to Fairfax and I haven't been home long enough to get a phone yet, but take my pager number—703-999-0999 ***and*?**"

"***And*** what?" She asked him.

"What do I have to do to get the digits baby sing a lullaby?" He asked her, laughing.

"Yeahhh," Jade said, in a daring tone. Mitch began singing—

> "*I'm a big handsome guy,*
> *And I ain't too shy,*

What do I have to do?
To get some numbers from you"....

Mitchell was serenading Jade and she was laughing at him. "That's pretty good Mitchell. Since you were resourceful enough to find me, my home number is 708-9521.

"Thanks Jaaaade, call me soon. I really want to see you again and oh, you know who you remind me of?"

"Yes, I do. Goodbye Mitchell." She said, and hung up. The phone rang again. "Jade excuse me, but Bob asked me to buzz you when you finished your call. He wants to see you in his office." Michelle said.

"Oh right, I was supposed to with meet him at ten-thirty, shix I forgot." Jade jumped up from her desk and headed down the hall to Bob's office, wondering what he wanted with her anyway, he wasn't *her* supervisor. She went in and took a seat.

"Good morning Jade, I hope you don't mind Peter sitting in, and I guess you're wondering what this is about. I wanted you to know how grateful we are, and how impressed we were with you yesterday. I know news is not your thing, but you did such an outstanding job for someone who was caught by surprise. You're photogenic, you're articulate and you react well on your feet. Jade the camera loved you and so did we." Bob complimented her.

"Thank you Bob," Jade said, surprised.

"I asked you here today to make an offer to you. We'd like for you to consider applying for an anchor position we'll be posting soon. It'll be for the noon slot, and we'd love to see you in it."

"ME? Anchor?" Jade was caught completely off guard, she wasn't expecting that either!"

"Yes," Bob said, smiling. "You'd be perfect."

"I –I don't quite know what to say. I'm really not a news person, but I am flattered."

"Give it some thought Jade, but think about it quickly," Peter added.

"When would you need to know Bob?"

"Peter?" Bob looked at Peter who was in charge of programming.

"I want the position filled by the beginning of next month, so let's say a few weeks, Jade."

"Well, I'll certainly consider it," Jade was still in shock. "Won't I need to be trained or........."

"If you do what you did yesterday *without* any training, I'm not a bit worried," Peter said. "I'm sure you can read prepared text, and you'd be working with Traci, she'll be your writer. The two of you can work out your timing and speaking patterns and such. It won't be a big thing, you're a natural."

"Thanks Bob and Peter. I've got to think about this, but I'll let you know soon." Jade floated back to her office. What a surprise, but there was one thing wrong with that possible move. She couldn't stand Bob Norris! He was a pompous ass and everybody knew it. Because of that, she would have to give that offer some serious consideration. Working under him would not be easy. He didn't have a reputation for working well with people plus, her sports producer was going to freak!

It had taken two weeks before Jade and Mitchell coordinated their schedules. She agreed to have dinner with him at Harry Browne's in Annapolis. She had gotten excited. Mitchell made her laugh, she liked that about him. Jade called Wendy to tell her about meeting Mitchell, and the fact that she was considering an anchor position at the station. She always ran things past Wendy, Jade respected her opinions.

"No wonder I can't catch up with you," Wendy said, in her "valley girl" accent. "You've been a busy little *beech*. Are you really going to anchor Jazz? When do you start, I want to hear all about it." Wendy bombarded Jade with questions.

"Why don't you meet me at Tyson's Corner for lunch, I'll give you all the juicy details, Wendy. You can help me pick something out to wear for my dinner date with Mitchell too." Jade said.

"Okay what time?"

"If we do one o'clock, that'll give me a chance to finish up my desk." Jade told her.

"Good time. I'll be out of court by eleven today, and I can be on my way. Meet me in front of Clancy's, I'll see you soon."

Later, Jade ran down to the control room to check the traffic screen before she left in case there were any tie-ups, she made that a habit before leaving the studio. She took the elevator to the parking garage, jumped in her Beamer and headed over the bridge. Traffic was heavy, but there was rarely a time in D.C. traffic wasn't heavy.

Wendy stood in front of Clancy's looking as beautiful as ever. She was in a Navy Blue Christian Dior pantsuit, white silk shirt, pearls and Navy pumps. It always amazed Jade that Wendy didn't let her six-foot height prevent her from wearing heels. Her makeup was as usual, flawless. The boy-bob haircut she had gotten, complimented her beautiful features. Jade was still surprised that Wendy had cut her long heavy mane of hair, but she'd probably gotten tired having to keep it up.

"Heeey Wendy." Jade said, walking up the sidewalk.

"Miss Anchor woman. You loo-keen good mommy!" Wendy said, smiling. "I've missed you girl, we need to stop being so busy."

"And how's the world of criminal justice these days?" Jade asked, as they strolled through the mall arm in arm.

"You know, same old' same. I'm just trying to hold my own, and kick a little hinny on the side," Wendy said, laughing.

"I read you were involved in that big Bianchi drug case. That must have been scary. I know you don't talk about your cases, but answer me one question. *WHY* did they think they could come into D.C.—Chocolate City mind you, and do that?"

"I guess they were misinformed. They thought D.C. was ripe for the pickings, or whatever. What I want to know is the low-down on this Mitchell Dawson." Wendy changed the subject.

"Well, let me tell you about him while we eat. I feel like Chinese today, what about you?" She said, pushing Wendy into the door of Peking Restaurant.

"Damn, guess I do." They both started to laugh.

"Two please," Jade said, and the waiter took them to a table.

"So, what's this about Mitchell Dawson? I saw your interview with him, so I gather he's new to the Buckskins? Is that how you met him?"

"I did the interview with him," Jade said, "afterwards he asked for my number and I wouldn't give it to him. When I got back to the studio that afternoon, there were *a zillion* red roses all over my office, dozens of them Wendy. I can only imagine how much that must have cost him. Anyway, he called me the next morning at work and asked me to have lunch, we're *just* hooking up. You know, he's on the road with the team, and I'm busy too."

"So, what do you know about him Jazz?"

"Not much," I'll find out more about him at dinner, I guess."

"Good luck and be careful." Wendy said, sarcastically.

"What?" Jade asked, pouring soy sauce over her rice.

"You know, the Buckskins are notorious for being dogs Jazz, and that's a fact. I know you're not a fool, but watch your back."

Jade told Wendy about the offer she had gotten for the anchor position. Wendy offered to look over the contract for her since it was more in-depth than her present one.

Jade and Wendy left the restaurant, and went into Nordstrom's to pick out an outfit for the dinner.

Jade spotted a green silk three-piece pantsuit with a long jacket, but Wendy had something else in mind for Jade's date. She had exquisite taste and Jade valued her opinion.

"Now look at this little number," Wendy said. "This is baaaad!" She picked out a Jonathan Logan off-white knit dress that hugged in all the right places, cut low in the front and in the back. Jade tried it on and came out of the dressing room to show Wendy.

"Wear it my sist'ah with your Vanessa Williams looking self." Wendy started laughing because she knew the comparison annoyed Jade to no end. "You're really excited about this guy, huh?

"Well, it has been a while since I've been involved with anybody. I thought I'd never get over Marconi, but I'm cool. I run into him quite a bit and when I see him, it's all gone. I wonder why I ever bothered. Dog! Speaking of dogs, what happened with you and Eliot?" Jade asked.

"Don't even say his name to me Jazz, I mean it!"

"Damn, is it that bad?" Wendy was visibly disturbed by the question.

"This is neither the time nor the place, and I've gott'a run anyway. I just hope you're not trading one dog for another Jazz." Wendy said, rolling her eyes and dabbing her lips with her laced handkerchief. "Hey, I just had an idea," Wendy said, excited. "Let's call the girls and have a hen party like old times. Jill has to go to Los Angeles so she'll miss it, but everybody else should be free. What do you think?"

"Sounds like fun, just let me know when." They gave each other mock kisses on the cheek. As Wendy walked away, she hollered back to Jade.

"Don't let me have to send you a bag of Purina now."

Jade was laughing thinking about how funny Wendy was, when her mother called upstairs breaking into her thoughts.

"Jade, Keith's here for breakfast."

"I'll be right down Ma," she said, getting out of the shower.

TWO
WENDY

WENDY HAINES KNEW dogs! Big ones, small ones, smooth ones, tall ones, mean ones, nice ones—they all flocked to her like she was a steak bone. She felt a couple of them had even mistaken her for a fire hydrant.

Her last "dog" was Eliot Roberts. He was a tall, attractive, attorney she'd met in the courtroom. They had just won a case and he was opposing counsel. She sat second chair that day. After the trial ended, he introduced himself to her as she packed up her valise.

"Good afternoon, I'm Eliot Roberts. I don't think I've had the pleasure," he said, extending his hand.

"I'm Wendy Haines." She shook his hand.

"Attorney Haines, could I interest you in a late lunch? I'm starving to death, and I can't begin to imagine why Judge Blair had us work straight through the lunch hour without a break."

HILL FOXES

"Maybe he wanted us to finish, so it wouldn't be continued *again.* Thanks for the invitation, but I need to get back to my office." She said, smiling.

"May I have a rain check then?"

"We may be able to arrange that."

"Great," he said, grinning. "Let me take your card."

"I'll take yours," Wendy said, cautiously, "I'll call you when I can get away." He handed her his card. "Now you can reach me at these numbers, but this is my car phone, I don't usually give that out," he said, scribbling a different phone number on her pad. "I look forward to seeing you again." He smiled as he walked away.

Wendy watched him walk out admiring his physique. He was indeed a handsome man. She guessed he was at least six-five. She was six-two in her heels, and he stood well above her. His temples were mixed grey, and he had long eyelashes with big puppy-dog eyes. She looked at the number he had scribbled on her pad. "Huh."

A week later, while sitting at her bar having a well-deserved drink, she decided to give Eliot a call and see what he was all about. She reached for her note pad and dialed the number.

"Hello", he answered.

"Hi, this is Wendy Haines. Did I call at a bad time?"

"Perfect timing, I just left the West End racquetball club with some friends."

"I see you're keeping fit," she said. "How've you been Eliot?"

"I've been great, just busy."

They talked for over an hour. He told her he had come to D.C. shortly after finishing law school at Duke. He had contemplated staying in Durham, but was offered a job at Calvaconti & Greene so he came to Washington. He lived on Capitol Hill near Lincoln Park and liked jazz, racquetball and old movies. He invited Wendy to a concert at Wolf Trap to hear George Michael perform that coming weekend, she accepted.

On the day of the concert, Eliot picked her up in his SUV. She was surprised that he had come equipped with a lawn blanket, and wine and cheese for their outing. He seemed to be very thoughtful and attentive.

They stopped by Hogate's after the concert, had huge seafood platters, and more wine. Wendy and Eliot hit it off quite well, she liked him.

The first six months of their relationship had been wonderfully romantic. Wendy awoke one beautiful Sunday morning and tip-toed downstairs to make coffee for Eliot. He was sleeping, they had made love most of the night. She smiled thinking about how he

HILL FOXES

had made her laugh when he asked her what she'd do if he came by one night in a pink rabbit suit beating a drum. Wendy didn't get it—she didn't know what he was talking about. "You know, the Energizer Bunny, dah?" He said, laughing. *Eliot had a slight tendency toward being corny, real corny.*

They spent that Sunday after a huge country breakfast, propped up on pillows in bed while they worked on their individual cases. Eliot was scheduled to meet with his guys at the fitness center later that afternoon for a game. He started gathering his papers. "I need to go and get some exercise baby so I can keep up with you in this bed, you're about to wear me out."

"Look who's talking," Wendy said, looking over her glasses laughing. "Who was it that kept pulling on me all night every time I fell asleep?"

"Must have been the bunny." He whispered.

"Keep it up. That bunny's going to be beating his own little *drum*."

Eliot showered, took the sweats from his gym bag and got ready to go to the West End.

"Keep sweet Wendy, don't work too hard today. I'll call you later, I'm sure I'll be up all night. I've got a potential career-making case in Judge Frederick's courtroom tomorrow," Eliot said, standing at her front door. He kissed her and went out to his car.

Wendy went to the kitchen to wash up the breakfast dishes and put a load of laundry in the machine. When she finished, she went back upstairs to continue working on her case. *"Oh dag, Eliot left his briefcase."* She sat it aside and paged him but didn't get an answer. He was probably on the racquetball court. She got back to her work and as the evening progressed, she decided to page him again, no response. Wendy got into her car and drove to M Street to his club. She didn't feel like going, but she knew how important that trial was, and he would need his paperwork for court. She parked with no problem, on Sundays, the meters were free.

"Good evening," she said, to the desk receptionist. "I'm looking for Eliot Roberts who's probably on the racquetball court.

"I'll see if I can locate him for you," he said. He paged for Eliot. After a few minutes, a guy stuck his head out of the door. "Eliot's gone home," the man said. Wendy thanked him and the desk receptionist and headed for Capitol Hill to Eliot's house. Her pager hadn't rung, so she thought he probably hadn't missed his briefcase yet, nor was he in his car to hear the car phone.

Wendy rang the doorbell. She had been standing there for a while before a man answered the door. "Martin?" She asked, surprised. "What are you doing here?" She walked past Martin and into the living room. Martin was a paralegal who worked at Eliot's firm, but she never knew them to be friends.

From the living room, Wendy saw a woman in the kitchen cooking, in her bra and panties. "Who is that, and where is Eliot?" Wendy asked Martin. She was about to give him her impersonation of a fire breather!

"He's not here right now," Martin said. "That's my lady friend and we're about to have dinner, you're welcome to join us." He seemed a little nervous.

"Uh-huh." Wendy said. "Tell Eliot I stopped by Martin, I'll call him later." Wendy left and as she drove, she felt something was wrong with that whole scene. When she got home, she looked inside Eliot's briefcase. The identification tag inside the case said—Eliot R. Roberts, 200 Beach Drive, NW, Washington, D. C. *But that's not his house address.* She got back into her car and went downtown to the District Courthouse. She flashed her ID to the Security Guard and entered the building. Since she was an attorney, it wasn't unusual for her to be there on a Sunday, she'd be one of many working in the building. She went to the records room and pulled the big blue book open. Richard—Richards—Robert—Roberts—

<u>Roberts</u>, Eliot F.   *200 Beach Drive, NW, DC 20012*
Attorney at Law   *$159,500. Property Ass. $825,000.*
Spouse: <u>Audrey B.</u>   *200 Beach Drive, NW DC 20012*
Financial Analyst   *$75,000. Gov't. Accounting Office*
Dependents: **03**

<u>Roberts</u>, Audrey B.   *200 Beach Drive, NW, DC 20012*
Financial Analyst   *$75,000. Property Ass. $825,000*
Spouse: <u>Eliot F.</u>   *200 Beach Drive, NW, DC 20012*
Attorney At Law   *$159,500 Calvaconti & Greene*
Dependents: 03

<u>Dixon</u>, Martin G.   *200 11th Street, NE 20003*
Paralegal $40,000.   *Property Ass. $695,500.*
Calvaconti & Greene   *400 Third Street, NW DC 20001*
Dependents: **00**

"That slimy, lying, M** F", Wendy whispered. She drove back home in a fury! She brought the briefcase back inside and opened it on her desk. She went through every piece of paper in it. She was trying to piece together just what was going on. As she began looking through the papers, her phone rang—the caller ID said *Roberts, E*. She didn't answer. She continued going through the papers. From what she could piece together, the dog was **married** to Audrey Roberts, and there were **three**

children. The house on Capitol Hill was in Martin's name. He lived on Beach Drive with his family, NOT on Capitol Hill where he always took her, and where they stayed sometime. The house being Martin's, was another whole mystery, how could a paralegal afford to live on Capitol Hill? The phone rang again, she didn't answer. Wendy needed time to think about what she was going to do. She called Noel.

"Noel, Wendy."

"What's shaking girl?" Noel asked.

"Where are you working tomorrow?"

"I won't know until I get to work, my case got a continuance."

"What do you know about Eliot Roberts?"

"You mean *your* boo Eliot?"

"Yes. I'm beginning to think he's dirty."

"I don't know too much about him, what's wrong?"

"I'm not sure yet, I'm trying to get to the bottom of it. I'm trying to find out *first,* where he lives."

"Where he lives? Haven't you ever been to his house? Noel sounded surprised.

"That's just it. I stay there often, but for some reason, that house is in Martin Dixon's name. Martin is a paralegal at Eliot's firm."

"Him I know." Noel said. "I'm not what you call a good friend of his, but he and I talk occasionally."

Wendy began telling Noel what happened and why she was asking.

"WHAT? The sneaky bastard!" Noel said. "Married!" You've been going with him for how long now?"

"Six months! Noel, I must be slipping. I was so busy I didn't take the time to do my homework."

"Don't beat up on yourself now. Let me snoop around and see what I can find out, I'll let you know." Noel said.

Just as Wendy hung up, her phone rang again—*Roberts, E.* "*I might as well get this over with,*" *she thought.*

"Hello."

"Hey, Wendy. I left my briefcase in your bedroom," Eliot said, sounding inconvenienced.

"You did?" Wendy answered, acting surprised.

"Yeah, baby, I thought it was in my car all this time, until I went to get it."

"That's funny Eliot, I'm in my bedroom and it's not here in fact, I'm sure you took it along with your gym bag, honey." *Hell will freeze over and thaw out again before you'll ever see this briefcase again, she was pissed!*

"Let me look again, but I know it's not there. I've got to have my notes for court in the morning. This is one of the biggest cases I've ever had. By the way, Martin said you stopped by the house?"

"I was out and about. I thought maybe I would

treat us to dinner at Mr. Henry's." Wendy said, nonchalantly. Martin and his girlfriend, I assume, were cooking dinner. His girlfriend was very comfortable, she was walking around in her bra and drawers," she said, sarcastically.

"I let him entertain at my house sometimes when he's trying to impress one of his more affluent lady friends."

"Damn charitable of you Eliot." Wendy said, still being sarcastic.

"I'm going to look in my car one more time," he said, changing the subject. "Wendy please check around again, if you don't mind."

"I will, but I can assure you Eliot, it's not here, baby." Wendy was enjoying making him squirm. "I hope you find it. I know how important the case is to your future. I'm going to get a shower and get to bed early honey, goodnight." She hung up.

Wendy walked through the metal detector the next morning. She stopped to be waned by security at the courthouse hallway. She started down the escalator toward the cafeteria to get coffee and a bagel. Wendy had over-slept, she'd been awake most of the night. She was pondering over what to do about Eliot's lying ass.

"Good morning Wendy," Noel said, setting her tray down at Wendy's table.

"Hey, Noel." She said, dryly.

"I'm glad I caught you and you look—like—shit!

"Gee, thanks a lot Noel. I didn't sleep too well."

"I'm glad I caught you before court," Noel said. "Got some information out of Marcus last night, and what's funny is, I doubt he even knows he gave it to me." She was whispering. "It seems like there are six guys, all married, all work here in the court system. They sat Martin up in that house on Capitol Hill. They each pay equal portions of the mortgage for the use of the house, primarily to entertain their women, girlfriends or whatever. Martin gets to stay there free. He's responsible for maintaining the house and keeping the schedule for them—you know "keeper of the house"? Anyway, Martin lets each one of them choose time slots they want to use the house, and they check with him in between times for any vacant spots. I guess it basically works like a time-share situation." Noel whispered.

"Kiss my ass!" Wendy whispered. "So what happens if a woman pops by unexpectedly like I did last night?"

"That was my question too. Martin is *always* their excuse. He's there while his apartment is being painted, or he's entertaining someone he wants to impress or whatever."

"Huh, that's exactly what Eliot told me, that

HILL FOXES

Martin was trying to impress some affluent woman, and he let him use his house, lying dog!"

Wendy and Noel rode the escalator upstairs to check the distribution schedule. Eliot's case was being continued. Apparently he couldn't get it together fast enough for court that morning. Wendy took pleasure in knowing that fact. Her mind wandered all day. She couldn't believe he had made such a fool out of her. Wendy hated women who dated married men, and here she was involved with some woman's husband, how disgusting! When she got home that evening, she got settled and went back out. She parked two blocks from the house on Capitol Hill, and dialed Eliot from a phone booth.

"Hey sugar," she was boiling inside. "How about if I come over and fix a nice home cooked meal?"

"That sounds good Wendy, but I'm trying to piece information together for my case, I asked the judge for a continuance this morning. I still don't know what has happened to my briefcase." He said, sounding pitiful.

"Honey, did you check at the club?" She asked, pretending to be concerned.

"Of course I did, they haven't seen it either."

"Wow", Wendy said, almost laughing. "You sound like you could use some of my good cooking, I wouldn't disturb you. All you have to do is work while I cook your dinner." She wondered if he could hear her grinning through the phone.

"Thanks baby, but I think I'm going to concentrate on putting this case back together. I'm already in bed for the night, I just need to get this done and get to sleep."

"Okay, but I still think you'd enjoy a good meal," she said, grinning at the phone.

"I'll take a rain check, gott'a run now Wendy, goodnight."

Wendy started up the car and drove around the corner. It took all of four minutes to get there. She knocked on the door. Martin answered.

"Hey Martin, are you staying here now?"

"Just for the week until my apartment gets painted, Eliot isn't here right now though."

BEEEEP—*wrong answer*. "I'll call him later," she said, and left the porch. *In for the night, huh!* Wendy spent another sleepless night, but the next morning, she was up and dressed early. She fought traffic on her way over to Beach Drive. When she got to the address inside Eliot's briefcase, she parked on the corner and her question was answered. There was Eliot F. Roberts, Esquire, in the flesh!

He was loading the back of his car with two children. One looked to be eight, the other maybe six.

There was a woman standing just inside the screen door of the house waving goodbye.

Wendy drove off toward District Court. *"You're going to pay Eliot Roberts, you're going to pay big time!"*

THREE
NOEL

NOEL DOSS WAS disappointed. She felt sad for Wendy, and infuriated with Eliot. How dare he try to pull that off. D. C. was entirely too small. Surprisingly, Marcus hadn't realized he'd given up as much information on Eliot as he had. Noel knew how to get it though, she knew exactly when and how. She never came right out and asked. She waited until he was engrossed in work. He was writing his closing argument for court, she slid his slippers off. She began messaging his feet, and after a few minutes asked him the first question. She warmed scented oil between her hands, and moved up to his legs. Five minutes later, she asked him the next question, and so on until she had all the information Wendy needed to know. Marcus was so busy working he didn't even know he had been in a conversation.

Noel brought Marcus a flute of Sherry. It always relaxed him before bed. He was staying overnight, and she was just happy they were spending some time together for a change, Lord knew she needed some.

Marcus Holbrook was constantly busy! Determined to become a judge, he involved himself in a multitude of organizations he felt would enhance his career; 100 Black Men, Alpha's, NAACP, and the NCBL—National Council of Black Lawyers. He also dabbled in local politics, holding a seat on the D.C. School Board. *Always* busy, but Noel loved her Marcus!

Noel began thinking about how they met in the courthouse cafeteria during that snow storm.

"Is this seat taken?" He had asked her.

"No it's not," she answered, biting into a sandwich.

"Nasty morning out there," he said, making conversation. "I hear they've closed some agencies already."

"I heard," Noel said. "They usually stagger the closings. I imagine they're getting the school kids home first."

"I'm sorry, I'm Marcus Holbrook."

"I'm Noel Ross."

"I think we've worked the same courtroom a couple of times, I know you look familiar," he said.

"Yes, we have."

But, that's not why Noel knew Marcus. Working in the District Courthouse was much like being in a small town, topics of gossip and people's personal business was public knowledge.

Not so very long ago, Attorney Marcus Holbrook's personal business qualified as "the Tid-bit" of the month!

His wife Lila had come to the building with their two children, and demanded to see Marcus. Marcus was involved in a closed hearing, the Marshall wouldn't let her go in and she freaked! She had an arm load of Safeway grocery bags, a young baby, and another child by the hand. She began to rip open the grocery bags and throw the containers of her baby's powered Similac all over the hallway, screaming that she needed to see her husband.

"They poisoned my baby's milk," she was screaming. She insisted "*they*" were trying to kill her baby and she needed Marcus to help her. It took two Marshalls to subdue her and from what the rumor-mill said, those two Marshalls were going to be sore for a while! They called DCPD and a rescue squad to have her transported to the Psych Ward at Columbia Hospital for Women.

Another time, supposedly in the Law Office of Simmons-McAlpine & Meghetti, she turned the place out. She went into Attorney Simmons office and completely trashed it, claiming that he was personally responsible for trying to destroy her family.

That he was covering up an affair Marcus was having with Sandra McAlpine, one of the partners. The receptionist called the police and they carried her to jail. Marcus was not in the office, nor was Attorney Simmons at the time, but needless to say, Attorney Simmons strongly advised Marcus get her some immediate help. Marcus ended up paying an enormous sum of money to have Simmons office redone. A lot of his personal items could not be replaced. The thing that hurt Simmons the most was the fact that Lila had destroyed his leather couch. It had also sat in his father's law office when he was a child, it was a memento. Lila ripped it to pieces with a box cutter.

When Lila appeared before the court for the various charges, including destruction of private property, she appeared before Judge Cheryl Roland. Judge Roland was aware of the situation and was sympathetic. She was willing to work with Marcus in getting help for Lila. To everyone's astonishment, Lila accused Judge Roland in front of the court, of conspiring to have her put away so she could have an affair with Marcus too. Judge Roland ordered Lila be taken to St. Elizabeth's Hospital for evaluation.

Yes, the courthouse was all a-buzz about Marcus and his crazy wife Lila. Marcus continued his work, despite the tremendous strain he was under. Lila was diagnosed Paranoid Schizophrenic. Marcus had her transferred from St. E's to a private hospital in Maryland, where she could receive the help and medication she needed. A few months later, Lila returned home. By then, Marcus had hired Mrs. Prince, a sixty year old woman, who cared for the children as well as their home.

Things seemed back to normal. Lila was much better and Mrs. Prince was a great help around the house to Lila. Marcus felt Mrs. Prince wouldn't pose a threat to Lila, being an older woman. The boys were adjusting to Lila's being home. Brent was six and Bryan, almost a year old.

Mrs. Prince served breakfast in the breakfast room one morning, it was before Marcus and Brent left for work and school. Lila picked up her plate and hurled it at Mrs. Prince, hitting her in the face. Food flew all over the room, and the baby began screaming. Lila claimed Mrs. Prince had put something in her breakfast. That's when Marcus realized Lila wasn't taking her medications, so he had her re-admitted. He just couldn't trust Lila around the children, there was no telling when she'd go off. At some point, Lila signed herself out of the hospital and made it a living hell for Marcus and everybody in the neighborhood. He wanted to help her, but he wouldn't allow her in their house. He feared for their babies, as well as himself. Lila threw bricks through the windows, banged on the door all hours of the night, and the profanity she used out in front of their house was horrendous, embarrassing.

Marcus eventually moved from their home. He took Mrs. Prince and the boys to live at Tiber Island Towers, a security protected high rise in Southwest Washington, Mrs. Prince became a full-time live in.

Things must have been better at the Holbrook's. The rumor-mill hadn't buzzed lately about Marcus and his crazy little wife.

Noel knew Marcus alright. As if by some divine master plan of fate, Noel was assigned to a big case Marcus was on that lasted for months. It became routine for them to have lunch together in the cafeteria every day, and as they became better friends, Marcus began to confide in Noel. She learned the whole story about him and his wife. Noel was a good listener and a good confidant, he needed one. As they became closer friends, lunches became dinners, and then dinners and drinks at her house. Before long, Noel and Marcus were engaged in a full-time love affair. Underneath that hard exterior of Marcus', he was a thoughtful, gentle man, and Noel Ross had fallen hard.

Months after, they had taken their relationship to yet another level. Marcus called Noel one night and told her to pack her bags. "We're going on a trip."

"What?" She asked, confused.

"Pack your bags Noel. I want you to go somewhere with me." He was excited. Noel was baffled because it was so unlike Marcus to be spontaneous. She packed her bag, took leave, and boarded a plane. She had no idea where he was taking her, but she trusted him. Noel and Marcus landed on the beautiful islands of Turks and Caicos.

"It's been years since I've been able to get away," Marcus said, smiling.

"I think you deserve a break Marcus, and this is the most beautiful place I've ever seen." He picked up their rental car and drove to a house Marcus had arranged to get on time-share. It was wonderful relaxing on the beach, watching marine life, feeling the warm breezes, and just being together, uninterrupted.

"I hope this meets with your approval Noel." Marcus said rubbing Noel's sun kissed thigh as they gazed at the clear blue skies on the beach. "I know I don't spend as much time with you as you'd like, but I miss you too. I just hope this makes up for some of my absences, but Noel, I'm serious when I tell you I *am* going to get to the top one day. I had a setback in my life I hadn't counted on, certainly nothing like what's happened but it did, and there's nothing I can do about it. I've tried to keep my head up and persevere. I've spent this last year trying to do damage control and rise above it, I hope in time people will forget. I know I don't have the right to ask you this right now, but I ask for your trust, I ask for your patience because when I get to where I'm going, I want you there with me Noel."

Marcus pulled out a ring that rivaled the tropical sun above them! "*Marcus*," Noel whispered. She was speechless. It was the biggest diamond she'd ever seen.

"I'm asking you to bear with me while I try to put my life back in order, and I promise to make you my wife."

FOUR
JILL

"**WOULD YOU LIKE** coffee Noel?" Jill asked, pushing the serving cart down the aisle beside Marcus and Noel. Marcus and Noel had taken a commuter plane back from Turks & Caicos to Miami, drove up to West Palm Beach and spent the day, then headed back to D. C.

"I'll take orange juice, but you can give Marcus the coffee." Noel said.

"I could have upgraded your seats to first class if I'd known you were going to be on this flight," Jill whispered to them.

"Thanks," Marcus said, smiling. "Maybe next time, this was a last minute thing."

Jill was happy for Noel. That ring was something to behold, uh-uh-uh! The girls were going to die! Jill was smiling. She closed her eyes and said her little prayer as the landing gear dropped for their approach to National airport. As quiet as it was kept, of all the airports Jill landed in, National was still the one that scared the living daylights out of her.

"Thanks for flying with us today," Jill said, to Noel, Marcus, and the other passengers exiting the cabin door. "I'll see you at Wendy's pajama party right?" Noel asked.

"I'm afraid not, I'm working for someone on a Los Angeles flight. "Congratulations again you two."

After finishing up her paperwork, Jill gathered her flight bag and headed for the terminal, Julius was meeting her out front. He had a run to drop off two passengers at National, and he could take her at home. Julius was standing by the limousine in the loading zone looking like a movie star when she came out. *Damn he's fine!*

Julius was average height, slim with a nice build. He looked strikingly handsome in his Chauffer's uniform, starched white shirt, shined black shoes, black designer shades, and always, manicured nails.

"Good morning Sunshine," Julius said, smiling at her.

"Good morning Julius," she smiled back. He gave her a quick kiss on her lips, opened her door and they were off.

"Tired?" Julius asked, looking at her through the rear view mirror.

"No, not really, I got to bed early last night." She smiled, thinking about how wonderful her date with Michael had been the night before in West Palm. She was in bed early, alright.

Jill and Julius talked on the way through the city about the latest reply he'd gotten from an insurance company. He wanted to buy his own limousine and start a service. He had been busy doing the ground work. Julius pulled up at Jill's garden apartments in Fort Chaplin on East Capitol Street. It was almost a straight shot from the airport and in inclement weather, or if she didn't want to drive to National, it was close to the Metro train.

"I've got a pick-up in a half hour, I'll call you later," Julius said, giving her another brief kiss.

"Okay honey, I'm going in and get a nap."

Jill opened the door to her condo and went straight to the bedroom to get out of her uniform. She *was* tired, good and tired! Michael had really rocked her world the night before. He was the cutest little honey, and she always enjoyed his attention whenever she stayed over. He always wined and dined her, then tried to screw her brains out before she left. They had an understanding—he was her "in-town" guy whenever she was "in-town". There was no pretending that their relationship would ever go beyond that besides, he was married.

HILL FOXES

She'd met Michael through Gina, her co-worker. Gina shared her four bedroom house with Jill and two other flight attendants on their crew, whenever they laid-over in West Palm Beach. Michael was Gina's older brother. He helped her out with some of the small maintenance tasks around her house. Michael was in the hallway on a ladder outside the bedrooms one day. He was changing a light bulb when Jill came out of her bedroom in her panties—that's all.

"Oh, I'm so sorry," he said. Jill jumped back inside the room and closed the door. She came back out in her bathrobe to apologize to him.

"I didn't know anyone was here," Jill said, embarrassed.

"I didn't either! I'm Michael, Gina's brother."

"So you're Michael, I'm Jill."

"Jill, I finally get to see you."

"Yes, and I'm afraid you got to see all of me," she laughed.

Jill started the water for a shower and smiled, thinking about Michael. She picked up the phone and called Wendy. Wendy was in court so she left a voice message…"You little horny tramps go ahead and party without me, I'll be in Los Angeles. Call me."

FIVE
LAUREN

LAUREN LIFTED HER waist-length locs, pulled them across her shoulder, and braided them into one long piece. She was rushing to do a photo shoot at the Baltimore Inner Harbor, she was late. It was an extremely windy day. She knew before she got to Baltimore, that shoot wasn't going to happen. Her client wanted to do the shoot outside on the street with the Harbor as the backdrop.

"I suggest we try another day." Lauren told the manager in charge of the Boutique.

"Do you know how much cancelling's going to cost us? Can't we just get it done today?" He whined.

"I don't see how," Lauren said. "The models, as well as your props, are going to get blown away. Let's be realistic, it's not going to work. Please don't be angry with me, be angry with Mother Nature."

After finally persuading the manager to cancel

the shoot, Lauren got into her truck. She had called ahead to see if she could get an appointment at *Le Loc Salon*, a salon specializing in Locs and Braids. The girl told her she would squeeze her in since it was just a shampoo. Lauren drove down BW Parkway back into D.C., then up to Georgia Avenue.

"Hello everyone," Lauren greeted everyone as she walked into a salon full of people.

"Hello," the clients and employees responded in unison.

"Assaslam Aleikom, my Sister," Mustafa Saleem the owner greeted her. The salon was filled with beautiful Black women, natural locs adorning their heads. There was one man and one upset Caucasian woman. Mustafa tried calming her down. "Be patient, that's one of the teachings of the process. It's one of the spiritual lessons of locking My Sister—Patience," he told her.

"That's the problem", an older woman sitting next to Lauren whispered. "*If* she was a *sister* the process *would* be natural—*it ain't natural for her*." Lauren smiled. "I hear you," she said to the woman.

"How can we assist you today my beautiful Sister Lauren?" Mustafa asked her.

"Today, I just need my hair shampooed."

"Haadiya, would you please be kind enough to get Sister Lauren washed?" Mustafa asked.

Lauren lay back in the chair at the sink for Haadiya to wash her hair. As warm water ran through her scalp, Haadiya added coconut scented shampoo and gently began washing. She tenderly messaged her scalp and temples; it was all Lauren could to do to stay awake. This woman's touch was so soothing, an involuntary moan escaped Lauren's throat as Haadiya began to softly scrub her scalp with her nails. When Lauren was finished, Mustafa thanked her for her patronage, and quietly whispered a reminder of the promise she'd made to have tea with him.

"I will," she whispered. "I've just been so busy."

"You don't seem too busy now. Why don't you let me take you to the Harambee House?"

"Well," she thought for a minute, "okay I guess so." She had time since the shoot in Baltimore had been canceled. Mustafa grabbed his satchel, and asked Haadiya to hold down the Fort until he returned. She seemed to be second in charge there.

Mustafa suggested they take Lauren's truck. He'd made an appointment with Sheyhe Ford to pick up his truck from the salon for repair.

Lauren drove them to the Harambee House, and once inside, they were seated at a table by a bay window. She began to focus in on Mustafa the man, instead of Mustafa the hairdresser. He was tall, with a

HILL FOXES

honey-brown complexion, beautiful shoulder length locs, and a thick mustache surrounded perfect white teeth. He wore a Dashiki in African print over his pants, and leather sandals. Mustafa wore a diamond stud in his ear and expensive looking gold bangles on his muscular arm.

"So, tell me something I don't know about you, Sister Lauren." Mustafa asked, blowing steam away from his cup of Oolong tea.

"Well," she said, "that might take a while since you don't really know me."

"I beg to differ with you my sister," Mustafa said, looking into her eyes. "I know *everything* about you. You're a queen among women. You're gentle and warm, nurturing and giving, loving and kind, you're sensitive and sensual. You Lauren, are an incredibly, phenomenal woman."

"Wow! You think that's who I am huh?"

"I *know* that's who you are, and I'm strongly attracted to you. Maybe we can begin to see more of each other?" Mustafa asked, softly.

"Maybe." Lauren and Mustafa sat and talked quietly at the table looking onto Georgia Avenue, as quiet jazz played softly in the background. Mustafa ordered more Oolong tea for them while they talked. Before they knew it, it was late afternoon.

"Oh, my gosh," Lauren said, looking at her watch.

"I had no idea it was this late. We'd better go so we can get you back to the salon."

"I've enjoyed this exchange with you Lauren, I hope this won't be the last time," he said, waving for the waiter.

"I've enjoyed talking with you too, Mustafa." The waiter laid the leather check folder down on the table and Mustafa opened his satchel. He placed his head in his hands. "Lauren, you let me walk out of the salon without my wallet, ahhh, I'm so embarrassed."

"I've got it," Lauren said, taking the American Express card from her purse.

"I'm sorry Sister. I'll give it back to you when we get to the salon. Would you please leave the young man five dollars? You know they're working Howard students and I always like to leave a nice tip."

Lauren drove them back to *Le Loc*. When they got there, she noticed that Sheyhe Ford hadn't come for his truck yet, or maybe they had been there and had already returned it.

"Oh my goodness, there's Mrs. Johnson in my chair," Mustafa said, excited, looking into the salon window. "I was enjoying your company so much I forgot I had an appointment. I'll call you tonight after we close, maybe we can get together again." He jumped out of the Pathfinder and rushed inside. Lauren headed home to call Wendy for the details of the slumber party.

SIX
BREA

BREA SHREE JONES awoke to the ringing of the Monastery bell in the distance of her Northeast D.C. home. She stretched, and wondered what new revelations that day would bring. Her life some months ago, had been a whirlwind of crazy, and she was trying to put it back in place.

Brea threw on some sweats, went downstairs to grab a bottled water from the refrigerator, and headed out the door for her morning run. She did a few warm-up stretches out on the porch, and couldn't help but feel sad when she looked across the street at her neighbor's house. Miss Palmer wasn't out front sweeping imaginary debris from the sidewalk anymore, so she would have a bird's eye view of everything and everybody on the block. Brea thought she'd never admit it, but she missed Miss Palmer, nosey ol' Bat.

Brea adjusted the volume on her headset, tuned in to Donnie Simpson's morning drive, and began her run. Running gave Brea a feeling of freedom, and for some reason, it seemed to clear her head. As each foot hit the pavement, she tried to stomp out any memory of Melik Iverson from her mind. He'd left an indelible scar on her heart and the memories just wouldn't go away. Brea's mind drifted back to one of her first encounters with Melik, while she ran. *He had scheduled a meeting with her and her agent Damon Whitehead in D.C., to discuss the possibility of Brea signing with Melik's recording label, Natural Element.*

Brea was a celebrity in her own right; she was an internationally known runway and fashion model. Her heart's desire however, was to sing. Melik Iverson was going to make that happen for her.

The year before, Brea arrived at a downtown restaurant for the meeting with Natural Element, and her agent Damon, at four o'clock.

"Who's coming from Natural Element for the meeting?" Brea asked Damon, holding her breath in anticipation of the answer. She hoped it would be Melik and not one of his producers.

"It really doesn't matter. Melik is pulling the strings either way." Damon said. He ordered a glass of wine but decided she didn't need any. He wanted her fresh for her appearance that night. Damon asked for the menu and

ordered from the lunch selection because for whoever was coming, it would be lunchtime in Los Angeles. A waitress approached their table escorting MELIK! Brea's heart began to beat fast when she saw him. He was as fine as she had remembered when she auditioned for them.

"Melik," Damon said, raising from his chair and extending his hand. "Of course you remember Brea."

"Yes, I do," he said, smiling. He bent down and kissed her cheek. "How are you both this afternoon?" Melik took the seat opposite Brea. Damon ordered wine for Melik, and the meeting was underway. Melik made an offer let's just say like the gangster movies, one that was hard to refuse. With the exception of a few bumps, Damon said he thought they could work something out, the terms seemed quite amenable.

"This calls for a celebration," Melik said, smiling. "You can't imagine how happy I am that you're going to join our little family Brea. The two of you should join me for dinner at the Jefferson Hotel tonight?"

"I'd love to Melik, but I have an engagement tonight at the Basement in Georgetown," Brea told him.

"Why don't you join us for the show and have dinner there with us?"

"I'd love to," Melik said, smiling at her.

The concert was a smash! Brea was accompanied by a local group, "Ice". She had been invited to sing with them on their gig at the famous Basement Club, and

Damon thought it would be good exposure for her. Their reserved tables had finally begun to empty after the nonstop champagne Melik kept coming to the tables for Brea, "Ice", their friends and family. After everyone was gone from the table, Melik looked at Brea and smiled with approval. "Well Miss Jones, at last we're alone. That was some "debut". I knew when I heard you audition in LA, you'd be fantastic."

"Thank you kind sir, but you know I was a basket case. I'm used to being in front of the public, but singing….."

"This is nothing compared to what lies ahead for you, you know that right?" Melik asked, helping with her wrap.

They left, and Brea offered Melik a ride back to his hotel. She stopped at the Tidal Basin before dropping him at his hotel.

"Have you ever been here before Melik?" She asked.

"No, but I've seen it on TV," he said, laughing. "It's as beautiful as I imagined."

"Let's get out and walk, then you can say you've actually walked the Basin." She grabbed her purse. He walked around to her side of the car, opened her door and they began to walk. He reached down and took her hand in his.

"Whew, this is an amazing city," he said. "There's one little thing, I'm not used to these temperatures," Melik said, pulling up his suit collar.

"Oh, I'm sorry," Brea said, apologizing. "Let's go back to the car, I forgot about that."

"Not on your life," he said, "I find it invigorating BUT, if I catch cold, I'm going to hang you by your toes young lady." They strolled around the Basin holding hands and he filled her in on what being in the music business was going to be like.

"Are you still cold?" Brea asked him after a while.

"It's a little chilly, but I'm okay."

"I think we need to get back to the car. God knows I don't want to take a chance on being hung by my toes," Brea said, laughing. They walked back to the car and she drove him to the hotel. He invited her up to his suite, but she declined his invitation. It had been a long day and she knew what would happen if she went with him. It was much too soon for that!

Melik eventually signed Brea and launched her singing career, after a nasty knock-down fight between Melik and her agent Damon Whitehead. Melik also signed "Ice" as her band. They all packed up and moved out to California. Brea moved in with Melik at his Blue Lakes Estates mansion, after their romance grew into an incredible love relationship.

He sent Brea and "Ice" on a cross-country tour that started in LA, and ended at home in D.C. at Constitution Hall. They were promoting Brea's first CD "Come with Me". It sold faster than weed, and climbed to the top of the charts. While they were out on tour, Brea accidently found out who the real Melik Iverson was.

The tour group was winding down in Brea's hotel apartment after finishing two shows in Greensboro. They were trying to decide what they were going to do about dinner that night. Brea's girlfriend Christy from D.C. had flown down to catch the show before it got to D.C., and to spend some time with Brea. Brea, Christy, and Brea's backup singers Courtney and Nicolette were sitting at the dining room table in the apartment.

"How long have you been touring Courtney?" Christy asked her. She seemed to be an experienced "road hog".

"Ah, about three years. I'm a Cosmetologist on my off time. One day I was doing Melik's girlfriend's hair, when she gave me a flyer to post in the shop. Natural Element was holding auditions for singers. I took my narrow ass right down there and auditioned, joined the union and started working." Courtney said. "I've been on several of Natural Element's tours over the last few years.

"Melik's girlfriend? So who was he dating then?" Brea asked, being nosey.

"Same person," Courtney said, pouring another glass of wine.

"Same person as who?" Brea asked, confused. Courtney must have assumed Brea knew who she was talking about.

"Now Brea, I know you ain't been living at Melik's

all this time and never met Denise." Courtney said.

"You mean his sister Denise?" Brea asked. Her eyes widened.

"Sister? Melik ain't got no sister." Nicolette said, smacking on a bag of pork skins.

Christy took over the conversation and changed the subject. As well as she knew Brea, she knew her friend had just been knocked off her feet. Christy and Reggie both purposely, began steering everyone out of Brea's apartment by ordering food from a nearby carry-out, and having it delivered up to Reggie's apartment.

"Who is Denise, and why did you think she was Melik's sister?" Christy asked Brea after they were finally alone. Christy was as confused as Brea looked.

"He told me she was." Brea said, softly, she was trembling.

"I don't understand," Christy said. "Does that mean you don't know her, or that she never came to his house?"

"Denise is always around somewhere," Brea said sadly. "I'd see her out at the pool, or I'd notice her car parked out front and it was no big whoop. Whenever I saw Denise, we'd wave to each other and keep going. You have to imagine Christy, just how large that property is, and I lived on the other side in the guest house. She and I were never formerly introduced. I've actually never talked with her. I figured at some point, she and I would get to sit down together and talk because she's from D.C. too."

*"Whoa. I'm like Courtney now, how did you **not** know Brea?*

"It happened! That shows you just how stupid I am…."

"No, you're not," Christy said. *"That shows me how slick he is, but that's a bit much! If he got away with that, he's slicker than a can of Johnson wax."*

Brea and "Ice" went back to D.C. after the tour ended. She contacted her former agent Damon Whitehead, for help. She wasn't sure if he would help her, they hadn't exactly parted as friends after the nasty fight between him and Melik. Brea wanted out of her contract with Melik and Natural Element. She couldn't stand the sight of him. Anyone who was tactless enough to have two women that close around each other didn't deserve to enjoy the rewards of her hard work, and talent. That unfortunate experience had devastated her.

Brea finished her morning run at Taft's school track. She got up from the picnic table she had rested on while she reminisced, and continued home. She made a mental note to call and RSVP Wendy for the slumber party.

SEVEN
JADE

THE DAY HAD finally come for Jade's date with Mitchell Dawson, and she was very excited. She filled the tub and dropped perfumed beads in the hot water, lighted scented candles, and put on some Marvin Gaye. Jade filled her wine goblet with Zinfandel, sat back and relaxed. She felt she deserved that treat after "her day from hell" at work. She reached for the ringing phone.

"Hey, Reds, it's Mitch."

"Boy?"

"Sorry J-a-a-a-d, its Mitch. Whach'a doing?"

"I'm getting ready to dress, is everything alright?"

"Everything will be better when I see you. You said off Taylor Street right?"

"Right. Are you sure you can find it? I know you're not that familiar with the city yet."

"I'll see you in about an hour." *Click*!

Wendy definitely had an eye for fashion. *I'm wearing the hell of this dress*, Jade thought, admiring herself in the mirror. The doorbell rang an hour later and there was Mitchell Dawson, big, bad, and Black!

"Hey," she said, grinning. "I almost didn't recognize you with your clothes on."

"That's right. You haven't seen me with clothes on have you. Like what you see?" He was posing and turning around in the foyer.

"Not too bad. Would you like a cocktail before we leave?"

"No thank you, baby, I don't drink during season."

"I wasn't thinking. I'm ready if you are."

"May I say how beautiful you look tonight J-a-a-a-d," he took her hand and turned her around. "Now I know who you look like, what's her name that was Miss America"…

"Yeah, yeah, let's go." She said, opening the door. They walked down the porch steps and there was a white limousine parked two doors down, it moved up in front of the house.

"Your chariot awaits Princess," he said, extending his arm.

"How nice." The driver opened the door and they got in. "Hey Jazz." It was Jill's friend Julius. "Well hello Julius, small world. It's good to see you."

"Would you like a drink Jade? They have a lot of

little bottles of stuff in the bar if you want something." Mitch asked.

"I'll take Zinfandel if there's some."

"Your wish is my command Princess." He poured her drink.

"So Mitchell, tell me how do you like D.C.?"

"From what I've seen so far, I like it better than Denver."

"Is Denver your home, did you grow up there?"

"No, I grew up in Fort Pierce, Florida. I'm sure you've never heard of it, it's a small town."

"No, I haven't heard of it, but I like Florida."

"What's not to like," he said, laughing. "I've been cold ever since I left there. I hear D.C. is rather mild in the winter compared to a lot of cities."

"This is still the South, so it's not so bad most of the time. We have good weeks and bad ones too." They chatted all the way to Annapolis while she drank a couple of glasses of Zin. Jade was trying to get a feel for Mitch since under the circumstances, no one knew him personally. She was pretty buzzed by the time they arrived.

Dinner was very nice. She was enjoying Mitch's company. He had a good sense of humor, and was a pretty good conversationalist, although he could have stood a little help with his social graces. Other than that, he seemed to be a fun person.

Mitch had come from a family that worked the orange groves. His parent's dream was for him to go to college. Football was his ticket out of Fort Pierce. He was very attractive, Six-five, 240 pounds and naturally, the physique of a football player. He was as dark as midnight, and when he smiled, you caught a glimpse of gold somewhere in his mouth.

Dinner was interrupted three times by people who recognized him. Jade thought they would have to get security for one guy who had obviously had too much to drink. He had the nerve to pull up a chair, sit his fat ass down at the table, and talk football. Mitch was polite. He answered questions and remained pretty cool. Jade was annoyed to no end. No matter how many times she cleared her throat, he kept right on talking. By then, she was pissed and her Zinfandel's were taking their effect. She was becoming annoyed with Mitch because he had gotten into a full-fledged conversation about the Defense. He was obviously enjoying the attention. Jade got up and went to the ladies room since it seemed like the man wasn't going to leave, and when she returned, he had gone back to his table.

"So Princess, I hope you're enjoying dinner." Mitch said, smiling.

"Other than that ill-mannered intruder, I think dinner was delicious, the atmosphere and company have been great, the champagne is divine, and I'm probably going to be sorry as hell tomorrow." She said, buzzed.

"Good, I'm glad I can make you happy. I'm going to get you back to D.C. before midnight and our chariot turns into a pumpkin or something. Truth is I need to get back in the house before they do the phone check."

"Oh, so you finally got yourself a phone."

"No, I don't have a house phone yet, they'll probably page me." He explained.

"Mitch, maybe it's the wine, but that makes absolutely no sense to me at all. How do you check somebody on a pager? You could be in Africa and answer your pager." *Jade smelled bullshit!*

He came around the table behind the back of her chair. "Are you ready baby?"

"Yes indeedy—I am ready." She said, sarcastically. She snatched her pocketbook from the floor.

Usually when you're going to a new place, it seems to take forever to get there and only a minute to get back. Not this trip! It took forever to get back into D.C. The trip back was void of conversation and the champagne kept telling her Mitchell Dawson was as full of sh**.

"Princess, you mighty quiet. Do you have some kind of attitude with me?"

"Should I have one with you?" She asked, rolling her eyes in the darkness of the limousine.

"I don't know why you would. So when can I see you again?"

"I really don't know Mitchell. You know how our schedules are," she said, as they approached her house.

"We have away games for the next two weekends, and then we get a week off. Why don't you invite me over and cook some of those collard greens and cornbread you say is your specialty?"

"Why don't you invite me to your house, and I'll cook them over there?"

"That sounds good, but you probably need to bring the pots and pans with you, I don't have any. Oh, bring the dishes and chairs too." He said, laughing.

"No problem, I can do that. Call me when you get back, I'll drive over to Fairfax and thanks for a lovely evening." Jade was trying to open her door before Julius even got out. She was tired of bullshit.

"Whoa, Princess, what's the rush? Let me walk you to your door." She was half way up to her porch before Mitch caught up with her. He grabbed her hand.

"Come on Princess, have I done something wrong?"

"No, I'm just tired—*and drunk*. I need to go in now Mitchell.

"Can I make a pit stop before I ride all the way back out to Virginia?"

HILL FOXES

"Come in," she said, opening the door and pointed to the powder room off the kitchen. *He will not slick-ass his way upstairs to my bed.* When he came out, she was standing at the door with the door knob in her hand.

"Jade, seriously what's wrong?" He asked, softly.

"Mitch, I'm tired and I want to go to bed." He took her hand, pulled her close to him and hugged her gently.

"Jade, I don't know what I did, but I apologize for whatever it was," he whispered. Jade got lost in the power of his big arms and his gentleness. He was warm, and strong, and he felt good. They stood embracing for a moment. She had laid her head on his chest. He reached down and put his finger under her chin and raised her head. She allowed her mouth to relax in preparation for the pleasure of his warm lips, and he kissed the tip of her nose. "Goodnight Princess," he said, and walked out of the door.

"I think you did the right thing Jazz," Wendy told her. "They can be as slick as chicken grease."

"I don't know, Wendy I can't seem to read him. On one hand he seems to be a dog, on the other hand, he's a gentle giant.

"Have you talked with him since?"

"No, but I'm going to call him later when I think he's free, I embarrassed myself. I think I need to apologize, too much champagne girl."

"I'd go with my first instinct. He's probably typical Buckskin Bull!" Wendy said.

"Are we still on for the slumber party?"

"Yep, it's on. I'm excited about all of us getting together. Everybody's coming except Jill.

Later that afternoon Jade dialed Mitch's beeper. He called back. "Yeah."

"Mitch this is Jade. Is this a bad time?"

"No baby, it's cool. I just got off the practice field and I was sitting in the whirlpool thinking about you."

See, there's the bullshit side I don't like. "I called you to apologize for the other night. Will you forgive me? To be truthful, I'd had too much champagne."

"Of course, Princess. As long as *I* didn't do anything to upset you. Miss me baby?"

"Just a little bit," she said, laughing. "Where are you anyway?"

"Buffalo. Am I going to see you when I get back?"

"Sure, don't you remember I'm coming over to Fairfax to cook you collards and corn bread?" She said, teasing.

"Right, we'll talk about that when I get back. I've got to go but I'll call you in a day or so. Stay sweet J-a--a-d-e, and stay out of men's locker rooms," he was laughing. *Click!*

Damn she couldn't figure him out.

EIGHT
WENDY

WENDY LIVED AT the edge of the park in upper Northwest D.C. Her house was typical of the homes in that area, large and majestic with beautifully manicured lawns. The homes there were well kept and the neighborhood was quiet and peaceful.

When Jade drove up to Wendy's, she saw Lauren's Pathfinder and Noel's BMW. She parked at the end of the street and walked back up to Wendy's house. When she got to the porch, the door popped open and they all screamed—"J-a-a--d-e!" Okay, so they'd already been in the booze.

"F-o-x-e-s-s-s," Jade yelled back. They had a group hug and everyone went inside to the basement. Wendy had fried chicken wings, a huge toss salad, deviled eggs, cold slaw, crackers, potato chips, and any kind of junk food you could imagine. Jade looked at the table and shook her head.

"Who the hell, do you think is going to eat this fried, fattening, ass-spreading, artery blocking sh**?"

"You!" Wendy said, looking at Jade.

"Damn right, now where's my plate?" Jade asked, walking over to the table. Noel was in the middle of the floor shaking her butt to Midnight Hour. They all jumped beside her and formed a line and began to sing…

> *I'm gonn'a wait til the Midnight hour,*
> *When my love come tum-ba-lin down,*
> *I'm gonn'a wait til the Midnight hour,*
> *When there's no one else around…..*
>
> …..*Wilson Pickett*

"Can't you just see that fine-ass Snookie Harris dancing to this? He was so fine my panties would be wringing wet when he finished dancing with me." Noel screamed.

"Your panties would be wringing wet if King Kong danced with you slut!" Wendy said. They all laughed.

"Speaking of Snookie, where is he anyway? Has anybody seen him lately?" Noel asked.

"He's where all the good men are around here, in Lorton Prison." Brea said.

"Nooo," Noel whispered. "What a waste of good man."

"Didn't you defend him Wendy?" Brea asked.

"Yeah, they had too much on him. He'll be there for a while. Who wants more wine? "Wendy asked changing the subject. "No one has to drive home, so drink up tramps."

"Did you steal my glass Lauren?" Brea asked, laughing.

"I might have, honey. I'm drinking whatever's near me tonight." Lauren said, slurring.

"Ladies," Wendy said, with her glass raised. "Here's to us, The *Hill Foxes*. We've been together through kindergarten, high school, boyfriends, husbands, hangovers, divorces, fights, and we're still together."

"Here-here", Jade said, raising her glass. "*Hill Foxes.*"

"So, Noel what diamond mine did Marcus get that ring out of, my Lord!" Lauren asked.

"No shiggidy," Brea said. They all huddled around looking at Noel's ring.

"When's the big day?" Jade asked.

"We haven't set a date."

"I didn't know you were engaged Noel." Lauren said.

"It's not exactly something we're shouting from the roof tops," Noel said, softly.

"And why the hell not?" Lauren asked.

"Marcus is still *legally* married. His wife was hospitalized for mental illness, and she checked herself out the facility. He hasn't been able to locate her since." Noel explained.

"What?" Brea asked, astonished.

"Oh, my goodness!" Lauren said. "What are you going to do Noel?"

"Wait. All we can do is wait until he can find her, but until then, I don't tell *everybody* I'm engaged. Marcus isn't interested in too many people knowing either, legally he's committing adultery." Noel told them.

"Damn, to a certain extent she's stolen your joy."

"Needless to say, this stays in the *Foxes Den* ladies," Wendy reminded them.

"Of course." They all said, agreeing.

"So what about your love life Jazz?" Noel asked her.

"I've been seeing Mitchell Dawson lately. Don't know where or if it's going anywhere, but I'm going to give him a shot."

"Wasn't he just traded to the Buckskins this year?" Brea asked.

"Yes. We've actually only had one real date, but we've been getting to know each other on the phone for quite a while now."

"Well good luck with that one," Noel said. "The

Buckskins aren't particularly known for their decency to women. Maybe since he just got here, none of their funk has worn off on him yet." They all laughed.

"And are you currently in love Brea?" Wendy asked.

"Hell no! Not in love—not dating. I'm on that new diet called "Man-fast". She laughed.

"Ditto, the Man-fast diet!" Wendy said, with her nose turned up.

"I'll drink to that," Lauren said. "I got one I'm going to claim on my income tax as a dependent this year. Anybody need a broke-ass *business man*?" Lauren asked. She almost fell.

"All right Lauren, I think it's time you cooled it. Let's feed the alcohol ladies." Wendy started handing out plates and they completely pigged out. After they ate as much as they could, they lay on the floor on big pillows trying to recover.

"Oh-oh-oh! " Noel said. "My song!"

"Have you ever been kissed from head to toe,
"Up your back down to your naaa-vel....

"I love anything the Whispers sing," Noel said.

"You know what I feel like doing? In unison everybody asked "**What Lauren**?"

"Did you ever used to call and mess with people on the phone? That was so much fun."

"Okay you're banned from the bottle b----!" Noel said.

B.J. MAYO

"I know, let's play a game and see how well we really know each other. We're supposed to be tight right?" Wendy asked them.

"Okay, okay I'll start," Lauren said. "Answer this y'all, who did I lose my virginity to?"

"How the hell would we know? When we met you, you were grown!" Noel said. Everybody laughed.

"Oh, that's right," Lauren said, looking pitiful.

"Well, Noel, who did you lose your virginity to?" Brea asked her laughing, because she knew the answer.

"Remember Noonie Nance? Girl, one night we were coming back from the Ballou game and he had his uncle's car. He drove to some dark secluded hole out in Maryland, and we did it in the back seat." Noel confessed.

"And all this time, I thought it was my brother Kevin," Brea said, surprised and confused.

"Oh, it *was* Kevin the *second* time I lost my virginity."

They all laughed at Noel for ten minutes.

"Nonnie Nance?" He was my first too," Wendy said, surprised, "and I know for a fact he was Jill's first too."

"Well just damn! What was he doing, screwing everybody in Wheeler Gardens?" Noel asked.

"No—no," Brea said, holding her hand in the air like she was testifying. "He didn't screw me."

"The little short-dick bastard." Noel said, laughing.

"It was little wasn't it?" Wendy said, and they all burst out laughing.

That hen-party was wild! They all had so much fun being together again. They ended up putting Lauren's drunken butt to bed while they continued to party. Somewhere between laughing and crying, Wendy pulled out some "Oou-wee" and passed it around. Jade was in total shock because she had no idea Wendy even smoked, and they were best friends. That was probably the point of her game. You really don't know people as well as you think.

NINE
NOEL

NOEL CAREFULLY WRAPPED the sandwiches in plastic wrap, and placed them in the basket. She felt a little anxious that morning about meeting the boys, Marcus had been so protective of them, and she understood. He was so absorbed in his work he rarely spent time with Brent and Bryan. Noel planned a fun outing for the day for them.

She glanced in the mirror one more time, making sure she looked presentable, *like little boys would give a hoot about her outfit, she thought.* Just then, the doorbell rang and she peeped out. Marcus, Brent, and little Bryan were there so she opened the door smiling.

"Good morning fellows, come in and make your selves at home."

"Good morning, Miss Noel," Marcus said, pushing the boys inside. "What do you say Brent?"

"Good morning Miss Noel," Brent sang out. Bryan had already spotted Noel's six-foot Giraffe, and made a bee-line straight toward her living room. "Oooooh," he shrieked, running toward it.

"Bryan!" Marcus said, running after him.

"It's okay, he can't hurt it Marcus."

Marcus took his youngest child by the hand, and led him back into the kitchen. "Boys this is Miss Noel, she's going with us to the park today. What do we say Brent?"

"Nice to meet you," he said, shyly.

"It's nice to finally meet you too," Noel told them. "Are we ready for some fun?" She gave Marcus the picnic basket, grabbed her backpack and little Bryan's hand, and they were out the door. Marcus secured the boys in their car seats and they were on their way. The day had been designed to entertain the boys, and to have Marcus spend some quality time with them. Noel thought they needed to see the fun side of their father, outside of their home. When Marcus came home in the evenings, he played with Brent and Bryan for twenty to thirty minutes before dinner, and that was it. After dinner, Mrs. Prince bathed them, got them ready for bed, and they said goodnight to Marcus. That was the extent of their interaction with him on any given day.

Marcus had staked out a place in the park that

was quiet enough for a picnic, but close enough to the amusements. He sat the picnic basket and drinks on the wooden table under the trees, while Noel spread the colorful blanket on the ground. The boys were running around squealing and rolling in the grass, like they had just been freed from state prison. *Poor little things, Noel thought.*

The first thing to go "left" that day was their clothes, they were covered with fresh green grass stains from rolling on the ground, Noel thought Marcus was going into cardiac arrest.

"They're boys Marcus!" The rest of the day consisted of swings, the merry-go-round, cotton candy, orange juice, a *bathroom break*, peanut butter sandwiches and milk, the sliding board, juice boxes, *bathroom break*, popsicles, and *bathroom breaks*.

When the day of fun had ended, Noel said goodbye to Marcus and the sleeping boys in the back of his SUV. She went inside, closed her door and dropped down into her plush sofa. *"My ass is worn out!!"*

TEN
LAUREN

AFTER WENDY'S SLEEP-OVER, Lauren took a few days off. She stood across the street from *Le Loc Salon* snapping pictures of the front. Mustafa wanted to promote his business by advertising in the newspapers rather than relying on their occasional handouts in the neighborhoods. D.C. City Council had passed an ordinance restricting handbills. It had become a litter problem. People snatched the handbills from their car windshields, and threw them in the streets. The ones placed at resident's doors, simply blew away and added to the trash problem in the city.

Lauren finished the shots of the front of *Le Loc* and went inside. She snapped shots of the salon's interior, and a few pictures of the patrons who had agreed to pose for the style shots. Those pictures would go around the walls as well as in the style book. Mustafa let patrons beginning to lock, look at the album for examples of style choices and patterns.

When Mustafa first asked Lauren about the possibility of her doing a photo shoot for him, she explained how her agency worked, and explained the break-down of their fees. "Oh, my!" He shouted. *She knew in advance he couldn't afford it, hell he couldn't afford to support his daily habit of herb.* He asked if she would do the shoot for him on her own. Lauren reminded him that her job at Banks & Shane, and the Washington Post, left her very little time to do his pictures. He asked her if she could possibly do it on her off-time, she agreed. Obviously he didn't understand she worked at the Post *on her off-time.*

Lauren began taking shots of Haaydia, she was such a beautiful woman and her locs were amazing. She was the quiet type, and always professional. Haaydia went back to the kitchenette and invited Lauren back. "I'm about to take a little break," she said. She pulled out rice, spinach and plantain from the refrigerator. "Would you have some?" She asked Lauren.

"No, thank you. I'll get lunch later."

"Ah, don't wait too long, we have to keep our temples nourished my Sister." She smiled.

"You're a vegetarian or a Vegan?" Lauren asked.

"I'm not sure if I fall into any particular category, I eat what makes my body feel good. Something to drink Sister?" Haaydia asked Lauren.

"I have water, thank you. I've been able to get what I think are pretty good shots inside and out. I told Mustafa that advertising was very expensive. I'm not sure if he can afford to have ads placed in the Post, we're talking thousands of dollars."

"I know." Haaydia shook her head, and smiled.

"Personally," Lauren said, "I'd go with advertising in the neighborhood publications. You'd be surprised how many people they reach. There are dozens of them all over town. It would be less expensive, most of them are free."

"I know," Haaydia said, swallowing her coconut milk. "Mustafa thinks big," she said, laughing. "He just has the salon's best interest at heart. He tries."

Six months had passed since Lauren and Mustafa had tea at the Harambee House, and she was gettin' it on the regular now. They had fallen into a comfortable kind of life. Most nights when she didn't work late, he came by for dinner. He loved to relax in her lounge chair by the TV while she cooked. She poured him a glass of Chablis and went back to the kitchen to turn over the smothered pork chops on the stove. She was telling Mustafa about the new job she'd been assigned. The Air Force was launching a recruiting campaign, and she would be doing the photography for it at the Pentagon.

"Mustafa, please go out on the balcony to smoke that." Lauren had complained more than once about his smoking in her house, it got into her clothes.

"Should I roll you one Lauren?" He asked, her pulling the patio door open.

"No, Mustafa. I told you it's not something I do *daily* like you, I only smoke on occasion, I don't have anything against smoking weed, I just don't do it that often."

"I understand. By the way this is the last of it. Think you can get with Rasheed tomorrow?"

"I don't know, Mustafa. I don't like dealing with him, he makes me uncomfortable. And since we're on the subject, are you going to pay me back for the last *four* times I got something from him?"

"Sure I am. It's just so hard for me to get away from the salon to score during the day." He explained.

What does getting away from the salon have to do with paying me my money back, she wondered.

"Score before you get here then," she said, annoyed.

"I'm sorry Lauren, I'll try to do better from now on," he said, then kissed her. They ate smothered pork chops, mashed potatoes, string beans and cornbread for dinner.

They snuggled up close in bed after dinner, and he made passionate love to her. "I hope you're not angry with me My Queen, I don't ever want to do anything to make you unhappy. You *are* my world." Mustafa told her kissing her lips.

What had become part of their pattern or routine, was the fact that Mustafa made it a habit to go home before eleven o'clock. He wanted to be fresh for his patrons the next day. He showered, took a fresh T-shirt from the drawer, put on his pants and Dashiki, and she walked him to the door.

"You mean the world to me Lauren. Sleep tight and be safe." He gave Lauren a deep passionate kiss.

"Don't forget to catch Rasheed tomorrow,"

ELEVEN
JADE

THE MONDAY AFTER the slumber party, Mitch called Jade at work. "Hey baby, how's my Princess today?"

"I'm bogged down as usual. Are you back from Buffalo?"

"Not yet, we get into BWI tonight around seven. Whatch'a doin' later?" He asked her.

"Later like when?"

"I guess about eight, eight-thirty. Instead of driving all the way back out to Virginia tonight, I thought I'd just stay at the BWI Marriott. You could meet me out there for dinner, how's that sound?"

"Uh-huh, I guess I can."

"Good, I'll call you when we land." *Click*!

Jade was trying on clothes in her head. At least she could be casual. Anybody there on a Monday would more than likely be travelers. She went home, showered, put on her Ellen Tracey slacks and matching sweater with boots. The phone rang.

"Hey baby I'm on the Fifteenth floor, 1502. On your way?"

"On my way." She jumped in her Beamer, popped in some Luther, and headed out South Dakota Avenue to the BW Parkway. That time of night, it should only take her forty-five minutes or so, she estimated.

She pulled into short-term parking and walked into the high rise hotel. "Knock-knock, room service." She said. She playfully stuck her thumb over the peephole. Mitch cracked the door and peeped out like he really expected room service. "Princess," he said, opening the door all the way. They hugged for a minute, "I missed you baby."

There he goes again! "You know Mitch I can't imagine why you miss me so much. We haven't spent that much time together yet."

"I knew when I first saw you, I was going to be crazy about you baby."

"I hope we can get to know each other better Mitch, but do me a favor, let's be honest with each other. I *hate* bullshit!" She said, walking to the sofa.

"I ain't gonn'a bullshit you baby, I promise. I hope you don't mind having dinner here in the suite, I don't feel like being bothered with people tonight. There's plenty of wine here in the bar if you want some."

Jade was getting a strange vibe from Mitch. She couldn't put her finger on it, just strange. He seemed kind'a funky or something. "I'd like something *non*-alcoholic, are there sodas there?" She asked, not wanting to repeat the disaster of their first date.

"If you want a soda, I can go down the hall to the machine, but I'm not breaking the seal on this bar just for a damn soda," he snapped.

"Excuse me?" she asked, irritated by his manner.

"That refrigerator bar has $300 worth of liquor in it, once I break the seal on it, everything in there is mine."

"I see." She said, calmly reaching over and snatching the seal off the refrigerator. *You just bought me a $300 soda bitch, she said to herself.* "So Mitch how was the trip?" She asked, popping the soda top. He just looked at her.

"Do I really need to tell you how it was? Didn't you see the game?"

"Actually, I didn't catch it, sorry."

"It was shit. I played like shit, that's how it was. I've had enough grief from the damned media and coaches for one night! I don't wann'a talk about it."

Woops, guess I pulled the wrong chain, she thought. Brea got up and walked out to the balcony. "Chilly night."

"What did you do while I was away baby?" *Snap heee's back*!

Attempting to pacify him, Brea ignored his offensive attitude. "I've just been working hard. I haven't had a chance to tell you about my offer to anchor the noon news." They sat down on the sofa and she told him all about it.

"That's good news. I'm happy for you. That's a step up right?"

"I guess it would be."

"Are you okay coming out of the sports department?"

"I've never been interested in being on that side of the camera before, too much politics, game playing and back stabbing. All I ever wanted was to do my job, get my pay check, and go home."

"I heard that. I'm proud of you Princess, I'm sure you can handle it," Mitch said, looking off into space. The room got silent. She felt his tension. She felt his distance even though he was trying to hide it. Jade guessed the game loss was causing it. She reached behind him and began messaging his neck. He closed his eyes, and she could feel the muscles in his neck ease up a bit.

"Umm, that feels good," he whispered. She got up and walked behind the sofa to begin messaging his shoulders. For some reason, Jade was getting turned on herself, he had the perfect body. His smell was intoxicating, his skin was as Black and smooth as velvet.

She let her hand slide inside his shirt and she began rubbing his chest, resting her chin on the top of his head. "Umm," he moaned. "You know what I think?" he whispered.

"What do you think?" She asked breathlessly.

"I think you're about to get yourself in some serious trouble," he said, removing her hand from his shirt.

Damn! She thought.

"You want another drink?" He asked her, getting up.

"No, thank you," she said, getting up too and going to the balcony.

"Jade, I'm sorry. I'm trying to clear my head and take my game-face off, it's hard. Bear with me please."

"It's okay, I understand." She felt sorry for him.

"I'm going to do something I never do this time of year." He opened the refrigerator bar and poured himself a glass of Pinot Grigio. They talked for a long while about college, people, nothing really. Jade could sense that he was relaxing. "Hungry?" He asked her?"

"I guess I could eat something."

He gave her the menu. "Tell me what you want, and I'll call downstairs."

Later, their Lobster dinners were brought into the suite's dining room. Mitch and Jade had an interesting discussion about D.C. politics. When they had finished dinner, he turned to HBO to watch "48 Hours". He put his arm around Jade and gently kissed her on her forehead, eyelids, and her throat. He gave her a kiss of passion, Jade felt herself melting. He grabbed her hand and led her toward the master bedroom. It would have been the right time for her to turn and run, but she let that pivotal moment pass. He stood back and observed her beauty. "My magnificent Princess," he whispered. He undid her hair and it fell to her shoulders. Jade shivered at his gentle touch as he pulled her to the king-size bed. She was amazed at how someone so big, could be so gentle. "We shouldn't do this yet," she whispered, but her body said otherwise. "It's okay baby, it's okay."

TWELVE
BREA

BREA SAT ON a stool inside the old warehouse on Florida Avenue near City Market. "Ice", the backup band on her two CD's, was rehearsing for an upcoming engagement. Reggie Ricks invited Brea to make an appearance with them for a show they were booked to do at Constitution Hall. They were opening for Frankie Beverly & Maze. Since their semi-retirement from recording, they had all decided to stay in D.C., and make appearances to open for the hundreds of entertainers that came through D.C. during the year. Brea and "Ice" had hit the music scene big with two CD's that had skyrocketed to the top, and a gold record. The breakup of their association with the famous record label Natural Element sent them packing back to D.C. from Los Angeles.

While Brea and "Ice" were out on tour, Reggie became Brea's confidant and protector during her ordeal with Melik Iverson, and fell in love with her. She saw Reggie as her friend and big brother. He understood she wasn't ready to jump back into a relationship, be it with him or anybody else, so he didn't press the issue. Melik had hurt her deeply and Reggie would continue being her good friend, he was willing to wait.

They rehearsed for three hours going over some of the songs from the first CD *Come with Me*. Reggie, the group's leader, thought they should make Brea's title cut from the CD one of the three songs they were being allowed to perform. Everybody knew it, everybody loved it, and it had made gold.

"So Brea when do you think you might start recording again?" Reggie asked. They had come to her house after rehearsal and were in her kitchen eating sandwiches Reggie picked up from Potomac Fish house on Rhode Island Avenue.

"I'm not sure, but I think I'll know when the time is right." Brea answered, softly.

"Yeah, I know what you mean. Damon is being real good about giving us our space right now."

"We're blessed," Brea said. "He's one of the best agents in the world, we're lucky to have him. He *is* being very patient with us all," she said, wiping hot sauce from her lips.

"Do you ever hear from his majesty Melik?"

"Yes," she said, taking in a deep breath. "I don't know why he insists on calling here, I have nothing to say to him in fact, I hate him."

They talked about their experience with Melik, she despised talking about that. She was trying to get him off her mind and out of her heart. Reggie thought if he got her to talk about it as much and as often as he could, she might talk her pain away.

Brea and Reggie finished their sandwiches and beer and began listening to some new music Reggie bought.

"I meant to ask you if you wanted to see a movie later," Reggie asked.

"I'm having dinner at my mom's tonight. You want to come with?"

"I'd like that." He'd go anywhere to be in her presence. "Do you think she'll mind if I come?"

"When my mother cooks, she cooks for the whole village." They laughed.

An hour later, Brea and Reggie pulled up at Brea's mother Connie's on 20th and Queens Chapel. Connie loved to cook, and loved feeding people. Connie had also invited Brea's brother Kevin and his girlfriend. Connie served them fried chicken of course, potato salad, Turnip greens, barbequed pigs feet, Croker, macaroni and cheese, rolls, her famous sweet potato pie, and it was only Wednesday.

"Miss Connie!" Reggie shouted. "Who did you fix all this food for?" Brea hadn't exaggerated.

"She cooks like this all the time," Brea said, laughing before Connie could respond.

"Awh baby," Connie said. "It ain't much, just somthin' I threw together right quick."

Brea's brother Kevin and his girlfriend Destiny ate like they were disciples at the Last Supper.

"Y'all eat up now," Connie said. Brea's mother had a rough time raising Brea and her four brothers in Wheeler Gardens. She basically did it alone on a cook's salary. Brea's father, Chauncey, left them when they were young, and never supported his five children. Connie was a tough woman though. She did it by herself.

"Miss Connie," Reggie said, wiping his mouth, "this is the best meal I've had since I can't even remember."

"Thank you baby, now get som'a dat pie." After dinner, Brea and Reggie left Connie's to go back to her house. A fan of Brea's recognized her getting into Reggie's truck.

"Hey! Brea Sharee! When you gon' drop another record baby?" He asked, grinning.

"Pretty soon," she said, smiling, "pretty soon."

When Brea and Reggie got back to her house, they drove up in front and parked, Reggie cut off the truck. "Brea, I'm not going to beat around the bush anymore. You know how I feel about you, and I'm not bringing this up to put any pressure on you. I know you've been hurt. I hate like hell you had to go through that bullshit with Melik. It was hard for me too, especially since I had to helplessly stand by and watch it happen. You don't know how bad I wanted to bust his ass up!" Reggie said, biting his lip.

"You know what I'm thankful for?" She asked. "I'm thankful you were there to have my back Reggie," Brea said, patting his thigh. "As for us?" I love you, but I love you like I love my brothers. Your friendship means the world to me Reggie. I wouldn't want us to mess that up."

"I understand. I just want you to know that I'm here." He walked Brea to her door. She invited him in but he declined. "Thanks for inviting me for dinner," Reggie said, hugging her. She tip-toed up to give him a little *"I hope I didn't hurt your feelings"* kiss, and he gently gave her the deepest, most loving kiss she'd had for a while. She looked at him for a moment, wrapped her arms around Reggie and kissed him back. "Brea Sharee Jones," he whispered, "You know I love you girl."

THIRTEEN
JADE

AFTER HAVING SPENT an emotionally crazy evening with Mitch at the BWI Marriott, the rest of Jade's week was loaded with work. She received a call from Kirk Rucker in Brathwell, about coming down to take care of some of her aunt Judith's affairs. She contacted Keith to let him know she was coming, and would stay the weekend through Monday. He had promised her after the funeral, he would take care of the house and the property until things were settled. Friday evening after leaving the station, Jade jumped into her Beamer and headed south. Keith said he would ready the house for her and would be there when she arrived, she arrived just before nightfall.

"Jazz, it's good to see you." Keith said, hugging her.

"It's good to see you too Keith," she said, smiling.

"I really want to thank you for helping me out. I can't possibly take care of things here and be in D.C. at the same time," she followed him into the house.

"I think you'll find everything in order," he said. Buddy can stay here in the house with you tonight if you want. He really misses your aunt and this house. I play hell getting that dog out of here when I close up."

"I can just imagine," Jade said, rubbing Buddy's head. Keith and Jade talked about the upcoming meetings with the lawyers and with Kirk Rucker, who would be handling the sale of the properties. They both decided to turn in early and start out fresh the next day. The next morning, Keith woke Jade and told her to throw on some clothes so he could show her some of the properties before meeting Kirk. She put on jeans, a T-shirt and sandals. "Why don't I stop by some of our old haunts on the way, I can show you how things have changed around here." Keith said. He was a handsome man, she thought looking at him. He was wearing a pair of walking shorts, a white T-shirt, sandals and Versace sunglasses. It was a long stretch from the white-sock wearing—daddy's pickup truck driving—country boy back in the day. She laughed thinking about it.

"What's funny?" He asked her.

"Just thinking about something," she said, smiling

as he drove her through the countryside in his Silver Benz. Keith began pointing out all of the things that were different since they were teenagers. "Everything's changed" he said, "with the exception of one thing." He pulled off the main road and down the winding path to what had been their secret place. It was the place they had secret picnics, the place he had given her a friendship ring and promised her he'd always be hers—*right*! The sign on the road said "No Trespassing".

"Oh, our secret swimming hole Keith!" Jade said, excited. "Won't we get in trouble being here?"

"I doubt that very seriously," he said, smiling. "It's mine now. I bought this lake and all the land around it—it's now called Lassiter Lake.

"No!" Jade was surprised.

"Yes. After all the mess going on around here in the county, property gouging, crooked land deals, and the worse, taxing these poor farmers out of their land, I had to do something. People are coming down here buying up the property and misusing it. We probably have more shopping and strip malls than we have people. This is my birthplace, this is my home, and I'll protect it until I die.

"Keith this is unbelievable!" Jade said. "I'm thinking about all the times we came here for our secret picnics. Do you remember Aunt Judith's chicken and potato salad baskets? I swore the only reason you brought me here, was so you could eat." They laughed.

"Believe it or not, you're the only one I ever shared this place with. This was, and still is, a very special place to me Jazz. You want to stay here on the lake for a while?"

"Yeah, and I just bet you happen to have a blanket like you always did." She said, looking at him suspiciously. "I could never figure out why you always had a blanket in the back of that old truck." She teased.

"Remember, you wouldn't sit on it and accused me of using the blanket for our horses and pigs?" He said, falling out laughing.

"Yes, yes!" Jade was laughing. "I didn't know where that nasty little blanket had been." Keith opened the trunk of his Benz and pulled out a blanket **and** a picnic basket.

"No! When did you do this?" She asked surprised. Keith spread the blanket on the ground and put the basket down. He took a white linen napkin and put it across his wrist and bowed. "Mademoiselle s'il vous plait." Jade sat on the blanket and took her sandals off. He placed two beautiful china plates, two crystal goblets, linen napkins and the most exquisite silverware she'd ever seen, onto a laced tablecloth over the blanket. He then brought from the trunk, two covered dishes that matched the china filled with chicken, potato salad, rolls and slightly chilled Merlot.

"Shall we dine?" He asked, smiling that kill-a-woman smile. "Now I can't make you eat, but I slaved over a hot stove all morning to fix this." He said, laughing.

"This is beautiful Keith, thank you." They ate, laughed and talked about old times when they were kids. He had his car CD on, and they listened to Abby Lincoln while they enjoyed the hypnotic sounds of Brathwell County's crickets, and the thick fragrance of honey suckles. It was taking Jade back to a place she had almost forgotten.

"I used to enjoy coming here Keith," she said. Ducks flew by and landed in the water.

"So how's your life been Jazz? I hope you've been happy. I've kept up with most of your accomplishments through your Aunt Judith."

"I'm happy, I have a good job, good friends and yes, I'm pleased with my life so far."

"So why haven't you ever married, if I may ask?"

"I've basically been concentrating on advancing my career, just haven't given it that much effort." Jade said, watching the ducks.

"I'm surprised a woman such as you, beautiful, successful and living in D.C., hasn't been snagged up yet."

"I'm not marriage bound, but I am seeing someone."

"Serious?" He asked.

"I think so. At least I think it's heading in that direction. We have our days."

"I understand he's a football player."

"Mitchell Dawson. He plays for the Buckskins and we met when I interviewed him." She said, wondering how the hell he knew about Mitch.

"Football player." Keith mumbled under his breath.

"Something's wrong with that?" Jade asked, defensively.

"I hope not, for your sake. I just know football players."

"You should," she said, annoyed at his inference.

"Jazz be careful, that's all I mean."

"What should I be careful of, lies? Should I be careful because he might not keep his promises? Should I be afraid he might run off with some little White gold-digging bitch, get married and forget about me?" Jade had snapped, and it may have been the wine, but all the hurt and resentment she had held inside toward Keith had surfaced from *somewhere* after all those years. Jade didn't even know it was there.

"Jaazzz! Slow down, where's that coming from?" Keith asked, shocked.

HILL FOXES

"I'm sorry Keith, I don't know. Maybe I don't need any more wine. I didn't mean to bad-mouth your wife."

"My *ex*-wife, I'm sorry if I upset you. I just know what goes on in the lives of ball players, I lived it."

Silence hung on the heavy air for a while as they watched the ducks playfully fly into and out of the water.

"Jazz, I'm sorry if I hurt you," Keith said, softly. "It was so long ago. I didn't intentionally hurt you, I loved you. I just got caught up in that life. Here I was, a poor country boy in college, hadn't been out of Brathwell but a few times, and I suddenly had all of this attention. Girls were coming out the woodwork, all kinds and yes, I was flattered to have the attention of the White ones too. They had always been taboo, and they loved my dirty socks. They ran after me like you would *not* believe. They did my term papers, bought me clothes and jewelry, anything I wanted. Now Jazz to a poor country boy that was mind-boggling!

"Once I was drafted into the NFL, all hell broke loose. The competition between women got fierce. I was like a hot piece of meat on the bidding block and yes, I made the *conscience decision* to go to the highest bidder. They had the sense to know I was going to be somebody one day and by then, I had learned to play the game. If I married money, it would put me where I needed to be, and that's just what I did, Jazz. I guess you can say, I sold my soul to the highest bidder, and I'm not proud of that now. The woman I married was not a gold-digger as you said, bitch maybe, but her family had ties to the Bulls franchise and I figured that was my ace in the hole. I wanted it that bad Jazz and you know the sad part? Love had absolutely nothing to do with it. Being married didn't stop me or the women, if anything it got worse.

After my injury, they let my contract run out and the Bulls management acted like they had never heard of me before. I was no longer an asset to them. My teammates acted like I had a contagious disease they might catch, and my lovely wife suddenly couldn't stand the sight of me. She filed for divorce, charged me with desertion and took my daughter. All of the so-called friends I had helped with my money buying cars, co-signing for loans—all vanished and that's what hurt the most. I'm not able to be in my daughter's life, the family took care of that. I choose not to see my daughter right now, but I love my daughter. Maybe when she's older, she'll understand why I didn't fight for her. I stay away from her because I don't want Kaila confused by the fighting and trust me, there would be fighting. Her grandparents are high-profile old New York money. The publicity alone would be a media circus.

"I don't know what you've read or heard, but Brooke and I had a pre-nuptial agreement, the only thing I truly lost was my daughter. I invested my money wisely, and I deliberately placed everything in my father's name. Brooke or nobody else could touch it. It took me a while to consolidate my assets but basically, I'm comfortable.

You weren't in that kind of world Jazz, I'm sorry if I'm offending you, but I know that world and I can't see you in it. I don't want to see you become another victim of it, football has many victims. I don't know how deep your feelings are for Mitchell and I'm not asking, what I *am* asking is that you be careful. I care too much for you to see you hurt Jazz."

Jade sat slowly taking in what Keith had said and she felt depressed.

"I'll admit there are times when I doubt him," she said. "I don't completely trust him, but that could be the same even if he weren't a ball player."

"Sure it could, I just ask that you consider what I've said." Keith told her.

"Oh, I do understand what you're saying Keith, I'm in a lot of locker rooms doing my job. I've seen how aggressive those women are."

"Who's going in first?" Keith asked, smiling that kill-a-woman smile.

"Going in where?" Jade asked him, confused. Keith scooped her up from the blanket and threw her into the lake!

FOURTEEN
JILL

JILL'S FLIGHT FROM Los Angeles touched down at Hartsfield-Jackson in Atlanta, Jill was dead on arrival! *Why, oh why, do passengers insist on bringing toddlers on cross-county flights—Ugh!*

Jill's plan had been to deadhead back to D.C., but Clark begged and pleaded with her to lay over in Atlanta.

Clark Tynes was a Mechanical Engineer for Eastern Airlines. He was tall with a medium complexion, sparkly eyes, a sexy physique, and he wore a clean-shaven head. Clark waited outside the terminal for Jill to come out. His wipers swished away at the raindrops beading up on the window. He jumped out of his BMW when he saw Jill, and escorted her back to the car under his umbrella.

"Jill, welcome back," he said, taking her bag.

"Hi, Clark." Jill slid into his car.

"We're having a few showers this morning, they'll be over soon," he said, pulling onto the interstate. "How are you? It's good to see you."

"I'm tired as hell. I worked all the way back from L.A." Jill was yawning.

"I'm glad I could get you to stay over. I haven't seen you in a while."

"I'm giving you fair warning Clark, I'm not going to be good company, all I want to do is go to bed."

"Don't worry I'm going to take good care of you." They sped down the highway a short distance, and then exited at the Westin-Airport Hotel in Riverdale. Clark had a suite already reserved for Jill's visit. They took the elevator to the suite and went inside. Clark poured her a glass of pink champagne. He had arranged for room service to draw a pink champagne-bubble bath, with pink rose pedals, in the Jacuzzi. "I want you to get out of that uniform and take a relaxing bath," he said. "I'll be here when you get done. Take your time, and enjoy."

"Um, that sounds good." She went into the master bath room, took her clothes off and slid her aching body into the warm bath. The water jets gently flowing, the relaxing effects of the champagne, and the soft music coming from the system, took her to the place she needed to be. When she had finished, she emerged with just a tad more energy than when she entered. Jill wrapped her smooth Mocha body in the luxurious hotel robe, and went into the master bedroom. To her surprise, she was greeted there by a masseuse who invited her to the massage table for a full-body message. That was an incredible experience.

"Now you can eat." Clark said smiling, as he rolled a food cart into the room after they were done. He joined Jill for the ham, sausage and grits, biscuits, coffee, tea and orange juice breakfast.

"You've outdone yourself this morning Mr. Tynes, this is pure extravagance." Jill was smiling at him.

"My next gift to you this morning is the gift of sleep." He was patting the huge bed. He pulled back the covers and she got in. "I'm going to leave to run a few errands, but I'll be back later." He gave her a warm kiss.

"I must already be dreaming," she said, laughing. Clark closed the master suite bedroom door and left. Jill buried her head in the soft feather pillow and within seven minutes, she was sound asleep.

Several hours later, she awoke and sat at the edge of the bed. Her feet sunk into the soft plush carpet. She opened the bedroom door and found Clark watching the news out in the living room.

"Good afternoon," she said, stretching.

"Good afternoon to you, Jill. Are you rested?"

"I feel a whole lot better than when I got here. Thank you very much." She sat next to him.

"Are you hungry? Can I get you anything?"

"I'm okay for now. I could use some of that Cranberry juice."

"I'll get that for you." Clark brought Jill an iced glass of Cranberry juice.

"Ah, this hits the spot," she said, letting the cool liquid trickle down her parched throat.

"I sure have missed your smiling face," Clark said, pulling Jill closer. He kissed her cold lips, kissed her throat, and gently pulled the belt away from her robe to kiss her breasts. Clark picked Jill up and carried her into the master bed room and took his clothes off.

"This is my last gift to you today," he said, and then he made adoring love to her.

Two hours later, Jill watched head lights from passing cars streak by out of the car window.

"I really appreciate my day of gifts Clark. I needed it, especially the last one." Jill said, squeezing Clark's arm on the steering wheel.

"I'm glad you enjoyed them. Are you sure you won't change your mind, please?"

"I wish I could, but I've got to catch this last flight back to D.C. tonight." When they got to the terminal, he helped her out of the car and gave her a deep kiss. "I miss you already Jill." He whispered.

"Thanks again for my special day. I'll see you the next time."

She walked through the terminal thinking about Clark. It seemed to her, he was getting more serious than they had agreed on. She had been as up front with him in the beginning as everybody else—*"You're my in town guy when I'm in town Clark, there's nothing beyond this."*

Jill boarded the Eastern Shuttle, stuck her head in the cockpit and had a little conversation with the Captain, then took her place in the jump-seat. She was dead-heading back so she planned to sleep all the way home.

FIFTEEN
LAUREN

LAUREN USED THE rest of her days off to finish the pictures she had taken for Mustafa. She and Haaydia were in the kitchen looking at the proofs. "Very impressive," Haaydia said to Lauren. "How long have you been a photographer?"

"Eight years. I started out free-lancing, until I was hired by The Banks & Shane Studios. I freelance now for the Washington Post's Style section part-time."

"Have you ever thought of opening your own studio?" Haaydia asked Lauren.

"I've thought about it over the years, but I don't know if I have the courage to take that risk. I *know* I'm going to have a paycheck *every* Friday. I like that feeling."

"Oh, you can do it my Sister, it's not so bad. If you were to own your own studio instead of working for

SIXTEEN
NOEL

NOEL REMOVED HER lunch tray from the cafeteria table in the District Courthouse basement. She was thinking about the outing she'd had with Marcus and his sons Brent and Bryan, at the amusement park. They had worn her tail out that day she thought smiling, and if that was any indication of what lay ahead, she'd need to step up her game and get into shape—fast!

She felt accepted now that Marcus had finally invited her into that part of his life. He was so protective of those children. She didn't see how he could exclude her if he intended her to be his wife, and a mother to those boys.

Noel walked out front of the building to one of the vendor's carts to buy a vanilla ice cream cone, and get some fresh air. Being cooped up inside that building nine hours every day was confining, especially on beautiful days. She was eating her ice cream and watching the sights of D.C., when who should rush pass her but Eliot Roberts, Wendy's ex. *Repulsive dog!*

Noel checked her watch, and then went back inside for her next case. This would be one of those days when she and Marcus would be in the same courtroom.

The court was called to order, Judge Reynolds was seated. Marcus immediately asked to approach the bench. He asked Judge Reynolds to recluse him from the case because of conflict of interest. One of the defendants was his wife, Lila Holbrook! *There she was!* Marcus' estranged wife Lila. Judge Reynolds granted the request, and the case was continued. Noel could see the look of despair on Marcus' face. He quickly glanced at her on his way from the courtroom.

Where had Lila come from? Why had she been arrested? Noel couldn't wait to talk to Marcus, but of course, she couldn't do it there.

That evening, after a grueling day, Noel drove her BMW out of the parking garage and headed home. Her head had been whirling with curiosity all day about Lila's case, but she never had time to read it, she'd had back-to-back cases. As soon as she got into the house, she heard the phone ringing.

"Noel," Marcus said, "I'm on my way over." He must have been close; he was there in five minutes. He came in and kissed her.

"Marcus, what's going on?"

"It seems like Lila has been in the area all this time! All this time, and I thought she was back in Virginia. That's where my investigator has been concentrating his search. She and two other residents of some women's shelter near 6th Street in Northeast were arrested for disorderly conduct. They've been hanging out in front of Woodies on F Street, panhandling. The customers have been complaining, so the manager called the police. They put up a scuffle and refused to move. Lila hit one of the officers with a bottle, and they were all arrested.

"How did you get that case anyway?" Noel asked, pouring him a glass of Sherry.

"Doing Art Spencer a favor. He was their court appointed lawyer but his mother-in-law died, he had to fly out to Columbus. It's funny," Marcus said, staring at the floor, "how fate presents itself. If it weren't for Art's emergency, I may never have found Lila." He downed the Sherry. "I need something a little stronger than this honey," Marcus told Noel. She poured him some Cognac.

"Marcus do you think she's better? She didn't do anything bizarre in the courtroom today."

"I don't think she even realized who I was," he said. "I went straight to the bench, she might have thought I was Art, she could only see my back."

Jill and Marcus talked about how he planned to proceed now that he knew where she was. He wasn't sure if it was wise for him to go to the shelter, or to have his investigator make the contact with her.

Noel was beginning to see a ray of hope in their future now. Maybe her luck was finally beginning to change, and Marcus could soon be free.

SEVENTEEN
WENDY

WENDY MET JADE in Chinatown for lunch.

"Girl, where *have* you been?" Jade asked Wendy.

"I'm here and there, why you miss me?" Wendy asked, biting into an egg roll.

"You're not even returning my phone calls Wendy, what's going on with you hussy?" She asked, concerned.

"I've been so busy Jazz, it's not funny. I've been swamped at work I spend most of my time in court."

"And you don't have time to even return a call to your best friend, damn. I think you're burying yourself in work on purpose. Now we both know, all work and no play makes Wendy an evil bitch." Jade said, laughing.

"True, but I'm going to do better, I promise."

"Now get mad if you want, but I think you *are* deliberately burying yourself in work so you don't have to face the Eliot thing. Is that what you're doing Wendy?"

Wendy took a deep breath and waited until the waitress left the table. "Maybe I am, and it doesn't help that I have to see him at work every day."

"How do you feel when you see him? Have you two talked?" Jade asked.

"No. I won't let him near me. He's called three times this week alone. I have nothing to say to him Jazz."

"You know Wendy, maybe you should speak to him, and you need closure. You just walked away without saying anything after you saw him with his family. Don't you want the satisfaction of telling him off about his sorry-ass? "

"Maybe you're right and yes, I'd love jumping into him." Wendy said frowning.

"Do it!" Jade said.

Jade and Wendy finished lunch and went window shopping, one of their favorite sports.

The next day, Wendy's phone rang after she left court. She was in the parking garage and had climbed into her car, ready to head back to Whitted & Whitted. It was Eliot. She looked at the phone and decided by the fourth ring, to answer him. "Hello."

"Hello," a voice said, from outside her window. Eliot was standing at her car.

HILL FOXES

"Are you stalking me?" Wendy's eyes were blazing like flames.

"No, Wendy, I'm not stalking you." Eliot said.

"What do you want?" She gave him a vengeful look.

"Why have you just walked away? Why won't you answer my calls?"

"What the HELL do you think?"

"Wendy, I miss you." He whispered.

"You are lower than creek scum to me Eliot Roberts…"

"Wendy…."

"Don't Wendy me." Her lips turned into a smirk. "Carry your sorry ass home to your wife and children, liar! You laid in MY bed, looked in MY face, and lied to me. Stay away from me Eliot Roberts!" She started her car, pulled up her window, and drove away leaving him standing in the garage.

EIGHTEEN
BREA

BREA AWOKE TO the sound of the Monastery bell ringing in the distance. She opened her eyes and smiled, wondering what the new day would bring. Carefully, she removed the heavy arm that had temporarily trapped her beneath the covers. Brea put on a robe, and went downstairs to start a pot of coffee. She put water in her tea kettle and turned on the stove. While she waited, she gazed out of the kitchen window and began to think about how her life was changing. It had seemed like only yesterday, she was deeply in love with Melik Iverson. Brea gave up her esteemed career as a model in order to pursue her life-long dream to sing, and Melik did make that happen for her. At twenty-nine she had already enjoyed prominence in the international world of fashion. She had recorded two CD's, had a gold record, and finished a cross-country concert tour that sold out to record crowds. Despite all of these impressive accomplishments, people would be stunned to know this seemingly successful woman, underneath it all, was an insecure, psychologically damaged, troubled soul who was constantly haunted by nightmares of her childhood. The dreams manifest themselves whenever she was extremely tired or stressed. She felt she had never truly been happy in her life, something was missing.

The teapot whistled loudly breaking into the silence of the morning, and her thoughts. Brea made a cup of tea with honey and lemon, and then poured hot coffee into another cup. She grabbed the tray and went back upstairs.

"Good morning," she said smiling.

"Umm, good morning," Reggie said, slowly waking. He propped himself up on his elbow.

"It's going to be a beautiful day," Brea said, sliding the drapes open across her window.

"It's already a beautiful day." He took the coffee from the tray and took a sip, "hot-hot!" Brea laughed at him while he went to the bathroom sink and rinsed his mouth.

"Didn't know I was going to need a toothbrush this morning." He said, self-conscientiously.

"I have extras," she said, grabbing a new toothbrush from the cabinet. Reggie and Brea went back and sat on the bed. Reggie sipped his coffee and smiled at her.

"Sitting here with you seems so natural." He was blowing steam away from his cup. "It feels like this is the way it's supposed to be."

"I'm comfortable too Reggie, but I've always been comfortable with you."

"I've prayed for the day that you'd realize how much I care for you. Do you know how much I love you Brea?" He asked, looking deeply into her eyes.

"I do." She said softly, feeling a warm closeness to him. Brea adored Reggie, she loved him, but she wasn't in love with him. And as if he could read her thoughts, he said—

"I'm not kidding myself. I know you're having a difficult time right now, but I'm thankful you're letting me show you what real love feels like. I have enough for the both of us."

Brea reached over and gently kissed his lips. She buried her head in his chest, and he held her. In that tender embrace, she felt his love, security and a sense of peace.

NINETEEN
JADE

TAKING CARE OF her late Aunt Judith's affairs, was more than she anticipated. Jade spent hours with real estate people, lawyers, and bankers. She realized it was going to take many trips to complete her business. Things had probably gone as smoothly as they had, because of Keith. He was directing her to all the right people, and she could see that he was well respected in that community as well,—it was, "Yes Mr. Lassiter, whatever you need Mr. Lassiter."

Convinced that Jade was going to die from malnutrition, Keith took her to dinner in town each night she was there. He invited her to dinner at his house the night before she drove back to D.C., and she was pleasantly surprised. Keith prepared Smoked Salmon topped with Angel Hair pasta, shrimp, and mushrooms with chives and chopped tomato. He served whole string beans braised in butter, and a slightly chilled bottle of Chardonnay. And if that wasn't enough, for dessert he gave her Chocolate Cheese cake with strawberries and whipped cream. They ate in the massive dining room to the glow of candlelight, and the soft sounds of jazz.

"Okay, so who cooked this for you?" She asked Keith.

"I told you I can cook woman, I'm a talented man."

Dinner was an absolute delight and so was Keith's company, Jade was thoroughly enjoying him. After dinner, he filled their glasses and they *retired* to the game room. It was huuuuge, the whole house was huge. It reminded her of a miniature "Tara", from Gone with the Wind. She expected to see Butterfly McQueen running through at any moment.

After his parents were gone, he told her, he bought out his brothers and sisters' shares of the old farm, to have it completely renovated inside and out to his specifications. He added a wondering garden, a tennis court and expanded the stables to accommodate the several show horses he had purchased. *Oh this man has bank!*

The fireplace stretched across the wall with the illusion of a fire. There was large Naugauhide leather sectional seating, and pieces of African art throughout the room. They lay at the fireplace on a thick Bear rug, and drank wine. She was surprised at how easy it was being with Keith. She loved Mitch, but she felt content with Keith, she liked that feeling.

"Excluding the circumstances," he said, "I've really enjoyed being with you these few days. I miss your Aunt Judith. She was a second mother to me. After tomorrow I'm going to miss your being around too."

"I've enjoyed myself, not to mention how thankful I am to have your help. You know, we spent some memorable times together what seems like a hundred years ago. I almost feel like the clock has gone back to that time." Brea said, looking into the fire place.

"Life is strange," Keith said. I wonder how it would have been if we had stayed together?"

"Who knows? Things would surely be different." She said, laughing.

"Seriously," he said, "the selfishness that kept me away from you in the first place is the same selfishness that wants to win you back." He reached over and gave Jade a loving kiss. "I know you have someone in your life, but I want you back in mine."

"Keith…."

"Shhhh." He said, as he kissed her neck. He gently pulled her top over her head and kissed her breasts. Jade felt like embers were smoldering in the pit of her stomach, she tried not to lose control. "Keith," she said pulling away from him. "I don't want to feel what I'm feeling right now." He didn't answer but pulled her back to him, and kissed her a kiss of desire.

"Just feel me." He whispered.

They had never gotten that far before when they were teens. He had said he wanted her as pure as snow on their wedding night—the one that never took place?

"I didn't think I had anything left inside for you," she whispered. "I loved you so much then, but this is now and I'm sorry Keith."

"Don't be sorry Jazz, be a woman."

"I can't do this Keith. I'm involved with someone I care a lot for, and it's not fair."

"What's fair Jazz? Who told you life was fair? What matters is how you feel about me, right here and now."

"I can't." She said, pulling the top back over her head.

Keith got up and poured another drink. "Can I get you another one?" He asked, politely.

"No, thank you. I've had more than I should already. I need to get ready for the drive back tomorrow." She said, getting up from the rug.

Jade thanked Keith for his hospitality and his help again, and he drove her back to Westbury Farm.

Traffic was God awful the next morning. Jade

meant to get back into D.C. earlier, before the gridlock started, but she left Westbury late. She was scared to go out alone in the pitch-darkness at the farmhouse, so she had to cut the porch light on to see. She'd call Keith and tell him to cut it off. She thought about Keith all night. *Please don't let him creep back into my heart*, she prayed.

She couldn't figure out why Mitch wasn't returning her calls or pages, she hoped nothing was wrong. She turned up her speakers and boogied all the way to work. She boogied down 14th Street, boogied to 1st and Massachusetts, headed into the parking lot, threw her hand up at Mike the parking attendant, and ran into the building. "Good morning, everybody." She said grinning.

"Who got some?" Anthony asked, standing at Michelle's desk.

"Not me." Jade said, laughing at him. "What's going on?"

"For one, Bob wants to see you in his office." Michelle told her.

"Thanks," she said, and went into her office first. She dialed Mitch's house and got no answer. She paged him and waited—no response. She went to Bob's office for an update. After meeting with Bob, she called downstairs to the sports desk.

"Daryl aren't you covering the Skins'?"

"Yep."

"Have you been out there lately?"

"Yep."

"Have you seen Mitchell Dawson?"

"I saw him. You know he was benched because of his leg, let's see, he's on injured reserve." Daryl told her.

"Thanks Daryl." Anthony came into her office and gave her kisses on each cheek.

"Hey sugar," he said. "How did everything go down South?" Anthony asked her.

"I got some things done. I've got much more to do though," she said. "Anthony have you been out to the Skins' camp?"

"Uh-huh."

"Did you see Mitch?"

"He was there with some big "thingy" on his leg."

"I haven't been able to catch up with him."

"You didn't hear from him when you were in the country? Anthony asked, surprised.

"No." Jade said, dryly.

"Whaaat? I ain't trying to be in your business or nothing, but that's some triff-lin' dog doo-doo."

"I don't know what's up with him, Anthony."

"Let's talk when I get back. I've got a shoot over at the Mall." Anthony said. "Let's do lunch."

"Later Anthony," she said, taking a swig of her bottled water.

HILL FOXES

Jade loved Anthony, he was a sweetheart. He was her best "girlfriend" on the job, although he didn't work with her anymore since she took the anchor chair. As far as anyone at the station knew, he was as straight as an arrow. He was very careful to stay *well* hidden in the closet. Only in the privacy of friends, was he "herself". Anthony was like any other man around the station. He was five-eight or nine, fair complexion, his hair was relaxed in a very close curl, and he wore his signature diamond studs in each ear. He was super neat, and everything was always in place plus, he smelled good all the time. Anthony was one of the best, and most qualified cameramen on staff.

Jade dialed Wendy's office. Her secretary said she was in court. Jade rocked back in her chair, closed her eyes and thought about Keith. *Don't let him in.* She forgot to call and tell him about the front porch light.

"Keith, this is Jazz. I was scared to go out in the dark this morning, so I packed the car with the porch light on and didn't cut it off." She said. "I also left all of my numbers on the foyer table so you can reach me wherever I am."

"All you had to do was call me if you were afraid this morning Jazz. I'm assuming you got back to D.C. okay?

"Yes, and I'm about to get ready for my show. Thanks for everything again Keith."

"You have a great day Jazz. Think of me once in a while."

Jade hung up and her thoughts remained with Keith. *Don't let him in.* He made her feel so warm, and so comfortable. She thought she made the right decision by not making love with him, Lord knows she wanted to, and that's what was confusing her. She was with Mitch. Where the hell was Mitch anyway?

Her intercom buzzed. "Jade make-up is on the way in, you cool?" Michelle asked.

"Send him in Michelle, thanks."

"Welcome back Jade." David said. "Well I'm just going to get you done and get out of your way. I never have much to do anyway your skin is so beautiful. You haven't been using your lip moisturizer? They're dry!" He said. "I'm going to put some moisturizer on, let it set, and then I'll apply your lip color." David said.

"I guess I've been neglecting my lips, my hair and everything else."

"Nothing we can't fix. He put on a rubber glove, dipped his finger into the solution, and slowly rubbed her lips. *What a sensual feeling she thought.* She closed her eyes and thought of the night before at Keith's in front of the fireplace. *Don't let him in.*

"Jade, why are you so tight?" David asked her. "I can feel it in your face. Do you need Steve to come in?"

"I don't think so."

"I think so, you have enough time. Let him work on you first, then I'll come back and finish." Steve came in and messaged her neck, shoulders, back and temples. He had relaxed her to the point she was almost snoring. By 11:55 Jade was alert, relaxed, and beautiful at the countdown. In 3-2-1—

"Good afternoon. This is News at Noon with Jade Zellmer and Gene Moore...."

After the show, she headed back to her office and found Anthony waiting. "Okay Miss Lady let's go eat. I'm famished, and I want to hear all the dirt."

"What dirt?" She asked. Just then, the intercom buzzed. "Jade the Fed Ex guy is here with a box for you."

"Be a sweetheart Michelle and sign for it, it's probably papers from those lawyers down in Virginia."

"I'll get it for you honey." Anthony said, going out the door. He brought the box back inside the office. "Let's see what this is before we go." Anthony said.

"Nosey ain't you," Jade said, laughing. She opened the box. Inside was a big Russ Teddy Bear holding a card.

Welcome Back! Rusty and I Missed You!
Mitch XXXXX

"Oh how cute," Anthony said, sarcastically. Jade

hurled the bear across the room and grabbed her bag. "Anthony let's roll."

The wait-lines at the restaurants were so long, they went to Union Station to the Food Court.

"I'll be glad when these damn tourists go the hell home," Anthony said, rolling his eyes. There was a table in the corner, they took their trays and sat down.

"Okay, so what's wrong," Anthony asked, "and don't bother to say nothing, 'cause I know you. Is it Mitch?"

"Part of it is, along with some other stuff. I'm really hurt that he isn't returning my calls and thinks he can send me a stupid bear, and that makes it okay."

"You know how I feel about the bitch, so don't even get me started." Anthony said. "What I been meaning to ask you is, who *was* that big juicy piece of chocolate running around at the funeral. You know, the one sitting next to you that couldn't keep his eyes off you?"

"That's Mr. Keith Lassiter," Jade said, laughing. He was my first serious boyfriend, and he's a close friend to the family."

"Ummm-huuum! He was guarding your ass like you had on 24-carat gold bloomers." Anthony said, and snapped his finger.

Jade was laughing. "Anthony you're crazy. He is a sweet man though. He was trying to rekindle our

HILL FOXES

little love-connection while I was there this weekend, but I didn't because of Mitch, you know."

"No, I don't know. "F" Mitch!"

"So, did you give him some?" Anthony asked Jade.

"Anthony!"

"You better give him some, life's too short. We have a little time, let's go upstairs and look in the Shoppes." I need something to wear to the Maze concert this weekend. I can't seem to find anything in my closet that works, and I have a new date taking me," Anthony was grinning. Anthony never talked about his personal life, so Jade found it endearing that he had confided in her. They browsed the Shoppes, oowing and aawing at the new fall fashions. Anthony grabbed Jade's hand and yanked her inside Chardet's Boutique. He walked straight to a Burnt-orange mini-dress by Liz Claiborne, and pulled it off the rack. It had a long multi-colored scarf with colors of orange, yellow and brown.

"This dress is smokin'!! Jade said. "Let me see a six please," she asked the sales woman. Anthony examined the fabric, and then inspected the workmanship.

"Yep, this is worth every dime. You might have to sell your car to get it, but this is nice. I like Liz's shit anyway," Anthony told her. Jade went to the dressing room and came out to get Anthony's opinion. "Is this the bomb or what?"

"It's the bomb! Are you getting' it?" He asked, excited.

"I don't know. I think so, but I'll have to come back. My cards are still in my suitcase in the car." Jade said. "Look at the time, let's get back to the studio.

The long day had finally ended. Jade took North Capitol over to Michigan, and over the Taylor Street Bridge. There was no place like home. She unpacked, and made a cup of Chamomile while she listened to her messages.

Jade, this is Kirk. I spoke with Keith this morning, and I'm going to get started on assessing your properties. If you have any questions, give me a call...."

She dialed Keith's number. "Keith? This is Jazz, how are you?"

"Hey, Jazz, I'm fine." His voice was so delicious!

"I got a message from Kirk. He says he spoke to you this morning?"

"Yes, he's going to start the ball rolling, and by the way, I opened your account today. I gave them your letter authorizing me to act on your behalf. I'm sure there won't be any problems. Most of my large accounts are with them. So how did your day go?"

"Rough is only a mild description. I should have taken today off, but I didn't want to push it."

"So when are you coming home?" Keith asked.

"Home? You mean Brathwell County?"

HILL FOXES

"Exactly."

"I'm going to come as soon as I can, I need to stop and get a grasp of what's happening. My whole life has just changed. It's caught me completely unprepared."

"Have you seen Mitch yet?"

"No." *The question caught her off guard, why did he ask her that?* "Well Keith, I'm going to get settled and ready for bed. I'm mentally and physically drained."

"Dream of me tonight Jazz, I love you." He said, softly.

"Good night, I'll talk to you soon." Did he just say the L word? *Don't let him in.* She went into the den to check her email, and turned on Magic 102.3. "*This is Mike Julius with Magic After Dark.*" Damn his voice was so sexy she could listen to him forever… and a day!

She wondered if she should call Mitch—hell no, obviously he and *Rusty* knew she was back. She dialed Wendy's number.

"What's happenin' stranger?"

"No happs. I was going to call you a soon as I could get a break. I'm working on something, and I'll probably be up all night. Noel has tickets for all of us to the Maze show Friday night, Brea and "Ice" are opening for them. I'd like to support her and I want to see that show anyway."

"I just heard Anthony talking about it today, that should be fun. Is everybody coming?"

"As far as I know. I hear it's sold out, so they'll probably have to add another show. I really don't need to be going anywhere, with as much work as I have, but since the tickets are fr-eee, what the hell."

Jade told her all about her trip to Virginia and how guilty she was feeling for wanting to have sex with Keith.

"Little tramp." Wendy called her, laughing. "And you haven't heard from Mitch yet? Hate to say I told you so."

"Wendy, don't."

"From what you say, you should be financially set for life," Wendy said, changing the subject. "If you invest wisely, and resist going on your non-stop shopping sprees, you should be okay. What I want to know is why are you *still* working, you lucky B."

"I haven't actually sat down and figured out my worth. I guess it hasn't hit me yet, Wendy. You don't think I have to work, for real?"

"From the way it sounds, you don't unless you want to. If you think you want help, let me know. I can turn you on to my financial planner at the firm, he's damn good. I'm okay with some things, but finance is not my strong point." Wendy told her.

Thanks, but Keith is basically doing all that for

me. I guess it won't hurt to see what your guy says though. I'm tired—I want sleep. Talk to you later Wendy," Jade said, and she got into bed.

The rest of the week was routine. Mitch called Thursday while she was going over her script with Traci. She asked Traci to give her a few minutes while she took his call.

"Hello Mitchell." She said coldly.

"Hey baby, miss me?"

"I haven't had time to miss you Mitch, I've been busy."

"Baby, I know you mad, but you don't know what happened. I just had two weeks from hell. I'm injured and can't play, the doctor ain't telling me shit I want to hear, on top of that, my agent is f' n around with my contract. If that wasn't enough, last week some asshole broke into my truck and stripped it of everything—my car phone, my pager and my organizer. I couldn't even call you baby 'cause I don't have your number nowhere else but in the phone.

Jade was amazed! "Your ingenuity worked when you found out how to get me here at the station."

"Oh baby, did you get Rusty?" He asked, changing the subject.

"Yes I did," she said, looking at the bear on the floor in the corner of her office.

"You and those *Foxes* you hang with want to

come to Sunday's game? I can leave some tickets in will-call for y'all."

"I don't know. I'll check if I find time, and let you know next time you decide to call me." She was kind of letting him slide because he *didn't* know how to reach her in Virginia, then she thought, hell no. The station phones work, he could have left a message with Michelle.

"Come on Princess, I was just about to give you my new number." He begged.

He had time to get new a number but he didn't have time to cancel the old one? "I've got to go Mitch, later." *Click.*

Friday night, Jade, Wendy, Lauren, Jill and Noel met in the lobby of Constitution Hall. They rushed to find seats as they arrived customarily late! The lights were going down when they got inside.

Ladies and Gentlemen, Please put your hands together and make some noise for Washington D.C.'s own home-grown sister from Southeast D.C., the award winning, beautiful and talented Miss Brea Sharee and the cool sounds of D.C.'s own"Ice".....

The audience went wild! "Ice" opened the show with an arrangement of "Inner City Blues" that had people rocking in their seats. The second number featured Brea singing a cut from her CD, *Come with Me,* and just like Reggie said when he chose it, everybody knew it, loved it, and sang all the words to it.

Now, D.C. was going to give props and respect to Maze alright, but they wanted to hear more of their home folks. Brea encored with *Dindi,* and Reggie laid out the instrumental part on his trumpet, they made beautiful music together.

At the end of their set, was an intermission. The *Hill Foxes* gathered outside in the lobby.

"Let's get some wine ladies," Noel said, "my treat. I'm just so happy we could all get together, and I'm happy to get the hell out of that house for a change. I need this break!"

"So how's everything going with Marcus?" Jade asked.

"Waiting." Noel said, disgusted.

"Brea said she'd meet us out here before the Maze show starts." Jade told them.

D.C. was like Paris. If you wanted to see the latest fashions, the brothers and sisters were going to show up in full gear, at any gathering where there were more than two people, and they hadn't disappointed. They were all sipping wine and watching out for Brea when Jade saw some *wench* walking toward her in her dress—the dress she tried on in Chardet's. The wench was switching and swaying her hips like some model on a runway. The orange, yellow and brown scarf was draped backward around her neck, and it gracefully flowed as she moved. *She did look good, Jade had to admit.* Jade went to tap Wendy to show her the dress when she noticed the wench was holding onto the arm of David—her makeup man from the station. *And Oh My God!* "Jade are you alright?" Wendy asked her.

"I'm okay," Jade said quickly, as the couple walked past them. *The wench was **Anthony** and he was with David!* Anthony looked Jade in her eyes and his look said—*please don't*—and she didn't.

Ladies and Gentlemen, the Nation's Capital proudly welcomes to the stage of Constitution Hall, the one—the only—Frankie Beverly & Maze!

"*Silky, silky Soul Singer,*

Silky, silky Soul Singer….."

Everybody was enjoying the concert singing along, popping their fingers and having a ball! After the show ended, they all stood outside and watched the parade of fashions, and talked to old friends out for the evening. Since they were all charged up and ready for some fun, the *Hill Foxes* decided to go to Mr. Henry's at Pennsylvania Avenue on Capitol Hill. Brea had heard from Frankie that Roberta was in town, and was going to be there to do a set for old time sake. They all squeezed into the little establishment to eat, get bombed and call it a night at two o'clock.

TWENTY
JILL

JULIUS COLLINS PLACED the dishes from the late lunch into the sink. "I hope you enjoyed," he said, pulling one of the curls on Jill's curly mop of hair.

"That was quite delicious, honey."

"Why don't you lie down for a while, I'll wake you when I get back, I won't be too long. I only have a couple of trips on schedule." Julius kissed her and left.

Jill lay down in his bed. They had spent the afternoon together. It was so seldom they got to do that. She brought her things with her so he could take her to the airport for her seven-thirty flight. Jill was thinking while she lay there, about the time she found the expensive tennis bracelet in his bathroom. *"I thought it was yours," he had said.* She suddenly became curious and started looking around. She looked through his drawers in the bedroom—nothing. She looked through the papers in the desk—nothing. She checked his caller ID-clean. *He must have cleared his calls, why?* Before leaving her house that morning she'd called him. That call wasn't there either. *The hell with this.* She got back into bed and went to sleep.

Julius came home several hours later and woke her.

"Wake up sleepy-head," he whispered in her ear.

"Um, what time is it?" She opened her eyes.

"Early," he said sliding his hand underneath the sheet. He ran his hand up her leg, pulled at her silk panties and kissed her. She reached up and pulled him down into bed with her.

Later, Julius sped down Constitution Avenue, they were late. He dropped Jill off at National and she ran inside the terminal. She boarded the plane and began working. After take-off, she demonstrated the emergency equipment to passengers as they headed for Miami. After finishing up the inventory report, she grabbed her bag and walked through the long terminal. As she made her way upstairs on the escalator, she thought about Julius. Something was going on with him, she felt it. He was probably doing what they all did, whoring around with some street booty.

Jill walked through the automatic doors and down to passenger loading. She waved and the Black Jeep Wrangler pulled up. Bryce Cooper jumped out and gave her a big hug. "Hey baby, give me your bag." She hopped into the Jeep and they merged into traffic on the hot muggy evening.

Bryce drove into the parking garage of Madison House. Jill stayed there whenever she had a layover in Miami. It belonged to Cheyenne Foster, an attendant from Miami, on her crew. This was one of the times they were working opposite each other. Cheyenne should have just landed in D.C. and she'd be staying at Jill's condo in Fort Chaplin.

Bryce walked with Jill inside the condo. "Are you off tonight?" Jill asked Bryce.

"Yeah, I worked a double so I have a few days off. It's good to see you, you look wonderful." He said. "I'm sorry I was working when you were here last time."

"Schedules, what would we do without them," Jill said, laughing. Bryce was part of Florida's Sheriff's Department. He was a beautiful tan-mulatto looking honey-bun of mixed heritage, that loved being with his little chocolate-drop Jill! He poured two glasses of chilled Chardonnay he brought with him while Jill changed out of her uniform.

"I feel like getting into the hot tub," he said. "I had a rough 24."

"Please do. Cut it on and get it started." Jill had changed into a tropical colored long wrap and sandals.

Underneath, she wore a hot-pink bathing suit that popped against her smooth chocolate skin. Her thick black curls had started curling tighter from the humidity in the air. They took their drinks and the bottle of wine to the pool deck. The area was hidden by tall privacy fencing and palm bushes. Jill lighted citronella candles around the pool. They got into the hot tub, sat back and relaxed.

"Hum, just what these bones need." Bryce said, closing his eyes. "How's your world Jill?"

"My world is pretty good Bryce, I guess I shouldn't complain."

"How's your man Julius, and how's that working out?"

"He's up to something. I have a strong feeling."

"What has he done now?" Bryce was aware of her suspicions of Julius.

"Nothing? She said, unsure how to answer. "I don't know, can't really put a finger on it. How's Saundra?"

"Eh-she's the same. Still bitching, moaning and complaining, but she wouldn't be Saundra if she wasn't."

They talked about their relationships with Julius and Saundra. Of course Jill had set the boundary of her and Bryce's relationship when they first met, so it wasn't a problem. Jill told him, *"I love being with you Bryce, but you're my "in-town" honey when I'm "in-town", there's nothing beyond this."*

"I'm always happy when you're here Jill. You're like a breath of fresh air." Bryce said, cuddling her chin.

"I enjoy being here with you Bryce, and if things weren't so crazy, I'd almost swear you were my soul mate."

Bryce reached over and gave Jill a long kiss of passion. She held onto to him and nibbled tiny bites of love-kisses on his neck, his shoulders and chest. He slipped the straps of her bathing suit down, and lightly brushed her breasts with his warm lips. Jill felt a real connection with Bryce, she loved being in his world.

TWENTY-ONE
JADE

WASHINGTON HAD BEGUN to display her magnificent array or colors, officially announcing the start of fall. Days were warm and beautiful with quiet reminders of summer, evenings were chilly and cool, with the intimidation of a winter impending.

Jade mistakenly mentioned the Buckskins tickets, and what did she do that for. Noel was hounding her like a bill collector. "Come on Jazz, get the tickets from Mitch, it'll be fun. I'd rather go before it gets too cold." Noel begged.

"Alright Noel, I'll see if I can still get them but it's going to be up to you to get the *Foxes* together. I really don't have that kind of time."

"No problem. I think it would be easy for us to meet in Eastern High's parking lot, if we're early enough, we can get a space and it's free."

HILL FOXES

"Whatever arrangement you make is fine with me." She dialed Mitch's new number.

"Yeah!"

"Mitch, this is Jade. If you still have those tickets, the girls want to come to the game."

"Whatever you want Princess, I'll leave them in will-call, you know your wish is my command. Whatch'a doing tonight?"

"Nothing, what's up?"

"Feel like some seafood?"

"That sounds good, what time?"

"I'll swing by your house about seven-ish. I've been here in town all day today anyhow."

"Fine, I'll see you at seven."

"Anthony sweetheart," she said, over the phone, "I have tickets for the game Sunday, would you like to go with us?"

"HELL YES, how much are the tickets?"

"They're complimentary tickets from Mitch and we're all meeting in Eastern's parking lot at 12:30."

"I'll be there with bells on."

"Anthony," Jade said, giggling, "Will I recognize you?"

"Kiss my ass, Jade. I'm telling you for the LAST time, I wouldn't have bought the damn dress if I thought you were really going to get it. I have told you three times…"

"Anthony, Anthony, stop! I'm just messing with you," Jade said, laughing and falling all over her desk.

"Jade?" Anthony said.

"Yes?" *CLICK*!!

Jade loved teasing Anthony. He was so funny, and she thought he really did feel bad about buying the dress. She was smiling when the intercom rang again.

"Jade?"

Now what! "Yes Michelle?"

"There is a Kirk Rucker on line four."

"Thanks. Good morning, Mr. Rucker."

"Kirk, please," he corrected her. "How are you today?"

"I'm well Kirk, any good news for me?"

"Yes, I think so. I have a few interested parties, but I'm not clear on the area you plan to sell."

"I'm interested in selling the land west of the farm," she told him. I really don't know how to explain the exact location."

"I understand. How soon would you be able to come down and identify it for me?"

"I can't come this weekend—on second thought maybe I can. I'll come down after work Friday, meet you Saturday morning if you're available, and get back to D.C. Sunday," she said planning out loud. *The hell with that game, I need to handle my business!*

"That should be fine. I'll meet you at ten." Kirk said.

HILL FOXES

She left a message on Keith's machine that she was coming down. She figured he was in school that time of day. Jade imagined she could take care of business, and be back in D.C. by game time. She called Wendy to invite her to go down to the country with her.

"Ohh—I got you." Jade said, surprised that Wendy had answered. "I don't know where you keep disappearing to Wendy."

"Busy. I've been up to my thongs with this case, girl."

"I need to ride down to Virginia this weekend, come go with me. Take a break for a day?"

"Noel called. I thought we were all going to the game?" Wendy asked.

"We can be back in time for the game. I need to take care of some more business with the property."

"No, woman can't do. I'm swamped and actually, I have no business going to the game. How's Mr. Keith?"

"He's great. We talk a few times during the week, I find myself thinking about him all the time."

"Really? Has something happen to you and Mitch?"

"No, I care about him too, is that possible or am I tripp'in?"

"No, that's just the trollop in you, "Wendy said,

laughing. "It's possible for you to like each of them a different way. One satisfies one set of needs, and the other satisfies another set. Personally, I wouldn't have that problem. It would simply boil down to the *Johnson—wink-wink.*" Wendy fell out laughing.

"Wendy, damn!"

"Speaking of Johnson's, are you protecting yourself, especially since you're dealing with that whorish Mitch?"

"I'm only dealing with Mitch and why does he have to be whorish?"

"Goodbye Jazz," Wendy said, disgusted.

"You know Wendy, you sound just like Keith. "

"Sounds like Keith has good sense. You need a reality check girlfriend, I'm gone, see you Sunday."

Wendy could be brutally honest and she was usually right about things. Jade hoped this time she was wrong.

Mitch arrived at Jade's house at Seven-thirty in jeans, a heavy sweater over a plaid shirt, and tennis. Jade decided to wear something similar.

"Hey Princess," he said, bending down to kiss her.

"Hey, Mitch." They hugged for a minute.

"I miss you, I really do," Mitch whispered. He could be so sweet when he wanted to. "Hungry?"

"Famished, are you ready?"

"Your chariot awaits Princess." He helped her

into his Burgundy Bronco trimmed with gold piping, and they headed to Southwest. He suggested the buffet at Hogate's so they could sample a little of everything.

Fans were waving and grinning at him. They took a table overlooking the water. It was still warm enough to enjoy, and their waiter was so excited Jade thought he was going to pee all over himself.

"My name is Mark, I'm going to be your waiter tonight," he said, grinning. "How was I lucky enough to get two celebrities tonight?"

"No, you only have one." Jade said, pointing to Mitch.

"Oh, I get it Miss Williams, you're not here." He winked.

Mitch started to laugh. "See I told you."

"Don't start, it's just dark in here," Jade said.

"I almost forgot to tell you, you know Tommy Hundley defensive back?" Well, we tease him 'cause he don't miss those Hollywood gossip shows. He told me they already got me linked up with Vanessa Williams. They say we been seen out on several occasions." Mitch was laughing.

"Ohh, that's awful! That woman is married. She's probably catching hell from her husband Ramon. You would think people would recognize me from my own show, they've plastered my face all over town."

"Yeah, I saw you on the side of a metro bus the other day," Mitch said, laughing. Just then, three young girls that looked to be about high school age approached their table. The tall attractive one came close. "Hi Mitch, I thought you were going to call me?"

"Hello, how are you?" He said.

"I'll be much better when you call," she said, smiling and they walked away.

"Well, just damn!" Jade said feeling disrespected.

"Don't." Mitch was holding his hand up, "Don't."

Jade was so annoyed, she just shook her head and started dipping her shrimp into the sauce.

"I don't know them. I figure it was probably a dare from her little girlfriends." Mitch said, quietly. Jade didn't feel like dealing with the incident so she said nothing. *They were kind of young, so Jade considered Mitch's analysis.*

When Mitch brought her back to the house after dinner, it was around ten-thirty, she invited him in.

"You know I can't stay long, I need to be back in Fairfax before they call."

"Thanks for dinner Mitch, I enjoyed the evening. I rarely get to see you." She said, snuggling close to him.

"I miss being around you too, but you don't have to put me out yet, I have a few minutes." Jade put on some smooth jazz, got herself some wine and made him a Cappuccino. They sat by the fireplace and talked. He placed his arm around her and gave her the sweetest kiss. Although he hadn't earned her full trust yet, she led him by the hand upstairs to her bedroom. He was so gentle, she held onto him like he was trying to escape. She reached into her nightstand, pulled out the condoms she got at Dart Drug taking heed to Wendy's advice about protecting herself.

"What's this?" Mitch asked her. "You got something?"

"No, we should have been doing this all along."

"Why start now, the cat's already out the bag."

"I want the "cat" to be assured of nine lives Mitch."

"What are you trying to say, I got something?"

"Mitch, let's just use it okay?"

"F*** no!" He jumped up and went into the bathroom. When he came out, he grabbed his jeans and began stepping into them.

"Mitch, why are you acting like this over a condom?"

"I thought you loved me Jade." He was angry.

"I do love you Mitch, but I still feel we need to use protection."

"Fine –whatever–I'm outta' here," he said, stomping downstairs and slamming her front door.

"F* you too", she mumbled beneath her breath.

She poured another glass of wine and wondered why Mitch was so upset? Wasn't he used to using condoms or had he just been screwing whoever came along bareback? Maybe he did, and that's what scared her.

She got up from her chair and checked her messages. She saw that Keith had called, twice. It was late so she decided to catch him before school the next morning. She had just drifted off to sleep when the phone rang. "Hey baby," the low voice said.

"Keith? Sorry, I had fallen asleep." She mumbled.

"Keith? Who is Keith?"

"Mitch!" Her eyes popped wide open. I thought you were the guy that works the night desk at the station."

"I'm sorry, Jade you're right." Mitch said.

"We do need to protect ourselves. If you *love me* you'll do it." She said.

"I don't want to get into that with you again tonight Jade, I *said* I'm sorry." *Click!*

Friday after work, Jade headed straight for I-64 and Virginia. She left a message on Mitch's machine telling him she would be back in time for the game on Sunday. She didn't feel like talking to him. She managed to escape the heaviest Friday traffic once she got through Dale City. Most of the commuters had already exited, and the drive south was simply beautiful. The trees were brilliant reds, oranges and gold. They looked magnificent against the golden sunset. She stopped on the way to buy Keith a thank you gift.

She drove up the dark, tree-lined winding road that led to Keith's property, about seven-thirty. The trees were as tall as buildings and must have been hundreds of years old. The road ended in a circled drive at Keith's front door. He employed a gentleman by the name of Ben. He worked in the house and lived in the guest quarters. Keith, Ben, and Buddy met her at the door. She waved and when she popped her trunk open to retrieve Keith's gift, Ben lifted her bag out and took it inside.

"Jazz," Keith said, hugging her. "Good to see you."

"Good to see you too, Keith." Jade said, smiling and it *was* good seeing him.

"Would you like to come in first, or would you like to go straight to Westbury farm?

"It seems like Ben wants me to stay or he just hijacked my bag." Jade said, laughing.

"I don't know why you *don't* stay here."

"I don't want to impose on you anymore than I already have. I planned to stay at the farm but I forgot my keys, I came here first to borrow yours." She explained.

"I'd love to have you stay here Jazz, it won't be an imposition."

"Well, let's go to the farm first and I'll see." Ben brought the Jeep around to the circle and they drove over to Westbury. They drove down the dark roads with only the moon to guide them. Buddy rode with his head stuck out of the window while Jade listened to the feeble song of the crickets. It sounded like they were weeping for the end of their season, and their inevitable demise. It made her feel sad.

When they arrived at Westbury, Keith got out, opened the door, and turned on the lights in the house before he came back for her. He checked around as he did every day.

"I've placed all of the mail, minus the bills, on the desk in the study," he said. "There are still sympathy cards coming in."

"Thanks, I'll grab them and take them home. It's still hard to believe they're both gone," she said, looking around. "This house used to be so full of life and love."

"I know. I miss them too. I'd like to think Judith is somewhere smiling because we're here in this house together."

"Would you believe I used to hate this place?" She asked him and he gave her shoulder a squeeze. *Don't let him back in.*

"Do you want to check around upstairs?"

"Yes, my mom wants me to look for daddy's jacket he thinks he left when we were here for the funeral."

HILL FOXES

"Did you want to go up by yourself?"

"You can come with me Keith."

Since Aunt Judith's unexpected death, Jade had been in and out of there always in a rush. She peeked into her little room where her teddy bears still sat and began to get depressed. From somewhere, and Jade wasn't sure where, the flood gates opened and tears started forming. She felt so sad all of a sudden looking around the room. It reminded her of her youth and her innocence. Keith came into the room and noticed her tears. He took her in his arms and gently rocked her. "Shhh," he said. "Let it out, this is something you probably should have done a while ago, you just wouldn't give yourself the time. I miss them too sweetheart. I wouldn't be where I am today had it not been for them." Keith bent down and kissed her tears.

"You okay?"

"I'm okay," she said, half laughing. "I don't know what got into me, I'm sorry."

It had started to rain. The raindrops were hitting hard against the windows. "Is there anything else you want to do here?" Keith asked. "You're going to stay with me tonight and that's that."

"No, I can come back tomorrow." They went back downstairs and Jade waited for Keith to cut off the lights in the house. They started out and Keith called for Buddy.

"I don't remember where he went," Jade said.

"I know where he is, he does this all the time." Keith went back upstairs to get Buddy off Aunt Judith's bed.

When they got back to Keith's, Ben had set the table for dinner. He was a big athletic looking man and appeared to be about their age. "Are you ready for dinner now?" Ben asked.

"Are you ready now Jazz?"

"Sure, if you are."

"Ben, if you have something to do, I'll get it."

"I'll serve you and Miss Jazz."

"Just Jazz, or Jade please, Ben." She said. He smiled.

Ben must have thought she was related to the Queen of England. He had prepared Roasted Peppers, Grilled Zucchini and Egg Plant marinated with garlic, for appetizers. Cucumber soup with a Caesar salad, and the entrée, Blackened Swordfish, served with Red wine. What-a-meal! When Jade thought she was completely stuffed to the gills, out came a flaming dessert.

Jade and Keith talked during dinner about their business. They would meet with Kirk the next morning and ride out to identify the property she wanted to put on the market.

"I've worked with Kirk several times before."

HILL FOXES

Keith said. "If you don't mind, let me steer the conversation. I like his work, but he's trying to make a buck like everybody else and you have to watch him."

"No problem Keith. You know I don't know a thing when it comes to land values, especially land around here."

They *retired* to the game room and sat on the sofa drinking wine, listening to Mark Murphy playing in the background.

"I am stuffed!" Jade said.

"I hope you enjoyed dinner."

"So, it was Ben who fixed dinner when I was here before?" Jade asked, laughing.

"I fixed your dinner when you were here before. Ben could probably learn a few things from me."

"Seriously Keith, didn't Ben fix that meal?" She teased.

"Once again, I cooked that meal. When I hired Ben, he had previously worked for our Commissioner. I had been to several of the Commissioner's functions at his home, so when the Commissioner transferred from the area, I hired Ben. He does other things around here too. He's quite the handy man. I'm sure I'm less formal than his former employers and basically, we have an arrangement. I let him do his thing, he lives here free.

"Oh, I see. One thing's for sure, he knows his

way around a kitchen." Keith was gently running his hands through Jade's hair as they lay on the sofa enjoying the ambiance. The last thing Jade remembered was Keith pulling a soft spread over her.

"Keith, I'm sorry, I must have fallen asleep." She looked around and she was in his bed. "How did I get....."

"Shhh, close your eyes sweetheart," he said continuing to stroke her hair. She awoke the next morning in Keith's arms, head buried in his chest, warm, totally content and fully dressed. She became conscience of her body pressed against his, one thing lead to another. There should have been a law against the kind of sweet love he made to her that morning, and she thought all this time she had been loved? Uh-uh.

After they lay in each other's arms for a while, Jade began to come back to reality. *What the hell am I doing? Am I not in a relationship with Mitchell Dawson?* She never thought to bring those damn condoms with her after her sermon to Mitch on the importance of being protected. She tried to justify that by thinking Keith's life style was probably less risky than Mitch's, but she had been with Mitch, and it was Keith who was being put at risk.

"Penny for your thoughts?" Keith said.

"I'm thinking you put something in my wine."

Jade said, laughing. "I'm also thinking I surely need a shower."

"Our meeting with Kirk is at ten, you're okay with that?"

"What time is it now?" She asked.

"Seven-forty, relax." He said, looking at the clock. "Jazz, I want to ask you something without invading too much of your privacy, but are you still seeing Mitchell?"

Oh damn! "Keith, I'm going to be honest and you might not like it. I'm still seeing him and I'm not sure where my heart is right now," she said dreading his reaction.

"It's no secret I want you for myself Jazz, I've told you that. I'm willing to do whatever it takes to get you back. I let you get away once, but I won't make that mistake again. And just so you know? If you think you love Mitchell, you're sadly mistaken sweetheart.

"How would you know that?"

"Trust me, after being with you this morning, you're not in love with him, I felt your soul. I waited for this all these years, and so did you. You can deny your feelings for me verbally if you want, but ask your body.

"I'm uncomfortable discussing this Keith."

"I'm going to put it aside for right now, but we *will* talk about this again. There's a lot involved here Jazz. Would you like me to start your water?"

"If you want to spoil me," she said, smiling and grateful he had changed the conversation.

The bathroom off the master bedroom suite was as large as the whole first floor of her house. All of the fixtures were Black and Gold, the Roman tub, toilet, bidet' and the sinks. The walls were mirrored. There was a TV and a telephone on the wall, both Black. Keith filled the tub with bubbled water, sprinkled with rose petals. She laid back and closed her eyes. *I could do this!*

They dressed and came downstairs. Ben left bagels and cream cheese, juice, coffee and fresh fruit for breakfast. The phone rang and Keith answered.

"Hey man, no problem. She's here and we're getting a quick bite of breakfast. Why don't you come here, it's closer. Later." He hung up. "That was Kirk, he's on his way. I thought we'd take the horses. Some of that area is pretty rough. Do you mind?"

"Horses? Keith, are you crazy? Do you know the last time I was on a horse?"

"It's like riding a bicycle, Jazz."

"Then, I'll take the bicycle for a hundred please."

"You'll be fine. I'm going to let you ride Misty, she's very gentle." Keith said, laughing.

Kirk arrived at ten sharp. "Hey man, you remember Jade."

"Of course, good morning Jade." Kirk shook her hand.

Ben brought the Jeep around and they all got in and rode to the stables. Keith helped Jade onto Misty.

"Oh, Keith, she's beautiful." As they began to ride through the trails, it brought back memories. As they rode, Keith did most of the talking. Jade identified the property she wanted to sell and Kirk marked it off.

The ride was invigorating to say the least, by the time they got back to the stables, Jade could already feel her muscles tightening up, there was going to be a problem. "You were a good girl, Misty," Jade said, as she stroked the horse. Ben stayed to take care of the horses while Keith drove them back to the house. Jade said goodbye to Kirk, "You have my numbers, thanks again."

"Keith," Jade said, as Kirk drove away, "I can't move."

"Aw, woman, what you need to do is run down to the road and back, keep those muscles moving." He was laughing.

"I see nothing funny Keith, I knew this would happen." He helped her up the steps of the porch by her hand. "You act like an old woman. Let me put you in the Jacuzzi." He took her off to an area near the game room. It was glassed in up to the roof, with a solar heating system. He started the water, and brought her a thick terry bathrobe and some thick towels.

"I can't sit in her with all this glass. I'll be too uncomfortable Keith."

"Now, who do you think's going to see you in here? I've already seen your little birthday suit, and Ben only peeps on Tuesdays, today is Saturday." Keith said amused.

"Funny, ha-ha! Just get out."

"Do you need help getting in or do you need me to stand guard?" He asked, laughing.

"Just get out!" Jade nervously undressed and quickly got in. She sat back and looked out at the falling leaves. Keith turned on some music. *He thinks of everything*, that's why she was falling deeper and deeper. How was she going to look Mitch in the eye?

"Would you like champagne Jazz?" Jade sat straight up! She covered her breast and let out a little squeal.

"I'm on the intercom you nut," Keith said, laughing.

"Have you ever had to fish a dead body from your Jacuzzi?" She asked him. "You scared me to death." He knocked and brought her drink in. "Enjoy, and if you need anything else, just press this little button here on the right and Ben will be right in. I've got some calls to make." He left laughing.

"Thanks, I'm fine." She sat there a minute listening to the music and it hit her—*Ben will be right in?* Oh, he's crazy!

Ben prepared lunch, and they ate in the game room. They had smoked Turnkey and Swiss cheese sandwiches, on White Mountain bread that had been brushed with butter and garlic, a hot cup of soup, chips and drinks. Keith watched the Virginia Tech game as he worked on some test papers. "I hope you don't mind coming to our game tonight." He said.

"No, it should be fun. It's been a long time since I've been to a high school game. I'd love to see your team play."

"Would you like to eat out tonight or would you rather eat here?"

"Whatever's good for you, works for me."

Jade and Keith spent the afternoon together talking and enjoying each other's company, they had a lot of years to catch up on. Keith left around four to go to school, Jade drove over later. Keith was a good coach and they won their game. She waited for him outside while he cleared the locker room of his players.

"Did you enjoy the game sweetheart?" He asked her and kissed her forehead. Just then, one of his boys coming out of the building said, "Awh, coach got a girlfriend."

"All right guys, let's clear out and go home now, I'll see you Monday."

"I made reservations at Antonio's, feel like going?"

"That's fine, but are you sure you don't want to cook for me tonight or is Ben off?" Jade was laughing. He slapped her on her butt and pointed her toward the truck. "Just follow me smarty." They got in their separate cars and drove into town. They parked into the curb and walked hand in hand into Antonio's. "Lassiter", he said, at the door. They had been there several times, so Keith requested the same table by the window, the waiter knew them.

"Good evening Mr. Lassiter, Mrs. Lassiter." He handed them the menus.

Jade looked at Keith and whispered, "Did I miss the wedding?"

"No sweetheart, because if there had been one you'd never forget it." He ordered for them. Sweet potato soup-their specialty, a salad with dried cranberries, walnuts, dried cherries and pieces of pear on a bed of lettuce and a vinaigrette dressing. The entrée was Chicken Frangelico.

Antonio's was small and intimate, on weekends they had live music. Keith took Jade's hand and led her to the dance floor and they danced a slow dance of love.

"You know what? I've had a wonderful time, but I haven't spent any of it at Westbury." She said, holding onto him.

"Guess you're going to have to come back, huh."

"Actually, I didn't have anything else planned other than the property this time. I'm getting up early so I can hit the road. I need to be back by in D.C. by eleven."

Keith looked disappointed. "I hope you'll take the time to make some decisions Jazz," he said, softly. "I need you."

Keith drove the winding, dark road back to his house, and she followed. It was a good thing she could follow him, those roads were dark, winding and narrow. Keith's mood seemed to have changed once they were back in the house. He poured them a glass of wine. "I guess we should get to bed early so you can be rested in the morning." He kissed her and they held each other for a while. "Let's close up and go to bed." He said.

TWENTY-TWO
LAUREN

LAUREN PACKED UP her photography equipment and got ready to go home for the evening, she had decided not to work at the Post that night. She felt like crap, and it had taken her until well after lunchtime to shake off her monstrosity of a hangover. The night before, she had consumed an entire bottle of Chablis. She was depressed and had come to the conclusion that there just wasn't any hope of finding a decent man. Whatever had she done in life to deserve what kept happening to her? Her ex-husband Troy had treated her like she was a non-person, just a meal-ticket and a place to lay his head while he did whatever he wanted. He was abusive, and evil, she tolerated him for as long as she could—longer than most women would have. She finally reached the end of her rope. He had shared with her yet another STD, the *third* one that year. It was a wonder

HILL FOXES

she wasn't sterile! After she asked him to leave her condo and never come back, he packed up, moved out and emptied her bank accounts.

Now, here she was again. In love with a Nation of Islam imposter named Mustafa Saleem, A.K.A. Freddie James Johnson, who smoked herb like a chimney, ate pork like a heathen, and drank wine by the gallon. Despite all of his flaws, he treated her like a queen and loved her like a goddess. The problem with that, he wanted her to be part of a harem.

Lauren had refused to take any of Mustafa's calls, she was still dumbfounded. Haaydia had opened her eyes to what was right in front of her, and she had completely missed it. She couldn't understand how Haaydia could support Mustafa's need to have someone other than her, the thing she called man-sharing. Lauren examined her deepest feelings like Haaydia had suggested. She did love Mustafa and deep down she knew Mustafa loved her. Did that make her pathetic? Did that make her one of the biggest fools this side of the Mason-Dixon Line? The one thing that truly disturbed Lauren was that Mustafa hadn't trusted her enough to tell her about Haaydia, yet Haaydia knew all about Lauren. It had all been her own fault, she had ignored the obvious and simply missed it and now, she missed him.

Lauren laid across the bed in her condo. Her

thoughts had been consumed with questions about herself and what she was going to do. To anyone else, it would have been a "no-brainer". She could just hear the girls criticizing and judging her now, especially Noel, but they didn't know her pain. They didn't know how Mustafa had "fixed her", an insecure, abused, broken woman. They only knew the part of her she let them see; the fun-loving party girl. That was far from the truth.

Lauren reached for the phone. It was still early and she could probably catch Mustafa closing the salon, she promptly put the phone back in its cradle. What was she going to say to him? How was she going to confront him and salvage what little dignity she had left? Yet she needed him to know how his dishonesty had hurt her. It wasn't what he said, it was what he hadn't said. She needed him to know that she actually felt he and Haaydia had conspired against her. She needed him to know how it was hard for her to accept that she had shared her man without her knowledge or consent.

She picked up the phone again and dialed Mustafa. "Mustafa, if you would be kind enough to stop by here before you go in, I'd appreciate it. We have issues that need to be discussed once and for all."

When Mustafa walked into Lauren's house, she looked at this man and lost all sense of space and time. She walked into the embrace of his strong arms, felt his gentle touch, felt the soul of the man who fulfilled her every need. Without a spoken word, his penetrating eyes answered all of her questions and she—Mustafa's Queen, surrendered to her King.

TWENTY-THREE
JADE

THE TRIP BACK into D. C. was quiet. It was a beautiful Sunday morning, and unseasonably warm. When Jade got home, she changed into jeans, tennis and the Buckskin jacket Mitch had given her. She quickly grabbed some juice and headed to Eastern High School's parking lot to meet the girls and Anthony. They all hugged and walked down 19th Street toward the stadium. The streets were full of vendors, the parking lots were full of tailgaters, and the atmosphere was festive. There couldn't have been a more perfect day, a wonderful Indian summer afternoon. Die-heart Buckskin fans were ready to party! The balloon man yelled at them and gave each a balloon. "Y'all some fine *Foxes*, yes you are!" He said. Trails of smoke blew from the parking lots with the rich smell of charcoal filling the air. It was football Sunday in D.C.!

HILL FOXES

Jade stood in the will-call line waiting her turn.

"Mitchell Dawson," she said, and the man handed her the envelope of tickets. She gave everyone a ticket and there were four left. "Sir you gave me more than I need, are you sure you gave me the right envelope?" Jade asked him. Tickets to those games were non-existent and Lord knew, she didn't want to prevent anyone from getting in.

"Let me see", the man said, checking his list. "Mitchell Dawson, ten. I'll keep them Miss, in case he has other guest coming." She gave him the remaining tickets.

The *Hill Foxes* had good seats—"Good Seats!" Wendy yelled.

"She's made enough touchdowns to get these good seats," Noel said, and they all laughed.

"Don't get cute," Jade said, rolling her eyes.

"Anybody want a hotdog?" Anthony asked.

"Not at these prices," Brea said, "I ate before I came."

The band was jumping and everybody was getting pumped up for the game. "Look," Jill squealed, "The Buckette mascots. They're sooo cute. Big, too."

"Yep," Wendy said, "and in just two years you can look like that too."

"Shut up, Wendy Haines," Jill said, and they all stood up to let some ladies squeeze by on their row.

Tailgaters were beginning to come in, they were juiced up already and the game hadn't even started. The Bucksinettes looked as trashy as ever in their new cheerleading uniforms for that season.

Wendy leaned over and whispered in Jade's ear, "How did your business in Virginia go?"

"I'll tell you about it later," Jade said, "I'll just say this, I think I'm in love!"

Whoa!" Wendy said, stomping her feet on the ground.

The game was exciting. Mitch was getting a lot of play time. Each time he handled the ball, the fans next to them went wild screaming his name and high-fiving each other. Jade couldn't seem to get her head into the game. She was daydreaming about her visit to Virginia. She knew she couldn't leave Keith hanging the way she had, but truth be told, she didn't know who she wanted to be with.

"Awwwwhh!" The whole stadium moaned in unison and stood to their feet, bringing Jade back into the game. The announcer was saying that Mitch was down and possibly injured. The trainer was out on the field, and a fan sitting down from them screamed, "Oh no, my baby's hurt!" Simultaneously, the *Foxes* all leaned forward and looked down the row toward the ladies who had squeezed by, and who do you think Jade recognized? The young girls from Hogate's! The ones who had come to the table, and asked Mitch why he hadn't called. Jade's party was sitting in A1 thru 6, and they were in A7 thru 10—*the extra four tickets in the envelope.* Jade didn't say anything, but Wendy glanced at her and had probably guessed something was up. Wendy didn't say anything either.

Mitch wasn't hurt badly, a little shaken up, so they benched him for the rest of the game.

At the end of the game, the *Hill Foxes* decided to eat at Chef's table on Benning Road, not far from the stadium. Jade decided she wouldn't say anything to Wendy about the girl at the stadium. She didn't feel like hearing it. Maybe she did need to do a reality check. *Was* she being naïve about Mitch? After they had finished the buffet dinner, the girls hugged, thanked Jade for the game, and went their separate ways.

Jade drove down Bladensburg Road to South Dakota, thinking about Keith and Mitch. When she got to 20th Street, she turned at Newton when she noticed people were still on the tennis courts. Others were running around Taft's track, so she pulled over and parked to watch, it was such a beautiful evening.

"Jazz, is that you?" Someone was approaching her car but she couldn't make out who it was. "It's me Terry—Terry Brooks."

"Terry," she got out and hugged him. "I see you

still got that tennis racket in your hand boy." She teased him.

"Got to stay in shape, plus it's a pretty night. You waiting for somebody out here?" He asked Jade.

"No, I was just passing by and got nostalgic, thinking about how much fun we used to have down here. I'm on my way home."

"We did used to have fun here. Do you still run, Jazz?"

"Sometimes, I usually don't have the time."

"You should come down here and run, you'd be surprised who you'll see. Remember Dempsey? He was down here last week. You talk about a blast from the past. You know he did some time, but heee's back! Just don't give him your address." Terry was laughing. "He looks like he's been hittin' the pipe."

"Oh, that's too bad. So Terry how is it being *the* District's hot new Prosecuting Attorney?"

"How is it being *the* District's best news anchor?"

"It's a job," Jade said.

"My sentiments exactly. I see so many of our classmates messed up and in the court system, that job depresses me. I guess we were some of the lucky ones Jazz. Look, I'm cooling down so let me get back. It's good to see you again girl, think about coming down here sometime." He waved and ran back onto the tennis court. She started her car and drove home, checked her messages, email, and unpacked her bag. She picked up the phone to call Keith. She needed to hear his voice.

"Keith, hey." She said sadly.

"Hey yourself, what's wrong?"

"Nothing, I just miss you." She said, quietly.

"I miss you too Jazz. Can you come back next weekend?"

She smiled. "I don't know yet."

"I'd come up there if I were invited," he said.

"I would love for you to come, but I'm not sure I'm ready for you to do that yet."

..........Silence.......deafening silence........

"Keith?"

"I'm here," he said, in almost a whisper.

"I'm dealing with it—I am. I want to be honest with you about everything. I'm going to work it out Keith. I ask that you be patient, please. I had another life a short while ago, you just popped back into it and things are supposed to change immediately?"

"I'm sorry, I don't mean to put any kind of pressure on you, but you see in my mind, there shouldn't be a problem. You love me and I know you do. I'll be patient until you realize that, Jazz. Do you have any idea how I feel thinking somebody else might be holding you or making love to you?"

"Please." Jade said. They held the phone in silence

for a while and he finally said, "I love you, enjoy your week." He hung up. The phone immediately rang again. He had called to say he was sorry for being so abrupt. Jade answered.

"It's okay baby, I understand how this must feel to you." Jade told him.

"You do?"

"Yes, I can understand you probably feel bad about not being able to finish the game Mitch." *This phone shit has got to stop!*

"Thanks baby, but I'm okay," Mitch said. "I don't feel too bad about it. Did you and your girls enjoy the game?"

"Yes Mitch, all *TEN* of us did!"

"You brought the whole neighborhood, huh?"

"There were only six of my friends, I don't know who the hell those other b**** were, at least you could have seated them in another section!" Jade was fuming.

"What are you talking about, Jade?"

"You know damn well what I'm talking about, but just in case you can't figure it out? Somebody in the front office screwed up your seating arrangements, and had that little girl from Hogate's and her party sitting right next to us." Jade was screaming.

"What little girl from Hogate's?"

"Show me *some* respect Mitch, damn!" Jade slammed the phone down.

After a hot shower, Jade was still too mad to go to sleep. She poured herself a glass of wine to calm her down. Did she really have the right to be angry with Mitch? Was what she had done with Keith respectful to him? Hadn't she done the same thing she was accusing him of doing? Jade cared for both of them. Mitch appealed to her "bad-boy" need, whereas she was attracted to Keith's refinement, intelligence and power, not to mention she had loved him since forever. She had no intentions however, on letting Keith force her into a decision with his subtle dominance. He was the type that would lock her ass up and never let her out again. But while she was locked up, he would shower her with whatever she wanted or needed. She smiled.

Jade left at least six messages over the course of the next few days for Wendy, but she never returned the calls at home or at work. She spoke with Wendy's secretary who told her, Wendy was working on an important case. At least she knew Wendy was alive.

TWENTY-FOUR
NOEL

IT WAS AS if Marcus Holbrook had stuck his hand inside a sleeping hornets' nest, and disturbed the hornets. All hell broke loose after he discovered his estranged wife Lila Holbrook's whereabouts.

Lila had seemed lucid during her courtroom appearance, which suggested she might be on medications, but that was one of the requirements for staying in the women's shelter. According to the shelter's director, Lila complied with shelter policies most of the time, but there were times when she was off her medications and disappeared for weeks at a time. When she refused to take her meds, her Schizophrenia surfaced.

When Lila was lucid, she was able to make rational decisions, and had requested that the court give her custody of Brent and Bryan—she wanted her boys! Lila Holbrook was good and crazy, but she wasn't dumb. Before her mental breakdown, she was a working paralegal, studying to become a Family Law attorney in the evenings, and on weekends.

She hadn't been able to locate her two boys since Marcus had moved them from their Northwest home. She did know where Marcus worked, and it's anybody's guess why she never bothered him at the courthouse. There was however, a stay-away order prohibiting her from coming near the law offices of Simmons, McAlpine and Maghetti. She'd trashed their offices during one of her schizophrenic episodes.

"There's no way I'm letting that woman near my children," Marcus said, through clinched teeth.

"I understand honey," Noel said, "but be realistic. She has the right to see them, even if by supervised visitation. We're not going to worry about her gaining custody, her history speaks for itself, and a material change of circumstances hasn't occurred. She's not employed, she's been diagnosed and hospitalized, and she can't show that your custody isn't in the best interest of the boys.

"She's off her meds again," Marcus said.

"That's obvious, but we'll get through this."

Lila had been terrorizing poor Marcus. She was at the District Courthouse everyday screaming that

Attorney Marcus Holbrook had stolen her children. Court security and the Marshalls kept Lila as far away from the front of the building as they could. Lila had become a one-woman protest, constantly trying to slip past security, blending in with the crowds entering the building. *"I have the right to be here," she screamed to the security guard.*

"And I have the right to have you removed for disturbing the peace and disorderly conduct on government property." The guard told her. Lila was there from 8:00 a.m. to 4:30 p.m., just like she was on a real job, screaming that Marcus had stolen her children and asking anyone passing by to help her. It had been a nightmare for Marcus. The rumor-mill in the building had been rejuvenated by gossip of Marcus Holbrook's little crazy wife, and the buzz word was, "She's back!"

Friday of that week, the conclusion of the hottest case on the docket for some time, was scheduled. The District of Columbia vs. Reverend Blake Thomas, minister of one of D.C.'s most prestigious churches and a member of City Council. The local press was everywhere. They had camped out on the steps of the courthouse and the streets, awaiting Reverend Thomas' exit from the building. As soon as he came out, up pops Lila. Fearing she might be removed from the area, Lila silently carried a huge three-foot sign in her hands that read:

ATTORNEY MARCUS HOLBROOK STOLE MY CHILDREN!
Help Me Get Them Back!

Reverend Thomas approached the microphone that had been set up for his statement by Fox 5, and Lila had positioned herself on the steps behind him. There was no way in hell you could miss that sign on camera. Lady Luck was still sitting on Marcus' shoulder, and the Fox 5 reporter covering the press release, was non-other than Jade "Jazz" Zellmer.

"Oh, my Jesus!" Jade said to herself. "That must be Noel's fiancee's wife." Jade instructed Anthony her cameraman, to position the camera to exclude the view of Lila's sign. The camera rolled without Lila being in the picture, at least not on Channel 5.

"What am I going to do Noel?" Marcus asked holding his head in his hands.

"You're going to go about your business as you've always done." Noel said, trying to console him.

"She's killing me Noel! I can't stand this type of attention. All of my efforts to try to move my career forward are being jeopardized by her crazy antics.

That's because she is crazy, Noel said to herself. Marcus wanted to stay with Noel that night. He needed her warmth and compassion right then. Marcus' persona was that of a cool, calm, level-headed person, but Lila Holbrook was sending him over the top!

"I often wonder why this is happening to me. I followed the rules, I paid my dues, and I don't think I deserve this." Marcus laid his head on Noel's stomach.

"That, which does not kill us, makes us stronger." Noel said, rubbing his graying temple. She loved this man and she sympathized with him after all, the drama unfolding directly affected her future too.

"Just be strong." Noel whispered.

TWENTY-FIVE
BREA

BREA SHAREE JONES had been happy for the last few weeks. Her mood was good, her heart was light, and she hadn't been having those horrible nightmares.

She had a ball with the girls at the game. After they all split up and left Chef's table that night, she went home and met Reggie at her house.

"How did you enjoy the game?" He asked her grinning.

"That was fun! That's the first time I've ever been to a Buckskins game, and I've lived here all of my life. Have you ever been?"

"I've seen a few, I even thought about buying season tickets, but I'd have to sell my house." He was laughing.

"Jazz got us complimentary tickets from her boyfriend Mitch Dawson, or I probably wouldn't have been there," Brea pulled out a bowl from the refrigerator. They sat in the kitchen while Reggie ate a Tuna-Macaroni and Shrimp salad she had fixed.

"This is good Brea. You picked up some of Miss Connie's skills I see."

"I don't know about that, there's not much to making a salad", she said, tasting a spoonful of it. "I'm still full from Chef's table. So what's the earthshaking news you wanted to tell me?"

"It would be earthshaking, if I truly gave a ratsass. I got a call from Damon earlier this afternoon…"

"I see two messages on my caller ID from him," Brea said, interrupting Reggie, "what's wrong?"

"I'm trying to tell you baby. It seems like our old manager Bobby Knowles, is threatening to sue Damon and us…"

"US, WHO?" Brea said, raising her voice.

"Ice." He's complaining that he never received any financial compensation from the contract buyout deal between Damon and Melik." *The mere mention of Melik's name gave Brea chills.*

"Why not?" She asked, wide-eyed.

"Our agreement with Melik and Natural Element was negotiated by Bobby, your contract with Melik and Natural Element was negotiated by Damon. What I know about the details of those contracts could fit inside this piece of shrimp."

"Then, it seems to me, Bobby needs to be talking to Melik." Brea said.

"Damon said, not to worry he'd take care of it."

"I'll call Damon back later. There's always some BS being thrown up in your face. People just can't stand to see you successful."

Brea put the salad away and took care of the dishes. She felt one of her moods trying to creep into her space. She and Reggie went into the living room and sat on the sofa to watch the days NFL highlights. He put his arm around her, and she laid her head on his shoulder. Reggie was so happy with his life right then, he didn't know what to do. Brea was content, and had been slowly healing one day at a time.

"I can't believe this mess isn't over," Brea said.

"It's over. Don't start worrying about it. It's not going to happen. Even if Bobby tries to sue us, he's seriously out of luck. You can't get blood from a turnip."

Reggie told Brea not to worry, but she felt in her bones there was something in the air. She was good at that and she always trusted her "feelings". She would call Damon to find out if that was the whole story, somehow she didn't think so.

She stretched out and snuggled close to Reggie. He held her while she drifted into sleep...

.... and she drifted onto the third floor landing of

their apartment building. She always hid in the stairwell there when she was young. It was the place she went to feel safe, and to escape the fighting and cursing going on in their apartment by her mother Connie, and her father Chauncey. The apartment always looked like a disaster area when they were done. Her father was always drunk, and her mother Connie, hurled obscenities at him as well as small pieces of furniture. Those fights were often violent, and the police were frequently called to their home. Connie would threaten Chauncey with a knife when she got really mad. Brea was a sensitive child, they scared her. Someone was going to get hurt one day. Her four brothers didn't seem to care one way or the other. Connie had pushed Chauncey down to the floor and was standing over him with the butcher knife raised.....

"Baby, baby it's okay, you were dreaming." Reggie said, gently shaking Brea awake. Brea was sobbing and shaking uncontrollably.

"I'm sorry," she said, wiping her eyes. She told Reggie all about her nightmares, they came especially if she was stressed, and they had haunted her all of her life. Reggie wanted to know if she had ever considered seeing someone to get help. He thought it could be caused by some deep-seated crisis that had happened to her.

"I've thought about seeing someone, but I've always been too busy."

"Now that you're on hiatus, you need to take the time," he suggested to her softly.

"Maybe I will, the dreams are pretty bad Reggie and I wake up crying all the time." She told him. Reggie didn't want to leave her alone, what he had just witnessed scared *him*. To her, it was just another nightmare. To him it was quite disturbing. "Do you want to talk about the dream?" He asked hoping it would make her feel better.

"No, they've become part of my everyday existence."

"I'm staying here with you tonight," he said, firmly.

They watched TV for a while longer. He poured her a glass of wine, and they went upstairs to bed. Reggie cuddled Brea in his arms while she fell asleep. He enjoyed the softness of her, the sweetness of her smell, and he finally fell asleep himself.

The next day, Brea met Damon at Saundra's Lounge on Franklin Street. "Brea," Damon said, smiling when he saw her. He was at the bar. "I left you a couple of messages yesterday. I wanted to bring you up to speed."

"I've heard some of it from Reggie. Tell me what's going on."

He told her what she was afraid of hearing, more

mess from the Melik Iverson camp! Bobby Knowles was trying to make trouble for all of them. Apparently, he had never been compensated from the buyout and had unsuccessfully tried to get his share from Melik. Melik in turn, wouldn't deal with him, wouldn't even return his calls so he got a lawyer and wanted to sue. "I'm not sure what the agreement between Melik's label and Bobby was. I wasn't privy to that." Damon said. "When I bought your and Ice's contracts from Melik, there was nothing relating to Bobby Knowles in the paperwork."

So why does he want to sue you?" Brea asked confused.

"I'm sure his lawyer has told him that when I bought the contracts, I automatically assumed all of the conditions, agreements, outstanding debt and whatever went with them, and that's true. Negotiating recording contracts is part of my livelihood, and I'm good at what I do. Now it is possible Bobby accepted verbal promises from Melik, and I'm not sure what they might have been. All I'm saying is there was nothing in writing, it's not like I missed something."

"I knew I felt trouble in the air," Brea said, looking into space.

"I'm not overly concerned." It's just that it could be time consuming and messy. Everything was done aboveboard and legal. I have only one slight apprehension."

"What's that?"

"I did the buy-outs as one deal, instead of doing them individually. If his attorney is lucky enough to use that loop-hole, that could make your contract and Ice's contract with me null and void. Melik would love to hear that shit!"

"Oh pleeeease don't let that happen." She begged. They sat had a couple more drinks, hugged and left Saundra's. "I'll keep you posted Brea, but I'm pretty confident that I've covered all my bases." He kissed her forehead and they went their separate ways.

TWENTY-SIX
JADE

THE HOT STORY in town that month, involved one of D.C.'s biggest drug dealers Richard P. Sweet, better known as "Sweet Dick". He had been arrested after he was set up in a sting by DCPD, and Wendy's firm had been hired to represent him. Jade's station Fox 5 hadn't carried anything on it yet. *Maybe that's why Wendy's been so busy, Jade thought.*

"Sweet Dick" had been a classmate of theirs in high school. He was *the* lady's man extraordinaire, hence the name. *Jade smiled as she thought about him.* He had at least one girlfriend in *every* homeroom. He was voted "Most Likely to Succeed" their senior year, and graduated in the top percentile of the class—the boy was heavy! *"Big brains and other thangs"*, was what the girls used to say about him.

"Sweet Dick lived large in D.C., everybody knew him and loved him. He was a street legend. They say it was nothing for him to leave ten-thousand dollars at his church any given Sunday, to help people who needed help. How "Sweet Dick" got it, didn't concern them. "Sweet Dick" was a smart, intelligent man, and a sting was probably the only way they were ever going to get him. From the picture in the Post, he was still as fine as he ever was. Someone had posted what was described as D.C.'s largest bail security on record, and he was back on the street after being in jail all of an hour-and a half.

Jade was working at her desk and Michelle called on the intercom, "Jade you have a call from Mitch on line five."

"Yes Mitch." She sounded irritated.

"Hey Princess, you okay?"

"I'm fine and you?"

"I'm okay, I'm in Chicago. I thought I'd give you a call since I haven't been able to catch you lately. Are we cool? You miss me?"

"How's Chicago?" She asked, ignoring his questions.

"It's alright. Am I going to see you when I get back?"

"Why don't you give me a call when you get back, and we'll go from there?

"Okay baby, I'll call you when we get in, love ya'."
Click.

"Jade, Wendy's holding on line two," Michelle said.

"Ohh, Wendy damn! I thought I was going to have to call in the National Guard to find you. Where the hell have you been?" Jade asked her, relieved and annoyed.

"Been real busy, and I don't have much time to talk. What are you doing after work?" Wendy asked rushing.

"Nothing much, what's up?"

"Come up to the house for dinner and drinks. I need to talk to you."

"Okay," Jade said trying to read her. "How about 6:30?"

"Good time. Got to run, kisses." *Click.*

Wendy sounded like something was awry.

Jade drove up Riggs Road toward Northwest, trying to figure out why Wendy sounded mysterious. When she got to Wendy's, she luckily found a good park in front of her house, one of the neighbors was going to be pissed. She rang the doorbell, Wendy opened it and they hugged.

"I miss you Wendy." Jade said sincerely.

"I've missed you too, come on into the kitchen and pour yourself a drink. I'm whipping us up some dinner."

"You must really be on a hard case. I've been trying

to catch up with you forever. Jade sat down at the breakfast counter in the spacious kitchen.

"Jazz, do you remember "Sweet Dick" from school?

"Of course, I was just reading about him today. Is that what you're involved with? The paper said your firm was representing him."

"I'm involved alright, she said, looking tense. "You know I love you as much as if you were my blood sister don't you?" Wendy asked Jade. "There's a lot of crap getting ready to go down, I don't think you need to know about for your own good. Let's just say this—I'm scared." Wendy whispered.

"What's wrong?" Jade asked alarmed. She had never seen Wendy Haines that nervous—ever.

"Remember that game we played downstairs about really knowing a person? What you know about me as your best friend is just a prelude to my real life Jazz."

"Wendy what's wrong?" Jade asked her again.

"I said I wouldn't tell you yet, but Richard and I have been seeing each other for about six months……"

"WHAT?" Jade almost dropped her glass of wine. "You mean "Sweet Dick"?"

"Yes, and nobody knows. I can't afford to let anyone know, he's a known drug dealer, now here's the shit. I put this house up to help bond him out and the whole thing went wrong." Jade's mouth dropped open. "We had pre-arranged it so the identity of the person who posted the bail wasn't listed, but it is, and now it's a matter of public record. I'm so scared." Wendy was walking up and down the kitchen floor.

"Sit down baby," Jade said. "That was your money the paper talked about?"

"Some of it, most of it was his. I have his accounts in my name. I'm actually sitting on millions, Jazz. His cars and some of his properties are in my name too. Some snoopy-ass reporter is going to find out and I don't know what to do about it." Wendy said, pouring another glass of wine.

"Can't you say you did it because your firm represents him?"

That would have had to be cleared by the firm. This is strictly a personal thing, and I could get my firm in serious trouble. I know it's all going to blow up."

"Oh, God Wendy! What the hell were you thinking about? Why are you jeopardizing your career and your reputation?"

"The old L-word girl, I love this man. He's the sweetest man I've *ever* had, and I'd do it all over again. If he goes down Jazz, I'm going down with him."

"I don't know what to say Wendy, I'm in shock!"

"I'm so paranoid, I had one of my friends from

HILL FOXES

the Fifth District come in and sweep this house for bugs. Jazz grab your bloomers, this is going to be a big mess! Do me a favor and keep your ears open, let me know what you hear in your newsroom."

"You know I will," Jade reached out to hug her. "So where is "Sweet Dick now?"

"I talked to him a little while ago. He's going to chill about coming over here, I can't take that chance and he doesn't want me to. You know the best place for us to meet? In public, isn't that ironic? We have to hide in public." Wendy said, laughing.

"Right, because he's a client of your firm. Damn, damn, damn Wendy! What actually happened, I know there's another side of the story than what the Post gave."

"He went against his better judgment, made a deal with some guy from out of town himself. The agent *was* from out of town, Richard knows everybody in town so they couldn't use anyone from D.C. Since the courier was from out of town, he didn't want any of his lieutenants to do the deal. He and the guy met and made the exchange. The agent gave Richard a bag of marked money and left. When Richard came out of the apartment later that night, they were outside waiting for him. They took the bag out of his briefcase and arrested him." Wendy and Jade sat quietly for a while.

"I feel better now that I could tell you. I hope you're not disappointed in me Jazz, but you know what? I'd do it all again, that's how much I love him."

"Wendy and "Sweet Dick", Jazz whispered, dazed.

"Jazz, I'm going to ask you for another favor. This is going to be hard for me, but after tonight I want you to stay away from me until this is over. I don't want to put you in a position that could ultimately hurt you."

"Wendy, I'm not worried…."

"Trust me Jazz, there could be repercussions to you, you haven't even dreamed of yet. Don't call me I'll call you, as they say in the movies. So enough about my problems, let's eat." Wendy said, trying to brighten the mood.

"I've lost my damn appetite." Jade said.

Jade and Wendy drank the whole bottle of wine and nibbled at dinner. When Jade got ready to go home, she realized she had no business driving a car or operating heavy machinery. "Nooo chick, give me those keys," Wendy said, "you're spending the night." Wendy moved Jade's car into her garage so no one would see it. They talked about "Sweet Dick", Mitch and Keith until they fell asleep around one o'clock.

TWENTY-SEVEN
NOEL

THINGS HAD QUIETED down some at the District Courthouse. Lila had disappeared! She had stopped her one-woman protest against Marcus every day in front of the building. It was eerily quiet.

Marcus had attempted to have her served a few times at the women's shelter, but she eluded them and they couldn't catch her. The shelter director wasn't allowed to take the summons, so they continued to try to find her.

Noel was anxious for them to find Lila. She was simply tired of sneaking around with Marcus. They tried to keep their relationship and their engagement as hush-hush as possible, and she was tired of living like that.

Noel was dressing to meet the *Hill Foxes* at Takoma Station for drinks and jazz that evening. She drove up to 4th Street, found a good park and went inside the popular spot. She spotted the *Hill Foxes* seated at a table.

"The D.C. Hill Foxes," she greeted them grinning.

"Hey, Miss Noel," Jade said, hugging her. Noel went around the table cheek-kissing Jill, Brea and Lauren.

"God, I can't believe everyone made it," liquor please!"

"Girl, we all ahead of you, you're going to have to play catch up." Jill said.

"Where's Wendy, is she coming?" Noel asked.

"She's busy working." Jade answered.

"So what's going on sluts?" Noel asked them laughing. Everybody gave quick updates on their love life. Noel thanked Jade again for what she did at the courthouse.

"All in a day's work." Jade said, winking.

Lauren was quiet, she seemed depressed and she was drinking heavily. After she was prodded into giving her love-update, everybody sat quietly with their mouths hanging open.

"What?" Jill said finally. "So you're in a three-way?"

"Wait a minute, exactly what is this woman asking you to do?" Jade asked Lauren.

"I don't know if she's suggesting a three-way, as

much as I think she's asking me to accept that we're sharing Mustafa." Lauren told them.

"Excuse me," Noel asked, "what's the damn difference?"

Brea started singing, "*Lady, I'm calling to let you know your husband been cheatin' on us...*" Everybody started laughing.

They ordered appetizers, drank all sorts of exotic things, and laughed until midnight. The *Foxes* hugged, kissed and went their separate ways. "Until the next time ladies," Brea said waving.

The next day in court, Noel was going to meet Marcus in the cafeteria and *casually* "bump into him" and eat at the same table. As soon as he sat down with his tray, his beeper started buzzing. One of the Marshall's was rushing toward their table. Noel's eyes got big. Marcus glanced at his beeper and his home number was displayed. He looked pale. He jumped up from the table and the Marshall told him he was there to escort him home, there was a problem.

"Oh my God," Noel whispered. She grabbed her purse and followed them upstairs. That was what she hated about that whole secrecy thing—she didn't dare ask too many questions.

She found out later, that Lila had put on a wig and sunglasses, and in disguise, signed in as Mrs. Prince's daughter Carolyn at the security desk of

Marcus' building. Lila knew Carolyn from picking Mrs. Prince up after work, when they lived in Northwest. When the security desk called Mrs. Prince, they said Carolyn her daughter, was on her way up. Mrs. Prince thought it was just a pleasant surprise visit, nothing unusual.

Lila knocked on the apartment door and when Mrs. Prince answered, she knocked Mrs. Prince to the floor and started running through the apartment calling for Brent and Bryan. Brent was in school, and Bryan was playing in the den. Lila grabbed Bryan and headed for the door. Mrs. Prince tried to stop her, but the fall had twisted her ankle so badly, she couldn't hold on to Lila. Mrs. Prince hobbled to the phone and called downstairs to the front desk to alert them.

Lila rode the elevator to the basement floor, passing the main floor stop, with Bryan clutched in her arms. When the doors opened on the basement floor, security was waiting for her there too.

"Ma'am, put the baby down," the security guard told her.

"Get away from me," Lila screamed. Additional security personnel came to the basement. Lila flipped open a switch blade knife and lashed out at the guard.

"Get away from me and my baby!" She screamed. Bryan was so frightened, he started to kick and scream. In his kicking, he knocked the knife from Lila's hand and security grabbed her.

By the time Marcus got to Tiber Island there were police, a fire truck and two ambulances. The police for Lila, the fire truck for Mrs. Prince, then the ambulance to transport Mrs. Prince to the hospital, the other ambulance to transport poor Lila to St. E's hospital.

"I'm going to lose it Noel," Marcus said later that night after he told her what had happened on the phone.

"No, you're not Marcus. We're going to be okay." Noel was desperately trying to believe that herself.

Marcus was going to take off while Mrs. Prince recovered. Her ankle had been badly sprained, and she would need crutches for a while. It was going to be hard for her to keep up with the two boys in that condition, but she was a trooper. What she did do every day was to position herself on the kitchen stool, and continue her magnificent meals as usual. Marcus did the other chores around the house that needed to be done. Noel would have helped, but she hadn't been invited to.

It had taken several days to get Bryan settled, he had been frightened by the whole ordeal and kept asking if that lady was coming to take him. Bryan was too young to remember Lila was his mother.

Noel invited Marcus and the boys to her house to give Mrs. Prince a break a few times. She thought it would also give her a chance to possibly bond with the boys, at least that was her hope.

TWENTY-EIGHT
JILL

JILL TOOK A long stretch in bed, and then smiled as she listened to water splash against the glass shower door, Bryce was up early. He needed to be downtown on business by nine o'clock. He'd told Saundra he was going to be busy for a few days, so she wouldn't bug the hell out of him.

Jill usually worked a round-trip back to D.C. whenever she came to Miami, but had decided to take in a few days of well-deserved sun and fun with Bryce.

"Good morning Jill," he said, as she stuck her head inside the bathroom door. "Did you sleep well?"

"I did." She said. "I wish I could join you."

"I'd love you to, but I need to get out of here." He got out, grabbed a towel and rubbed the tiny beads of water from his sun-kissed body until the water disappeared.

"Did you want coffee?" Jill asked.

"I'll get some on the way, I don't have time." He pulled up his jeans and secured his holster. He stretched the South Beach Jazz Festival T-shirt over his head, and pulled it over his gun. "The sooner I leave, the sooner I can get back," he said, kissing her lips and rushing out the door.

Jill was going to enjoy a quiet day of *nothing* by the pool, and soak in some sun. She took a shower, put on a linen Sarong and some flip-flops. She pulled her thick curly hair up and tied it with a bright ribbon. Sitting in the kitchen, she waited for the coffee to finish brewing and dialed Julius.

"Hey baby," she said.

"Good morning. How's Miami?" Julius asked her.

"It's so good I think I'm going to spend a few days. Is that cool with you?" She asked in case he'd made plans for them to do something.

"It's cool. When do you think you'll be back?"

"Probably the day after tomorrow, I thought I'd get some shopping done, catch a little beach time— just chill. I wish you could join me honey." She said, secure in knowing good and well his job had him *locked-down*.

"I do too. I'm on a run right now so I'll call you back later. Have fun, I love you," he said, and hung up.

Jill stretched and filled her cup with hot coffee. All she wanted to do was relax out by the pool and catch up on her reading. On her days off in D.C. she never rested, she always found some reason to run the streets. The calm life-style of Florida screamed—*Relax!*

She pushed the search button on the Bose system radio looking for jazz stations, either WMIA or WDNA. While it searched, she perused the family photographs sitting on Cheyenne's rich mahogany room divider. They were an attractive family, her mother and father, her brother and there was a professional portrait of Cheyenne and some guy, a boyfriend maybe. She'd never actually heard Cheyenne mention anyone special before, but he was attractive. There was a beautiful large wall portrait of her hanging above the fireplace, possibly by the same photographer, and there was something about that portrait. Something kept drawing her eye to it.

Jill grabbed magazines from the shelf and went outside to the patio, stretched out in the lounge chair and thumbed through the books. A soft tropical breeze caressed her shoulders ever so gently, and the smell of salt water floated on the humid air. She turned to a page and there as big as day in an old Vogue was Brea, an exquisite picture of her in all black. *Wow was she ever beautiful!*

Jill felt her eyelids getting heavy and she began drifting. She was so enjoying the peace and quiet that she let her old friend Mr. Sandman, whisk her away.

The telephone woke her at 12:30 p.m. "Hey baby you hungry?" It was Bryce. He picked her up and they drove out to Apprion's on the beach for a late lunch, she hadn't eaten all day and she was starving. Jill ordered Grilled Snapper with rice and a spring salad. Bryce had Chicken Enchiladas with a Salsa salad, sour cream and tortilla chips. After they finished two Margaritas each, they walked hand in hand down the beach and played toe-tag with the ocean waves coming ashore. They talked about his job and his dreams for the future. Jill talked about hers, and before they knew it, the sun had set. They rode back toward Madison House in Bryce's Wrangler with a hot breeze blowing through Jill's tight thick curls. He stopped by and picked up carry-out dinners for them from Outback.

After finishing the meal, Jill and Bryce glided around the pool on floats drinking wine, while they star-gazed.

"I really enjoy you Jill, you're always what I need." Bryce told her smiling. He slid off of his float and swam over to hers.

"Don't do it," she said, giggling.

"Don't do what-this?" He asked, and tipped her

float over into the water. They played in the pool like two little children, splashing and dunking each other.

"Bryce, stop! Isn't that your pager?" He prepared for the attitude he was about to show Saundra. *I told her I was going to be busy!* However, the number displayed on his beeper was the Sheriff's Department.

"OH HELL! They're calling me in."

"Oh, Bryce I'm so sorry," Jill said, getting out of the pool. "There is one good thing, I'll still be here tomorrow."

"I just hope I will," he said, sarcastically. "With these emergencies, we never know how long it'll be. I've got to go check in, Jill." Bryce angrily snatched his clothes and started to dress. He wrapped his arms around Jill and held her for a moment. "I'm so sorry our evening had to end," he whispered. "I'll see you as soon as I can." He gave her a slow loving kiss, and left.

Jill took a hot shower and laid on the sofa in the living room listening to soft jazz. She was sorry Bryce had to leave, she felt closer to him than anyone. That *did not* fit into her *un-committal rule*. She loved Julius, but he kept giving her little hints of skepticism, lightly sprinkled with distrust. There was something strange about him, she couldn't quite figure out.

Michael was a sweetheart, she enjoyed the time they spent together whenever she was in Palm Beach.

Clark in Atlanta, as *fine* as he was, was showing signs of breaching their "agreement". He was falling in love with her, and love was simply not allowed.

Bryce was her special and favorite "honey-bun" of all, she really liked him, and she needed to remind herself of her own rule *–"it could go no further."*

She poured a glass of Zinfandel since she was *unexpectedly* going to be sleeping alone. She sat gazing at Cheyenne's photos—*Cheyenne!* Cheyenne hadn't come home yet, Jill paged her. "Lady C, where the hell are you?" Jill asked, wondering why she hadn't come home.

"Girl, I'm still In D. C., at Tyson's Corner to be exact. Are you back at your house now?" Cheyenne asked.

"No I'm still at *your* house. I decided to stay a few days. You don't mind do you?"

"Not if you don't mind my staying here a few days," she said, and they laughed.

"Make yourself at home Cheyenne."

They wished each other good visits, and hung up. Jill sipped her wine, walked around the living room enjoying the feel of her bare feet sinking into Cheyenne's plush carpeting. She looked at the novels on the shelf looking for a good book to read, but most of Cheyenne's books were murder mysteries—not Jill's taste. She admired the photos again. Cheyenne had framed them in silver, sea-shells and gold, all beautiful frames. That's it! She had wondered what to leave as a gift for Cheyenne. She'd buy her a beautiful picture frame the next day.

For lack of anything else to do, Jill closed up the house and got into bed. There was absolutely nothing on TV she was interested in seeing either. Jill pulled the covers back and got in. She dialed Julius but got no answer. "Humm." She plumped her pillow and started to drift off. Jill's eyes popped open, she abruptly sat up! She cut on the light and went to the living room. She turned on the lamp by the room divider and looked at the portraits again. She looked at the large portrait over the fire place.

"I--will—just—be--damned! You dirty little bitch!"

TWENTY-NINE
JADE

WENDY'S PREDICAMENT HAD taken Jade for a loop, she couldn't get over it. She never remembered Wendy and "Sweet Dick" being close in school, but maybe they weren't. What the hell was Wendy thinking? How did she get herself into that mess? Jade got depressed just thinking about it.

Jade got a call from Kirk down in Virginia with some good news about a possible deal. The client was in agreement with the restrictions Keith had insisted on regarding land use. The client was interested in building a home and raising horses. No stores, no malls, and no commercial buildings—those were Keith's stipulations. He was adamant about preserving the land in Brathwell County, the reason he had purchased so much of it himself. Whatever—all Jade knew, is that she was about to be PAID! She called Keith.

"Keith, it's me."

"Hey Me, I miss you." Keith said, laughing.

"I miss you too. I just spoke with Kirk about a client. I'm running down there this weekend to meet with them."

"I can't wait. You're staying with me, right?"

"I could, but when am I ever going to stay at Westbury? I feel guilty."

"What is it that you need to do there? I'm there almost every day looking after things. Aren't you satisfied with my services, Madame?"

"Of course, I am. I guess there's really nothing for me to do at Westbury when I think about it."

"My cleaning person goes in every Monday and dusts around, everything is fine there sweetheart." "I talked to Kirk too, he told me about the guy. I have one concern though. I'll talk to you about that when you get here."

"How's Ben, and how's Buddy?"

"They're both fine, and they miss you too."

"I'm on my way to bed so I guess I'll talk with you soon. I love you Keith."

"I love you more, goodnight Jazz."

Things at Channel 5 were moving right along. Jade was hounding her reporters and Traci about any information they might have on "Sweet Dick". She told them she was interested, because they had been in the same graduating class in high school. Wendy called her one day from one of the phone booths inside the court house, taking paranoia to new level. She said she was okay, that there was a lot going on behind the scenes. She wished she could share it, but the less Jade knew, the safer she'd be. She reminded Jade to let her know if she heard anything from the newsroom reporters and if she did, call her pager and put in 2255-669 which spelled CALL NOW. She would get back to her. *Wendy had been watching too many "I Spy" re-runs.*

Mitch and Jade went to dinner at Casper's out Pennsylvania Avenue one evening, and for once it was almost drama-free—almost.

"Mitch, I usually expect some bull** to happen before our date ends, surprise me tonight, please."

"I don't know why you so hard on me baby, I don't do nothin'."

"To show you how pleasant I'm going to be tonight," Jade said, "I'm not even going to mention the game incident with that young girl."

"I don't know what you're talking about Jade. Princess, what do I have to do to convince you that I love just you?" Mitch asked. "I'm not going to lie, women come at me all the time, but I love you." He reached in his pocket and pulled out a velvet box. Inside was a gorgeous diamond tennis bracelet from Minnelli's.

"Mitch, how beautiful, I don't know if I should take this." Jade told him, surprised.

"Why not?"

"Thank you Mitch," Jade said, holding her arm out so he could put it on. *Guilt is a bitch, ain't it.* He reached over and gave her a quick kiss. "I love you Princess."

Dinner was different. They ate soul food for a change. A number of the Skins were there for dinner, too. They came to the table and Jade met some she hadn't met before. Butch Bennett, the running back, came over after a while and announced, "Cinderella-time man." Everyone around them started getting up to leave. "Well, I guess it's that time baby," Mitch said. They gathered their things, Mitch tipped the waiter, and they walked outside. Jade drove, so Mitch walked her to her car. They hugged for a while, and then he gave her a long kiss.

"Thank you for the bracelet Mitch, it's lovely."

"I'm glad you like it Princess. You know we're away this weekend, so I'll call you when I can."

"I'll be down in Virginia on business this weekend, you might need to page me," Jade said, getting into her car. "Be safe Mitch." She started the car and let the engine run to warm. Jade noticed a woman who had been inside, come out and get into the car parked next to Mitch. He leaned inside and said something to her, and then got into his car. Jade decided to sit there a little longer and she watched Mitch pull out. The woman's car pulled out behind him, and Jade behind them. She watched their cars all the way down Pennsylvania Avenue, and when Mitch took the Richmond exit, so did the woman. Coincidence?

Jade couldn't wait to get home. When she got there, she thought she had waited long enough for Mitch to have gotten to Fairfax. She dialed his number. It rang, and rang, and rang. *For somebody who expected a phone check, he sure wasn't trying to answer*! She was about to hang up when Mitch answered like he was being awaken from a deep sleep.

"Yeah." He answered, hoarse and whispery.

"Mitch, I wanted to thank you again for my bracelet, it's absolutely beautiful. I didn't wake you did I, it's only ten o'clock?"

"Yeah, I'm tired." Jade could hear music in the background, people talking and laughing. Sounded like a party to her!

"Oh, I'm sorry, I hear you have guests. Don't let me keep you. I thought you said you were asleep."

"No, my homeboy got some people over, but I'm in bed." He said, trying to sound groggy.

"I'll just bet you are," Jade said, shaking her head. "Goodnight Mitchell."

HILL FOXES

Winter was settling in, the days were getting shorter. The aroma of burning firewood was in the crisp air, and people were walking a little faster to their destinations. Flowers left over from fall were frosted over in the mornings, and bags of leaves were at curve-side waiting for the trash man.

Jade left work and headed down to Brathwell County. She could have made the trip the next morning, but she didn't want to waste another minute away from Keith. Ben, Keith, and Buddy were waiting for her when she pulled up in front.

"Hi sweetheart," Keith said, hugging her.

"Hi, yourself." She gave him a kiss and went inside. Ben was at the car getting her bag out.

"What do you want to do first," Keith asked, "go over to Westbury, or eat dinner?"

"I came straight from the office. I'd rather take a quick shower and have dinner. Could we save Westbury until morning?"

"We can. Ben took your bag upstairs, so make yourself at home and I'll see you in a little bit." He kissed Jade's forehead. Ben was coming out of the master bath when she got upstairs.

"Enjoy Miss Jazz." He had already filled the tub and sprinkled the bath with pink blossoms. A decanter of wine and a wineglass sat on the marble ledge, chilled and ready. *They're going to spoil my ass rotten!*

When Jade finished her bath, she threw on some jeans, and a thick sweater, and went downstairs. She followed Keith's voice coming from the game room. He was on the telephone and when he saw her, he cut his conversation short. He got up from the desk, came over and gave her a big hug. "Enjoy your bath?"

"You're spoiling me Keith," she said, in a warning tone.

"If that's what I have to do to keep you here, so be it. "Hungry?"

"Sure am." He left for the kitchen. Jade looked around the room examining things she hadn't noticed before. The African art was remarkable. There were pictures of his family, millions of trophies and awards from high school, college and the NFL. It was all quite impressive.

Keith came back into the room. "It's going to be another twenty minutes," he was carrying a plate of appetizers. The fireplace had a real fire, and there was such a feeling of peace in that room. She took off her shoes and curled up on the soft sofa.

"Jazz, I took the liberty of telling Kirk to try and get the client to buy the whole plateau. He's interest in buying most of it, but the problem is the part he *isn't* buying. That's going to be worthless. It's not large enough to do anything with, and nobody would buy it. The next thing you know, he'd have something parked on it, or let his horses graze there, and after a while you won't remember whose it was. Happens a lot around here." Keith tried to explain.

"Suppose we fence the area in so he wouldn't have access?" Jade asked him.

"We could do that, but my point is that small piece would become wasted land. You could probably squeeze a small house with a front yard and back yard, but people don't do that around here. They want land around them."

"I understand. I'm so glad you're looking out for me, can you imagine me trying to handle this?"

"I'm sure he's playing a game, he thinks we'll lower the price on the other piece because he knows there's nothing we can do with it. He can bite my butt," Keith said, and Jade fell out laughing. "The only thing I like about this guy is that he's paying cash up front."

"What are we going to do?" Jade asked.

"Don't worry about it sweetheart, I'm going to handle it. And if all else fails, he can take his cash somewhere else."

"Dinner's ready you two," Ben announced. He started them with something like an egg roll stuffed with mushroom, cheese, hot peppers and a sweet sauce dip on the side. Then, he brought out a delicious Pot

B.J. MAYO

Roast with gravy, mushrooms, mashed potatoes, string beans and hot rolls.

"Ben, pack your bags. You're going home with me," Jade said, laughing. After dessert they *retired* to the game room with their wine. Jade sat looking into the fire, thinking how much she loved Keith's lifestyle.

"Penny for your thoughts," Keith said, putting his arms around her.

"I was just thinking how peaceful it is, and how much I enjoy being here." She laid her head on his shoulder. She was listening to a beautiful song. "Who's that?" She asked him.

"That's The Patti Wicks, awsome isn't she? I had the pleasure of meeting her after one of her performances in South Florida once." Keith said, and turned the music up with the remote.

"I'd love to borrow that Keith."

"I'll get you one sweetheart, I ain't parting with mine." They laughed and listened to Patti.

"Do you like fat women Keith?" Jade asked, softly.

"I don't know what you mean?"

"If I keep eating Ben's food, I'm going to look like Miss Piggy. I just wanted to make sure you liked fat women."

"If it's you sweetheart I'll love my woman fat." Keith was laughing.

"That's what you say now, and that's a good answer. What would you be doing if I weren't here?"

"Let's see, probably working out. I usually do that after football practice and checking Westbury." Ben came to the door, "I'm headed to bed, need anything?"

"No man, we're cool thanks. See you in the morning Ben." They sat on the couch and watched the fire and listened to music. Jade snuggled up close to Keith and yawned.

"I'm not going to do what I did before, unless you've already slipped those sleeping pills in my wine."

"I don't put sleeping pills in your wine woman, are you ready for bed?" Jade grabbed his hand and led him upstairs. They took their clothes off and got comfortable. Keith piped the music upstairs, and they held each other in the candle lit room. They kissed kisses of love and promise, and God knew how happy she was to be in the arms of this man. She reached into her cosmetic bag on the nightstand and grabbed the condoms. She had remembered them that time. Keith's look was so intense, it scared her. His jaw tightened, he took the condom and made love to her, but it was incredibly different from their first time. He was cold, emotionless, and forceful.

Afterwards, he went into the master bathroom, cut on the shower and got in and she thought, *here we go again—Condom Drama!*

Jade went to the bathroom and joined him in the shower. When she stepped in, he stepped out. "Keith did I do something wrong? She asked him, softly.

"I'm just tired," he said, toweling himself off.

"Are you sure? Is it the condom?"

"That *does* answer a question I had," he said, and went into the bedroom. She finished her shower and went into the room. He was already in bed, and his back was turned to her.

"You need anything?" He asked.

"I need you," she said, softly.

"Goodnight Jazz."

Jade lay in bed for what seemed like hours, she couldn't sleep. *I've hurt him. I was trying to protect him, but I hurt him instead.* Now that she had accepted the fact that Mitch was sleeping around, her intentions had been to protect them both. At some point she fell asleep. She turned over during the night and saw the candles still flickering. As her eyes focused, she saw Keith sitting on the chaise in the dark. He had been watching her sleep—now *that* was ekkie!

"Keith is everything alright?"

"Everything is fine, go back to sleep."

"Come to bed Keith, please?"

"I will." He had a glass of wine in his hand. Jade sat up in bed and propped her pillows up.

"You think I could have a glass too?

"Sure." He poured her a glass and took it to her.

"Thank you, come on in." she said, patting the bed. He sat his glass down on the nightstand and got in. They drank in silence. Jade glanced at the clock—three-forty. "Keith have you been to sleep?"

"No."

"Have I upset you that badly?"

"I'll be okay."

"Don't you think we should talk about it?"

"Not really. I had some things I needed to work out in my head, just like you're going to have to do."

"I know," she whispered, "I'm doing that. I just need more time."

"Take all the time you need sweetheart." When Jade finished her glass of wine she snuggled close to Keith. *Take all the time I need? What did that mean?*

The next morning Jade awoke alone, Keith was already downstairs. She dressed and went down. He and Ben were in the kitchen talking.

"Good morning, want some tea Miss Jazz?" Ben asked when he saw her entering the room.

"Good morning and it's just Jazz. I'll take some juice if you have it."

"Good morning Keith," she said, and bent down to kiss his cheek.

"Morning," he said, not looking up from his

newspaper. "What time would you like to go over to Westbury?"

"I told Kirk Ten." *Oh he's pissed, she thought.* The telephone rang and Keith grabbed it.

"Hey man…good…yeah, she's right here at the house…sure hold on." He handed her the phone, "Kirk."

"Good morning Jade. I'm sorry to have to tell you this, but the client had to go to Roanoke this morning on an emergency." Kirk said, apologizing. "I'm sorry you had to drive all the way down here for nothing, but there's not much I can do about it."

"Well, maybe I can get some other things done while I'm here and if he's available next weekend, I'll come back. Thanks Kirk, I'll touch bases with you during the week." She said, and hung up. "I guess you heard Keith?"

"*I'm* going to deal with this guy. I told you he's playing games. So what else do you want to do today?"

"Absolutely nothing!" She said, stretching her arms.

"Hungry?"

"Not yet. Just pretend I'm not here, and do what you do." She said.

"I've got a few things to take care of, and I'll take you to Westbury when I'm done. Make yourself at home."

Jade went to the game room, found a book and

began to read while Keith worked at his desk. Ben came in with a tray of country ham-biscuits and juice. Jade nibbled while she read. She still couldn't figure out what the hell happened to her when she came south of D. C., but she fell asleep and woke up two hours later. Keith was putting more firewood in the fireplace. She and Buddy had been knocked out.

"Keith, I swear you or Ben put something in my food." Keith gave her a faint smile. She knew he was still pissed at her, but she ignored his coolness and pretended she hadn't noticed. Maybe she could change his mood. She wasn't used to him being that way. "Let's ride over to the farm," he said, "I'll get your coat." Ben had already brought the Jeep around to the front and it was already warmed. *A girl could get used to this.* She smiled.

"Keith, you've been quiet all day." She tried to make him talk to her while they rode the winding roads. The trees had emptied their leaves across the fields, and their branches stood bare against the blue sky.

"Just thinking," he mumbled. They went into the house and he helped her out of her coat.

"Keith, do you keep the heat on in here all the time?"

"Yes, it prevents the pipes from freezing. It's not turned up high, just enough to knock the chill off."

"That makes sense. I'm going upstairs to get Aunt Judith's mink coat for mama."

I'll get the mail together for you." Keith said, going toward the study. They went over the bills, and Jade signed a few checks so he could pay them.

"Is there anything else you want to do while you're here?" He asked her.

"I guess not."

"Let's take a walk." Keith said, getting their coats. They walked outside and started towards the woods. It was brisk out but the sun felt warm. Jade took Keith's hand as they walked and it felt good, he had on leather gloves and his big hand swallowed hers.

Jade's beeper buzzed and like a fool, she looked at it. She didn't react to the call, but she was sure Keith guessed it was Mitch.

"Jazz, I overheard you tell Kirk you would be back next weekend to meet the client."

"If he can re-schedule the meeting I will, but I was thinking about coming anyway. I love getting away from D.C. and spending time here." She said, smiling.

"For the time being, I think you need to stay here at Westbury when you come. I'll prepare the house for your visit next weekend," Keith said, not looking at her. Jade tried not to reveal the pain his request made to her heart—it felt like a knife. She wasn't prepared for that, but she managed to say, "Okay." They continued to walk slowly while the only sound heard was the sound of their footsteps in the dry leaves. Buddy had run ahead and Jade was desperately trying to regain her composure. *I'm losing him.* All of a sudden, she felt defiant and decided to challenge his stance. "You know, I really don't have to stay here, I can go home this afternoon. I don't have anything else to do here." She said, arrogantly.

"Whatever." He said, not breaking his stride. *Whatever?* They walked back to the house in silence. Jade picked up the coat she was taking and looked around before they left. Keith was putting the inside lock on the door. She breezed past him, attitude intact, and he grabbed her hand. "I love you, Jazz. Just make sure you come to me soon." He kissed her a kiss of goodbye.

They went back to Keith's and she packed her bag. He hadn't begged her to stay like she had expected him to once she threatened to leave, that strategy hadn't worked. Keith disappeared somewhere within the house and Jade never saw him again. Ben took her bag to the car that was already in the circle, warm, and ready for the highway.

"Have a safe trip back Jazz," Ben said softly. There was the sound of regret in his voice. "Thanks." She jumped into her Beamer and headed north.

THIRTY
NOEL

NOEL WAS "WAITING to exhale," Marcus had filed papers for his divorce! His ingenious investigators had staked out the Center where Lila and other residents of the women's shelter received their medications. The weather was changing and Lila needed a place to stay, so it was imperative that she got her prescriptions filled to be allowed inside the shelter. During the warmer months, she hung out in the park, but the nights were colder now.

Marcus learned that the court had appointed Attorney Garry Mayo to represent Lila. The preliminary documentation confirming her mental illness had been presented, and they expected the hearing to be soon. Garry was a frat brother and friend of Marcus', so he expected everything to go smoothly.

Noel was getting excited. They had been through

hell and it was finally coming to an end. She was anxious to get started on her wedding plans.

Marcus wasn't bitter toward Lila she was ill, but he loathed the humiliation and pain she had put him and the boys through. Marcus, Noel, and Mrs. Prince were still troubled over the affects the near kidnapping had caused Bryan. Lila's attempted abduction of him had resonated with the poor little thing to a point of concern. He kept asking, "*Is that lady going to take me?*" There was no telling what Lila may have told him the short while they were in the elevator together that morning.

"Honey, have you thought about getting help for Bryan? Noel asked Marcus.

"Of course I've thought about it, but I can't imagine how they would get through to a child that young. I'm kind of taking the wait and see approach."

"They have ways of helping him by using methods on his level like play therapy, art and drawing, a number of things."

"I don't know." Marcus said.

"It may take some time, but he needs to feel safe again. Marcus, if I'm going to be part of your lives, those boys should be around me more. I know you have a lot on your plate right now, but we need to start including them into *our* equation. It's not just going to be you and me."

"I will," he said, without elaborating.

Noel wanted to make him realize there were other things affecting their future together. The boys, especially Brent, weren't going to understand her being in their lives out of the clear blue sky. She needed to be around them to gain their trust and their love in order for them to accept her. She couldn't show up one day out of nowhere and be "Mommy", it didn't work like that.

She wondered herself how long that was going to take. When was he planning to *include* her in their lives? It wasn't something that was going to happen overnight so did that mean a further delay in their marriage plans? Noel was simply growing weary.

THIRTY-ONE
LAUREN

LAUREN WAS FIGHTING demons from within. Every nerve and fiber in her body told her to dump that looser, and move on! All she needed in her life right then was another looser but stop—was he a looser or was she? Was she so desperate for a man she was willing to *knowingly* share him with another woman—his woman?

She felt she had been manipulated into that triangle. She didn't purposely go looking to join up with a" love-group".

Lauren was incensed, she was angry and most of the anger was directed at her.

Conversely, not in all of her thirty-three years had she met a man living or dead, who cared for her the way he did. She was his Queen, his Goddess of Love, and that's exactly the way he treated her. He sat her on a pedestal and worshipped her from the very throne he had placed her on. What warm-blooded-oxygen-breathing woman could reject that? He completed her and fulfilled her every desire. He assured her she was a woman possessed with great beauty and sensuality, and she was totally disgusted with herself for shamelessly letting him convince her of that. Now she understood what Haaydia meant, if having Mustafa in her life, in her world and in her bed, meant she had to accept Haaydia and God only knew who else, then so be it!

Lauren hurled the pillow that lay on the living room floor into a corner of the room, knocking over a vase of flowers. She slammed close the door of her condo and threw her recycle bag into the garbage shoot in the hall. The garbage shoot echoed the sound of breaking glass all the way down to the basement. She had contributed quite a few wine bottles to the recycle lately.

Her Pathfinder was already packed and ready to go on her trek to the Pentagon. She would be completing the photo shoot she was doing for the Air Force's recruitment project. She had met the most appealing *man-prospects* during her time there and would have been worthy of her exploration, had it been the year earlier. Right then, there was someone in her life that satisfied her needs so why was she so angry?

Lauren worked hard that day to complete the project within the guidelines agreed on, not stopping for food or drink. At the end of the day as she was being cleared to leave by Pentagon Security, her beeper buzzed. She found a phone.

"My Queen," Mustafa's deep voice greeted her. "Are you free tonight?"

"I could be, why?"

"I'd like to come by after closing if that's okay."

"Sure, if it's okay with everybody else." Lauren answered, sarcastically.

"There's no need to be unpleasant Lauren, if you'd rather I not come, I'll understand."

"Come then," she said. He had called her bluff.

Lauren drove through heavy traffic, crossed the bridge and headed up 14th Street toward home. She stopped and picked up a bottle of Pinot Noir, she had finished the bottle the night before.

Lauren was tired to the bone. She showered and sat on the edge of her bed rubbing her body in Cocoa Butter. She pulled the Caftan over her head, and lifted her heavy neglected locs of hair into a ponytail. Looking into the mirror, she saw that her slanted hazel eyes spoke to weariness and stress.

She answered Mustafa's knock and he entered into her space. What was it about that man that conjured up such wild feelings of both lust and hate from the pit of her soul? But then, she always felt a range of emotions whenever she saw him; happiness, hate, sorrow, forgiveness, anger and unadulterated love. When he took her in his arms, he could sense her pain.

"My love," he whispered in her ear. He kissed her with such sweetness he transferred his positive energy into her, and it felt so good.

"Would you like some wine?" She asked, pulling away from him.

"I would." He followed her into the kitchen and opened the bottle for her. "How was your day Lauren?" He poured her a glassful.

"I'm very tired," she said, moving into the living room.

"I'm sorry you have to work so hard. You look worried and thin. Are you taking care of yourself?"

"I am." She said, lying, "I'm just a little stressed."

"I hope I'm not responsible." He said, letting his finger trail down the back of her arm. She didn't answer, but downed the drink from her glass.

"I'm just trying to adjust or should I say, *accept* what has been put before me Mustafa. It's not easy."

"I'm sorry my Queen. I never meant to hurt you."

"Mustafa, what did you think your deceitfulness would do or did you care?" She asked, walking back into the kitchen to refill her glass. He followed her and took her hand.

HILL FOXES

"I wasn't being deceitful. What I thought is that you would feel my sincere love for you. Lauren you will never-*ever* find a man who will cherish you as much as I do." He said, looking into her eyes.

"You cherish too many," she said, taking back her hand and walking into the living room.

"I have room in my heart for that." He said, arrogantly.

Lauren was angry! She felt trapped. Yes, she could ask him to leave and never come back again, she'd done it before, but should she also ask her heart to stop beating? Her gold eyes narrowed to slits as the tug of war continued inside her.

"It wounds me to see you unhappy," he said, softly. "Above all else I want you happy, my Goddess."

Mustafa got up from the soda and walked to the patio door, he fumbled in his pocket. "Would you like me to roll you one?" He began unlocking the sliding doors.

"Alright, you can stay inside this time." Mustafa lit hers and then his own. They sat in silence while the aroma of the herb floated through the room. Mustafa messaged the back of her neck. The combination of his soft touch, and the marijuana was calming. It would be hard to explain to anyone how he ignited so many things in her at the same time. She wished she were stronger so she could resist him. Her inability to control herself only reassured her of her vulnerability. Was she vulnerable or was she desperate?

After a while, Lauren surrendered to her solace and laid her head against Mustafa's chest. Her nostrils filled with a sweet mixture of herb and Sandalwood oil, she closed her eyes. He took her hand and kissed the inside of her palm with his warm lips.

"I *do* love you Lauren," he whispered, trying to reassure her of his sincerity. He kissed her with such reverence she was suddenly whisked away to another place.

"I love you too Mustafa," she said, touching his lips with her finger. He lifted her from the sofa and carried her into the bedroom. He gently pulled the Caftan over her head, softly kissed her breasts and freed her locs, letting them cascade down her back. Lauren helped him pull the Dashiki over his head, and she tugged at the band of leather that held his locs in place. He kissed her, and she felt the heat emanating from him. She let her hand follow the outline of his muscular body, it was powerful yet supple, and through her trained photographer's eye, she saw a beautiful work of art.

Mustafa lifted Lauren's shaking body onto the bed, her whimpers of desire danced in his ears. She put her arms around her King; their bodies united and became one.

Afterwards, they lay in each other's arms wet with perspiration, and held onto each other as their passions subsided. There are no words to adequately describe their contentment.

Lauren kissed his lips. "Do you want me to start your shower?" She asked him, quietly.

"Not right now."

"It's after one," she said.

"She knows where I am." He said, softly.

THIRTY-TWO
JADE

JADE DROVE BACK to D.C. in a trance, she barely remembered driving into the city. The streets were busy with shoppers and weekend tourists. She rode past the Wharf and decided to stop in Phillips for a drink. She drove into the underground parking lot, and took the elevator up to the restaurant. She felt so alone. She had hurt Keith and Keith had hurt her, hurt her badly.

Jade took a seat at the bar and ordered a Vodka and grapefruit over crushed ice, and took a long slow drink. She desperately needed to talk to Wendy but wouldn't take that chance. She would respect Wendy's wishes and pray she was okay. Jade took another long drink and was about to finish that one.

"Fancy seeing you here," a voice came from behind.

"Terry Brooks. First, we don't see each other for

years, and then, we keep bumping into each other."

"How are you Jazz, mind if I sit down?"

"Please." She moved her purse.

"Are you alone? I don't want some hammer-head jacking me up in here." He said, laughing.

"I'm alone Terry, very much alone." She fought tears.

"That don't sound good. What are you doing down here in Southwest all by yourself, lady?"

"I was just getting off the road from Virginia, and decided I needed a drink or two or three. What brings you here?" She was downing the last of her drink.

"I went to the office today to do some work, and thought I'd come here for a meal, will you join me?"

"Thanks Terry, this *is* my meal." She said, trying to get the bartender's attention. "I'm not good company today."

"Tell you what," he said, "just come sit with me at the table and keep my company then." He was getting up from the bar.

"Just for a little while, like I said, I'm in a funk today."

Terry ordered the Seafood Sampler, a green salad, baked potato and a glass of Chablis. "What wrong Jazz? What's on your mind, you want to talk about it?"

"I feel like I've lost two of my dearest and closest friends, and I'm depressed about it." She felt the Vodka taking effect.

"I'm a good listener." Terry said.

"No, I'm not going to talk about it." She sounded like a first-grader.

"Okay, then let me order you a salad or something. You need to eat." He was concerned.

"Nooo, thank you."

"Do you ever see any of our classmates, Jazz?" Terry was trying to determine if she was high or just depressed.

"Not really." She said, waving for the waiter again.

"How's that fine Miss Wendy Haines. I see her in and out of the courthouse and *she's still fine*! Terry was grinning, his beautiful teeth glistened.

"I haven't seen her for a while." Jade said, sadly.

"I thought y'all were tight and stayed in touch?"

"We are, she's busy."

"So who are you seeing now, I heard you were with Mitch Dawson." Terry was biting a shrimp.

"I'm with him when I see him, and that ain't too often." Jade said, sarcastically.

"So why do you have the blues today, Mitch?"

"He's part of the problem. I should probably break up with him. We have such different life-styles, different schedules, it's just not working. You know what I mean?" She was almost lying on the table. "And flash—you're the first to know." The Vodka made Jade giggle.

"If it's not working Jazz, it's not working move on, life's too short. You've always been one of the beautiful people physically and spiritually, and you could have any man you want. Why waste time with him if it's a hassle?"

"You're right, I should move on. I miss the old days when your boyfriend was your best friend, and would stick with you through anything. People nowadays-another mind-set. It's every man for his or herself."

"We've gone our separate ways living in our own little worlds, but there's nothing like the love and support of your real homey's when you need them. I've never changed Jazz. I'm from the hood, still in the hood—by choice. I'll help my friends." He said and winked.

"You were always one of my favorite people Terry. We used to be as tight as brother and sister. How did I lose you?" She asked him, looking sad. "I miss you."

"I miss you too Jazz, I don't know about the sister and brother shit, but if that works for you, okay." He was laughing.

"You know what I mean Terry. We were always able to communicate." The Vodka was beginning to talk. "Waitress may I have a refill please?" Jade asked, as the waitress came over to clear Terry's dishes.

"Jazz, seriously, I know you're not a drinker so lighten up a little? You're not going to try to drive are you?"

"III'mm fine!" Jade said. The Vodka opened up the flood gates and tears flowed like a river. She was sitting in Phillips drunk and crying!

Oh shit, Terry said to himself. "Waitress, may I see the manager please?" Terry asked the woman.

"Is anything wrong Mr. Brooks?" The waitress asked.

"Everything's fine, I just need to speak with the manager. Jazz, give me your parking ticket."

"Terry, I'm okay stop worrying." Jade said, fumbling in her purse.

"Good evening Mr. Brooks, is everything okay here?" The manager asked Terry.

"Everything is excellent, as usual. I have a problem that couldn't be helped. My girlfriend ate some of my food and is having a reaction to something in my salad. What I'd like to do, is have you take her parking ticket and see that her car is secured until I can come back for it." Terry instructed him.

"Oh, no problem Mr. Brooks it's done, and I hope you feel better Miss Williams." The manager said, smiling.

Jazz started giggling uncontrollably. "That poor, poor woman," she said, laughing.

"Who is Miss Williams? Terry looked confused.

"Don't worry about it". She said, still laughing.

"Take my arm and let's go, I'm going to take you home Jazz." Terry was helping Jade from her chair.

"Terry quit! I'm not an invalid, you don't have to…ooops! On second thought, maybe you do."

They took the elevator down to the basement floor of the parking garage to Terry's Black Jag. He opened the door and helped her in.

"I love you Terry, you're my new best friend. The other ones can go to hell." She was still giggling.

"I love you too Jazz, where do you live?"

She must not have told him because she woke up at his house, in his bed. She looked at the clock in the strange room and it was eight-thirty p.m. "Ow, my head." She was thankful she still had her clothes on. Jade went to the bathroom then heard music, she followed the sound downstairs. There was a huge picture of Terry that was an enlargement from an Ebony article, "Most Eligible Bachelors." She saw a smaller one from the same article with Raymond Perry's picture. He was a judge downtown, and she thought. *Damn, my classmates have done well.* It was an excellent picture of Terry, he had been the class "pretty-boy" and he still was. Terry was about six-two and weighed around 190 or 195, medium athletic build, bronze complexion with dark curly hair and weird-colored eyes, with long eyelashes—the kind women had to buy! He had been their class Salutatorian.

Jade peeked into the living room and didn't see Terry, but found the source of the music. She walked through the dining room to the kitchen, and found him putting dishes into the dishwasher.

"Terry, I'm sorry and I'm so embarrassed. I don't know what to say except I don't do this all the time." She was leaning against the kitchen door.

"Jazz, please, I know that." He pointed to a chair at the breakfast table. "You're like family, don't be embarrassed. I just wanted to make sure you got home safely, but since you don't remember where it is, I brought you here. Young lady, here's where the lecture comes. You are a well-recognized television personality that cannot afford to do shit like this. End sermon."

"I know Terry, I know. I'm just so depressed."

"Want some coffee?"

"Got tea?"

"Got tea." He said, going into the pantry.

"I was admiring the pictures from the Ebony piece. Do you ever see or talk to Raymond Perry?" Jade asked him.

HILL FOXES

"We stay in touch. I'm often in his courtroom and we play tennis together quite often. That's my boy."

Terry and Jade talked until late. He pulled out old yearbooks and they started reminiscing about old times and talking about school. Surprisingly, after Jade found out *where* the hell she was when he took her home, they fell out laughing because she lived two blocks over from his house.

"If you want, we can ride back down to Phillips and pick your car up, or we can get it tomorrow."

"I'm still a little wobbly Terry. I'd rather get it tomorrow. Is that going to be a problem for you?"

"Not a big thang Black woman," he said, and reached over to give her a kiss of friendship. She reached over and gave him a kiss of appreciation that lasted a little longer than it should have, but what the hell.

"Good night Terry, thanks again." He waited for her to get inside.

The Thanksgiving holidays were approaching and Jade had been too self-absorbed to notice. "Good morning Michelle, the Thanksgiving decorations look nice girl. Did you do them?" She asked the receptionist.

"Traci helped me. I enjoy decorating. Don't forget we're having pot-luck next Tuesday around one-thirty. Are you bringing a dish?"

"I don't think you'd want to eat anything I made Michelle, for real." Jade said, laughing. "I'll bring bakery goods from Giant."

"That's funny Jade. Oh, you have a message from Mitchell to call him.

"Thanks, Michelle."

She took a deep breath and dialed Mitch's number. "Mitch, I got a message to call you?"

"Hey Princess, what's happ'nin, you miss me?"

"Same thing Mitch, work." She said, nonchalantly.

"Can you come over for a little get together party I'm throwing Friday night?" Mitch asked her.

"Is it a get-together or a party Mitch, there's a difference you know?"

"It's a pajama party, so wear your prettiest PJ's. Make sure you bring them *Foxes*, most of the guys on the team are gonn'a be there."

"Isn't this pretty close to the Dallas game to be having a party?"

"We just gonn'a party and have some fun, loosen up so we can whip Dallas' ass. Just the guests will be drinking."

"Yeah, right! Aren't pajamas a little risqué Mitch?"

"Just come and bring your girls. It's going to be fun." *Click!*

Jade called Noel and asked her to round up the

Foxes, find out if they wanted to go, and to find out who was *volunteering* to be the designated driver. She wished she could call Wendy, she probably needed a break. Jade called downstairs for Anthony.

"Anthony, would you like to go to a Buckskins party Friday night?"

"Do sinners in hell want ice water?" He screamed.

"It's a Pajama party, so pull out your best P.J.'s now. I think we're going to meet at my house."

"Oh, I can't wait." Anthony said, excited.

"Anthony, don't come out there in a night gown please." Jade said sniggling.

SLAM!

On her way home that evening, Jade saw Terry's big Jag sitting in front of his house. *It's so funny how she'd never noticed that house or car before.* Jade parked and rang Terry's doorbell.

"Hey, Terry."

"Come on in Jazz." Terry said, opening the screen.

"I was just passing and thought I'd say hi. You busy?"

"Not too busy for you, let me take your coat. Can I get you a drink?" He asked, hanging her coat in the closet.

"Uh, maybe a tiny one, I promise not to cry, plus I'm still hung over from Sunday." She said, laughing.

"I have Chardonnay or Zinfandel if you like." He brought two glasses from the dining room china cabinet.

He had been working at his desk. A fire was lit and classical music on his awesome sound system.

"Have I interrupted your work Terry?"

"Relax, it can wait. I enjoy your company and it's good to see you without the blues," he said, grinning. "Are you and Mitch okay now?"

"Slightly, but it's still early in the week."

"So what else have you been doing?" He asked.

"I've been running back and forth to Virginia taking care of the sale of some property my auntie left me."

"Do you have representation down there?"

"Yes, and so far he's doing a great job."

"Good. You know where to come if you need anything. Have you talked to your girl Wendy lately?"

"No, she's busy working."

"Do you know what she's working on?"

"Nope, sure don't." *Why would he ask me that?* 'Terry your house is so warm and comfortable, and it's so tastefully done. I love the way you hung the Ebony piece. Who framed that for you?"

"They did it as part of the deal."

"Eligible bachelor huh? Terry I don't know why I thought you were married all this time."

"I *was* once upon a time. You remember Becky Winslow? We married after Howard, and *that* didn't work out." He said, shaking his head.

"The old irreconcilable difference monster?"

"That too. Excuse my language, but the bitch was psychotic!"

"Ooow, that bad? What happened, on second thought *that is* a little personal, excuse my manners?"

"You don't know? Everybody knows." Terry said, and a look of sorrow crept across his face like a mask.

"Terry, if it's bad you don't have to talk about it."

"Becky got pregnant during the second year of our marriage." Terry started the story as he looked into the fireplace. "I don't know what happened, and as far as I knew everything was fine. She had a few problems and we couldn't have sex after the fourth month, but that happens sometimes. I got involved with painting and fixing the room for a nursery, buying baby clothes and stuffed animals, you know, the whole baby-coming shit. Pops made a crib for his first grand, we were all excited. I love children and have always wanted them, still do. Anyway, during her ninth month, they called me at the office and told me Becky was at the hospital. I was so nervous and excited that Raymond took me in his car. He teased me about being nervous all the way there. He kept saying *"okay big daddy, we'll be there in a minute."* He stopped the car at 4th and Rhode Island and bought some cigars and Brandy at that liquor store on the corner, and I totally lost it. I was going to whip his ass right out there on that corner. I almost hailed a cab and left that fool Jazz, it was just like a damn comedy show. All I wanted to do was get to the hospital to my wife, and this fool is playing around. So finally, when we get to Columbia Hospital to the third floor maternity ward they didn't have Becky's name on the admittance list. I told the nurse that a Dr. Marshall had just called me at work, and she told me Dr. Marshall was on the eighth floor. So me and Raymond take the elevator to the eighth floor and when we get off, the sign says Mental Health Unit. The nurse had called and told Dr. Marshall I was on the way up, and he met me at the elevator door.

Terry stopped talking and seemed to be trying to gather his composure. He seemed so sad and those beautiful eyes were all glassy.

"Did the baby die?" Jade whispered, softly.

"There *was* no baby. The eighth floor was the Psyche Ward and it was they who had admitted her.

"Terry what happened?" Jade asked almost in tears.

"She had lost the baby sometime during the third month and went right on with the charade. What

I've never understood is why? Why wouldn't she tell me?"

"Oh-my-God!" Jade whispered. "I'm so sorry Terry."

"I've never gotten over that, and I guess I never will." They both poured another drink and talked for the rest of the evening. She didn't want to leave until she felt he was okay again.

She kept thinking about Terry and Becky when she got home that night. She had always thought in school that Becky was strange. She checked her messages and there was one from Keith—

"Hey, just letting you know Jeff needs you to sign papers. Give me a call when you get in"—Beep One from Noel—

"We're getting a van for the party and everybody's going"—Beep

One from Mitch-

"Hey baby its Mitch, don't call me back, I'm in the streets."—Beep

"Hello Keith, how are you?" I got your message."

"Yes, Jazz. Jeff finally got this guy to agree to everything we want, he's ready to go to settlement. I guess you need to plan to come down or actually, it can be done over the phone if you're too busy."

"I'll give Jeff a call. How have you been?"

"Busy. I took Buddy to get his shots today."

"Aw, poor sugar. I'll be seeing you soon Keith, thanks and goodnight."

"Good night Jazz."

THIRTY-THREE
NOEL

BY D. C. standards, it was a warm winter day and government workers were escaping the cold greystone buildings to enjoy the sunshine at lunchtime.

Noel was between cases. She threw on her jacket and walked to John Marshall Plaza and bought a slice of pizza. She sat on the stone planter watching people come and go. Pan-handlers were a problem there, but she'd always give up a dollar or two to get rid of them.

"Ma'am, could you help me out?" Noel stuck her hand in her pocket to get the dollar bill she had folded up. *Oh my God it was Lila!* Noel handed her the dollar.

"Thank you."

"Are you hungry?" Noel asked her.

"No ma'am." Lila said.

"What are you going to do with that dollar?" Noel asked her, trying to gage her frame of mind.

"I'll save it for food. I don't use drugs."

"No, I didn't think that," Noel said, "I just wondered. Don't I know you? I work at the courthouse." Noel asked Lila, fishing.

"You might, I used to work at Simmons-McAlpine & Meghetti before I got sick."

"You were sick?" Noel asked, still probing."

"Yes, I'll probably always be sick because they tried to kill me."

"Who tried to kill you?"

"My husband." She said.

"Why would your husband try to kill you?"

"I caught him, and he was very angry with me for that."

"What did you catch him doing?"

Lila told Noel, she caught her husband with a woman in their bed. The woman was a partner at their law firm. Lila didn't go back to work because she couldn't bear being around them, so she took leave. The woman told everybody at Simmons, McAlpine and Meghetti that Lila had a nervous breakdown, and was hallucinating because Lila thought the woman had been in her house. The woman assured everyone she had never been to their house in her life, and told everybody Lila was crazy.

Lila said the only reason she even came home that day, was because she started her period and had soiled her skirt, she never came home in the middle of the day. She was too upset to go back to work and then she began to get sick. She slept all of the time and was very weak. Her husband hired a housekeeper-nurse. The nurse gave her vitamin shots to make her stronger, but the shots gave her horrible nightmares. She got sicker and sicker, so her husband had her put in a hospital and she couldn't get out. The medications at the hospital were so strong and made her so sick, she couldn't remember things. She was sedated most of the time.

After a while, she got better and they took her home. Her husband put her in the guest room. He and the housekeeper-nurse gave her pills and he told her if she didn't take them, she had to go back to the hospital. She learned to hide the pills under her tongue because she felt much better when she didn't swallow them.

Lila looked at Noel. Her eyes were tired and worn. At what seemed like the most lucid moment Lila had during the entire story, Lila whispered, "I'm not crazy, I know she was in my bed and I can prove it." Lila's nostrils flared and her eyes became wild.

"It's okay, really it is, don't get upset." Noel told her. Noel took Lila's frail hand and gave her a reassuring squeeze. Her little hand was so boney and cold. "Why don't you sit down beside me?" Noel asked her, moving over. Lila settled down and sat beside Noel and held onto Noel's hand. Lila looked down at the hand that held hers. "I used to have a ring just like that." She said, smiling. Noel quickly let go of Lila.

"Did you ever tell anyone you could prove she was in your house?" Noel continued questioning her.

"They don't believe me." She said, sadly.

"Who did you tell? How can you prove it?"

"I told my doctors."

"What proof do you have honey?"

"My lawn man knows. He said that wasn't the first time she'd been in my house." Lila's eyes came alive.

"Where is your lawn man honey?"

"I don't know." She said, looking into space.

"Do you know who he is?"

"Yes," Lila whispered. "James. James Wright."

Noel glanced at her watch. She needed to get back to work. "Are you cold?" She asked, watching Lila shiver.

"No."

"It's a little chilly. Take my jacket, I'll get it tomorrow." Noel took her jacket off and helped Lila into it. She slipped a $20 bill inside the pocket.

"Do you come here often?" Noel asked.

"Sometime."

"Maybe I'll see you tomorrow?" Noel watched

Lila walk down the steps to the next level and on to the street.

Back in the courtroom, Noel looked at her ring as she sat waiting for the judge. She'd never asked Marcus where he bought it. She thought that would be rude. All she knew is that the ring it was extremely expensive.

Noel thought about Lila and from deep within her own soul, she felt a *sliver* of truth was buried somewhere beneath all those bizarre claims. Was Lila truly crazy?

......*"Will the court please come to order! All rise for the Honorable Judge"*.......

THIRTY-FOUR
JADE

"**JADE, THE FED** Ex man is here with a package for you, do you want me to sign for it?" Michelle asked Jade over the intercom.

"Please." Jade was looking over the script and Traci came into her office. "Michelle asked me to bring you this package."

"Thanks." Jade opened the box from Frederick's of Hollywood and inside was a note from Mitch. *"This is you! I can't wait to see you in it Friday."—Mitch XXX*. Jade pulled from the box, a sheer, three-piece, god-awful-tacky-purple nightie she wouldn't wear in the privacy of her own bedroom, let alone out in public. Traci was on the floor dying laughing. "This m**f** has lost his rabbit-a** mind!" Jade cursed. She picked up the box and sent it flying across the room, and then she went to where it had landed and stuffed in the trash.

HILL FOXES

The girls and Antony gathered at Jade's house around seven-thirty Friday night. They never got a response from Wendy. "I have a bottle of champagne to get our party started while we ride over to Virginia," Jade said. "Everybody can have some except Anthony." She was laughing at him.

"I know you wenches fixed those straws so I would get the short one, I'm not stupid." Anthony said.

"Now, why on earth would we do that Anthony honey?" Brea asked, and they all laughed. When they got to Mitch's house in Fairfax, the party was well underway. The *Foxes* did their usual *entrance thing*.

"Woo, Frederick's of Hollywood is definitely in the houssse!" Noel said, shaking her head. The *Foxes* stood at the door in their customary elegance, and turned the heads of everyone in the party. Jade wore a beautiful mint green spaghetti-strapped silk gown that highlighted her eyes. Her hair was pulled on top of her head with dangling curls and diamond cluster earrings. Her shoes were clear-heeled mules with sprinkles of cut glass, and a full-length mink coat—all of the *Foxes* were in mink coats and they looked like class!

Mitch came running over to them grinning— "Damn, baby, y'all look good!

"I know." She said, taking off her mink. She

introduced Mitch to the girls and Anthony, who was by then in *hinny-heaven,* but he was cool. And someone must have blown a whistle, because no less than eight Buckskin players ran to Mitch's side. Mitch didn't know it, but he was officially on trial, he had to get it right with Jade that night.

"Hey gorgeous, haven't we met before?" Sam Jones asked extending his hand to Jade.

"Yes, I interviewed you at the beginning of the season up at camp." Jade reminded him, smiling.

"That's right, that's where it was. How could I ever have forgotten that?" He said, smiling. "Are you alone tonight if that's at all possible?"

Jade smiled sweetly and said, "I'm with my girlfriends." A woman walked up and yanked Sam's arm and Jade slowly moved away from them. She had promised herself not to be involved in any drama if she could avoid it.

The girls were all being occupied in conversation and Mitch was all over the place. He was wearing baby-blue satin striped Shorty-P.J.'s somewhat sheer, un-buttoned, displaying his "six-pack" and tiny waist. She had to admit, he was a handsome piece of sh**. Mitch came over and handed Jade a glass of wine. "You okay, baby?"

"Yes, thank you, this is a nice party."

"Damn, you look good enough to eat, but that's

not the outfit I bought you." He said, looking her up and down.

"Uh, no it didn't fit, sorry."

"Yeah, but you still looking good. I see my teammates sniffing 'round you but Im'a take care of that!"

"Just be careful yourself," she warned Mitch.

"Enjoy while I do my *host thang.*"

Anthony came over to Jade and whispered. "This is real nice. I presume the guests the HMO sent are their best representatives—and I'm *not* referring to health care, but the "Hoochie-Mama Organization." Jade laughed. "Boy you're a mess."

There were a few women however, that looked like they had some class about them, especially one at the patio door. Jade had been watching her pick up empty glasses and taking them back to the kitchen. She came out several times with trays of chips and horsd'oeuvres. *Was she the hired help?*

"Have you noticed that chick putting out the trays?" Anthony whispered to Jade. Just then, Lauren joined them bouncing to the beat of the music. "Now this is my kind a party—Heey! Some of these women must be from…"

"Watch your mouth Lauren," Anthony whispered. "We were just talking about that. Lauren was high—*again*!

"Grab your favorite lady while I change the pace a little taste!" The D.J. announced. *"I'm going for an oldie but definitely a goodie—"Don't Call me Brother" by the Commodores. Enjoy."*

"May I have this dance Princess?" Mitch came up behind Jade and grabbed her around her waist. They started to dance and she laid her head in his chest, wrapped her arms around him, and closed her eyes.

"Um, you smell good," he whispered. "Enjoying?"

"So far." *But it was still early, she thought.* "Thanks for inviting us. The girls are having a ball."

"What's up with your boy Anthony? He alright?"

"Sure, Anthony's fine," she smiled to herself. They bumped into the couple next to them. She opened her eyes to see the girl from the patio looking at her. Jade gave a quick smile, and put her arms around Mitch's neck.

"How long does this party last Mitch, aren't you afraid someone is going to check or something?"

"The phone guy is standing right over there by the door," Mitch said pointing. Jade looked next to them and there were those eyes fixed on her again, the girl from the patio. She wondered what was up with her. Toward the end of the song, Mitch wrapped his arms around Jade tighter, and lifted her from the floor and kissed her. "Mitch, you're so bad, put me down." When the song ended the girl was standing beside them staring, her eyes blazing. Mitch literally drug Jade over to where Anthony and Lauren were standing. "I'll be right back baby," he turned and went back to the girl.

"Oh, hell no! Jade said. *There will be no drama tonight, she reminded herself.* Mitch steered the girl toward the kitchen. Jade motioned for Jill and asked her to go near the kitchen to see if she could ease drop. Mitch didn't know Jill well and probably wouldn't notice her. A few minutes later, Jill returned all excited.

"Girl, that "Hoochie" is after your man." Jill said whispering. "You better go get him."

"What did they say?" Jade asked Jill.

"She's crying and he said, *"I told you my woman was coming, don't get crazy on me."* And she said, *"You told me you had broken up with her, that you were just friends now. That kiss didn't look like friends to me. I flew all the way here to be with you, where am I supposed to go now?"* And he said, *"Stay here like you been doing."*

"Oh, really?" Jade said, with a weird look in her eyes.

"Be cool Jade. Remember *who* you are and *where* you are." Anthony said, holding Jade by her shoulders.

"Anthony, I don't intend to do anything to embarrass you or myself tonight, trust me. I just need to find out something." Jade patiently waited for Mitch to go out on the patio. She moved toward the kitchen smiling sweetly, and speaking to people as she inched her way across the room.

"Hi, my name is Jade," she said to the girl extending her hand. The girl looked scared, like she expected Jade to punch her or something.

"I'm Star," she said, softly.

"Nice to meet you Star. Let's cut to the chase. Are you seeing Mitchell?" Star held up her hands. "I don't want any trouble." She said.

"Neither do I." Jade told her, calmly.

"I knew Mitch had a fiancée," Star explained," but he told me you had broken the engagement."

"How long have you been seeing Mitch?" Jade asked.

"For about a year. I live in Chicago, so I don't see him that much. I was aware he was with you when I first met him, but then he said you had given him the ring back. I would never have traveled here otherwise. So are you saying that you two are still engaged?" Star asked Jade.

"Never were."

"Aren't you from Florida?" Star asked.

"Nope, I'm from right here in the District of Columbia."

"Mitch told me he was engaged to his high school

sweetheart. He invited me to stay here this week and sent me a ticket to fly here last week."

"Star I was not—nor have I ever been engaged to Mitchell Dawson, must be somebody else. He and I have been dating for a while too and I've always suspected there were other women, but tonight just confirms that." Jade looked out into the room and saw Mitch coming in from the patio, Lauren grabbed him to dance. That move would buy her a few more minutes to talk with Star.

"Look Star, I'm not looking for any drama, I think we've both been played. I don't know what you're going to do, but I'm out of here." Jade said, turning to leave the kitchen.

"I'm sorry, I had no idea." Star said, looking as if she was going to cry again.

"Here's my number should you want to know anything else about that liar." Jade wrote her number on a napkin from the table. "A sist'ah should look out for another sist'ah." Jade went back and joined the girls in the party.

"Oww, tell me—tell me!" Noel screeched. "I see she's not bald-headed so it couldn't have been too bad." They all laughed.

"Actually she seems like a nice girl. She's been lied to just like I have. I'm ready to go home now, I'm done here." Jade told them.

Anthony went to gather the minks he had stashed in a closet away from the main rooms. Mitch came over when he saw them putting their coats on.

"Where y'all going? It's early."

"We're going back across the bridge Mitch, but thanks. This party has been a real eye-opener." Jade was so proud of her self-restraint she thought she deserved some brownie points.

"Aww baby, don't go, stay a little longer," he begged. Jill pulled Jade aside. "Look, I'm going to ride back with Mike Johnson, he's got to go out to Upper Marlboro so he can drop me off." She whispered.

"You know the rules," Brea said. "We come together we leave together."

"I'm not a child Brea. I'm cool, and I've only had one beer. I promise, I'll check in when I get into my house."

"Okay, grown lady. Let's go," Jade said. Mitch walked them to the door still begging. He grabbed Jade's hand and pulled her into his arms to kiss her. She took both of her hands and un-wrapped him from around her, and then walked away.

"I can't begin to tell you how proud I am of you Jade," Anthony said, looking through the rear view mirror. "You acted like the lady I always knew you were."

HILL FOXES

"You sure were a lady," Lauren said, "'cause she'd still be picking my toes out'a her tail."

"She would?" *Miss three-some*? "Stop and think about it. Was this her fault? She's been there at his house for a week, at *his* invitation, and I walk in, someone who was no longer supposed to be in the picture. Who looks like the intruder?"

"It's definitely Mitch's fault, he disrespected both of you, Jazz." Noel said. "Told you I didn't like him."

The trip back into D.C. seemed long, but Jade was glad she had a chance to catch Mitchell Dawson in action. She had put him on probation in her mind, all she was doing was waiting for one more" F" up, and he had delivered.

Jade got back home and took off her gown and put on some real P.J.'s. She didn't bother to check her messages because she was physically and mentally drained. The night had been full of surprises and had taken a toll. As soon as she found that right spot in her bed, Jill called. "Open your door," she said.

"What?" I'm in my bed and I'm tired Jill. You got home okay I see."

"Open your door," her voice was muffled like her mouth was close to the receiver.

"Aahh! I'm tired of you women for one night." Then she thought, maybe something was wrong with

Jill. Jade went downstairs and cut the porch light on, and peeped out. There was no one there. Ten minutes later, her doorbell rang and there stood Jill, Mike Johnson and *Star?*

"Come in," she said, surprised. *What the hell was Star doing there?*

"Mike, you and Star have a seat. I'm going to get something from Jazz," Jill said, pulling Jade into the kitchen.

"Giiiirl! You left before the fireworks and missed the show. Star turned the party out!" Jill whispered.

"What happened?"

"I'll call you later, Mike's got to go." She left the kitchen and pulled Mike out of the door with her. "Good night ladies." Jill said, grinning.

"Star would you like to put your things down?" Jade asked.

"I am so sorry Jazz. I know this is an intrusion but I'm desperate right now. Jill told me it would be okay with you if I came here."

"What's going on Star?" *I'm going to kick Jill's ass!*

"I tried to call National Airport to change my flight, but Jill told me they closed at eleven. I'm trying to get a flight back out to Chicago when they open in the morning. Jill's going to arrange it for me.

Why didn't she carry your butt to her house then?

"When were you supposed to leave?" Jade asked her.

HILL FOXES

"Monday morning, but I refuse to stay in that house with Mitch another minute. If you could just let me crash on your chair, sofa, anything for a few hours, I promise I'll be out of your way. I don't know anyone here Jade, and I don't have enough money to stay at a hotel. I didn't have anywhere else to go. You offered me help if I needed it, and I'd appreciate it." Star said, begging.

"Let me get you something to drink Star, how about Zin?" Jade poured them both a glass of wine. "I don't have a problem with your being here. Stay as long as you need. Are you okay? Did you and Mitch have words?" Jade asked trying to find out what the fireworks had been about.

"I'm okay," Star said. "I'm just hurt and disappointed that Mitch would do this. After you left, he *insisted* you two were only friends. I can't believe him."

"I think there should be a law that all men regardless of their first names, need to carry the name "Liar" as their middle name. John "Liar" Smith, Bobby "Liar" Miller, James "Liar" Williams and so on." Jade said.

"I just can't believe this is happening." Star said. "He's been very attentive and very thoughtful up to now. He sends me gifts, stuffed animals, flowers by the ton, just seemingly a good guy. I'm his "Princess", he says."

Princess? "I've been betrayed too Star, you're not alone. I just hope that if I were ever in your situation, in a place where I had no support, someone would reach out to help me.

Jade and Star talked for what was left of the night. Star was an intelligent, sensitive, kind person and Jade liked her. They compared Mitch's lies and excuses, and at times, were laughing their heads off.

Jill was able to get Star's flight changed through her employee connections and her flight was all set. Jade and Star decided to have a little fun before her flight left.

Jade called Mitch and asked him to please meet her at the airport. She had an emergency and desperately needed his help. "Yeah, Princess, I'll be there, just let me get some clothes on." Mitch was recuperating from the party and she had awakened him. "I'll be at Gate# 15, Eastern Airlines Mitch, please hurry." Jade said.

Half an hour later, Jade and Star went to Gate #15 and walked up on Mitch sitting in the chair. When he looked up and saw them together, he put his head between his hands and shook his head. Star and Jade laughed so hard they almost peed on themselves. Jade walked Star to her gate, they hugged and she was gone.

THIRTY-FIVE
JILL

JILL QUICKLY PACKED her bag and put her uniform in a zip up, and left a message on Bryce's cell. He called her back and told her he would be off in an hour. He asked her where she wanted to have breakfast.

"I've got to get back to D.C. today. I'm on my way to MIA right now so I can deadhead back, I'm so sorry baby," she told Bryce.

"I guess we weren't supposed to have our little rendezvous this time, first my emergency at work, now you've got to leave. I hope everything's all right." Bryce said, disappointed.

"Everything's okay," she said, not wanting to explain her sudden departure. "This trip just didn't work out for us. I'll call you as soon as I find out my next run here."

"If you can wait an hour I'll take you to the airport."

"Thanks baby, but I've already called a cab."

"Be good until I see you again Jill." The phone rang and the cab driver told her he was downstairs, she left Cheyenne's house for the last time. She would try to catch a nap on the plane since she hadn't slept all night.

Jill knew something in Cheyenne's photo kept getting her attention. Her brain didn't register it until she silenced her mind. In that lovely portrait and in the smaller pictures, Cheyenne wore a tennis bracelet *just like* the one Jill found in Julius' bathroom—the one he knew nothing of. That bracelet was too distinctive for it to have been a coincidence.

Jill checked in at the airport and boarded the plane. She knew Julius was doing some dirt, but with Cheyenne? How dare he! Yes, she had the right to be angry with him, for God's sake, that was her co-worker! As for Cheyenne, she was now history.

Jill wasn't sure if she should go home or to Julius' house. She caught the Metro train home because she remembered her car was at Julius'. She carefully put the key in the door of her condo, quietly went inside and **bingo**! They were at her dining room table eating. Jill stood there and looked at them. She thought Julius was going to shit! Cheyenne nervously tried to play it off.

"Jill!" Cheyenne said. "Julius just stopped by…

"Don't even try"! Jill said, calmly. The lie Cheyenne was *about* to tell implying that Julius had just *happened* to drop by, may have worked under ordinary circumstances, but not while they were undressed.

Cheyenne ran into the bedroom and put her uniform on, and threw her things in the bag. Julius hurriedly changed into his clothes as well. When they got to the door to leave, Jill stopped Cheyenne, "my keys please." Cheyenne handed Jill the keys and left.

"I'll pick up my car from your house later, Julius."

"Jill let me just say this…"

"You don't need to say anything to me—ever! You're insignificant to me Julius Collins."

Julius looked directly into Jill's eyes. "As long as I'm as insignificant as Bryce Cooper," he said, and walked out of her door.

THIRTY-SIX
BREA

BREA WAS FINISHING the first half of her run that morning to Langdon Park. As each footstep hit the pavement, they landed a little lighter these days. No longer did she try to stomp out the memory of Melik Iverson with every step, she had Reggie to thank for that. When she reached the park, she sat on a bench and took a swig of her bottled water. The morning was brilliant—bright and crisp. Brea loved running. It helped to clear her head, and allowed her to see things in a different light.

She smiled thinking about Mitch's party. She wanted to call Jazz and find out if the rumors about Star were true. *Poor Jazz, her bad luck with men seemed to equal her own.*

Things in Brea's life were going smoothly for a change. Her hiatus from the music scene had given her a chance to mellow out and get over Melik. Her new involvement with Reggie was almost therapeutic. Sure, her heart was still a little tender, but she was healing nicely, thank you.

Lurking in the shadows of their contentment however, was the impending threat of Bobby Knowles lawsuit. Brea's manager Damon had continuously tried to put her mind at ease about it. He didn't want her to worry, but worrying was part of Brea's make up, she worried about everything. Either Reggie wasn't concerned, or he didn't mention it to her on purpose, probably the latter. They hadn't actually heard anything new about it lately as far as *she* knew, but it was quietly humming in the background—not loud but like music in an elevator. You didn't hear it, but it was playing.

Brea started her return run home. She was going to have a busy day. She had promised to take her mother Connie out to Tyson's Corner to look at a coat she had seen in the newspaper, and Reggie had invited her to his house for dinner. He was going to make a big pot of spaghetti, a tossed salad and garlic bread—sounded good to her.

After a long day of shopping, Brea showered and took a quick nap before going to Reggie's, Connie had walked her little toes off.

Reggie had set the table by the time she arrived at his house.

"What can I help you do Reggie?"

"You can sit down and let me do this. Would you like a glass of wine?"

"Sure." She took off her boots and got comfortable on his sofa. He brought her the wine and sat down beside her.

"How was your day, baby?" He asked, putting his arm around her.

"A little busy."

"How is Miss Connie?"

"She's well. She found the coat she wanted so she's happy right now. She's probably at home cooking up a banquet to celebrate the coat as we speak." They laughed. Reggie's fingers softly caressed the back of Brea's neck, between that and the wine she was pretty relaxed. As time moved forward, their relationship was growing into something deeper than their "brother-sister friendship". Reggie loved her long before she ever knew it, but he never revealed it out of his respect for her and Melik's involvement. When Melik broke Brea's heart, it broke his heart too. It was difficult being there to witness what Melik was putting her through. It tore Reggie apart to see Melik dog Brea like he did, and there was nothing he could do.

Being there for her was all he could do, and possibly try to help her pick up the pieces.

HILL FOXES

"Would you like another glass of wine or are you ready to eat?" He asked.

"I'm hungry." She said, laughing. They went to the kitchen and enjoyed his specialty, spaghetti.

"Have you looked into finding a reputable psychologist or somebody about your nightmares yet, baby?" He sprinkled pepper on his salad.

"No, I'll get to it. I haven't been having the dreams lately. I know they're connected to my being stressed, so I'm trying to live a stress-free, drama-free life." She smiled.

"*Life* is not stress free or drama free Brea, so what are you going to do when they return?"

"I'll look into it Reggie." She said, trying to dismiss the subject. They went to the den after Reggie put the dishes into the dishwasher. He had rented a movie for them to watch. They stretched out on the long leather couch and Brea snuggled up under him. He was so happy he could make her feel warm and protected, and he loved that she was comfortable being up under him. He had been patient with Brea, not wanting to rush her, so he treaded lightly, he'd wait. He didn't fool himself into thinking it was going to be easy, he knew it would take time. What he was *also* happy about, was the fact that he'd made great progress towards gaining her trust and love. Her feelings for him seemed to have deepened. From what she had been through, that was a major accomplishment.

He kissed her cheek and took her hand in his. The warmth of his body and the scent of his Coty's Musk Oil began to awaken her senses.

Reggie gave her a loving, tender kiss and she responded. He had always been as gentle and understanding as possible whenever they made love. He moved over and pulled her under him. She raised her arms and wrapped them around his neck. He gently unbuttoned her shirt and undid her bra. She pulled him closer to her. Reggie was everywhere, her mouth, her neck, her breasts, her shoulders. He whispered in her ear the most beautiful things, over and over again. Of course, she'd heard these promises before in her life, but none of them were ever as powerful. She pulled him to her. His hands were doing the most incredible things and she was ready, she was pulling at his arms, pulling at his waist, she was ready for him to love her. He held back and put his finger to her soft lips then inside her mouth. He felt sure she was ready for him now, not just physically, but she was ready for *them*. He was going to make love to Brea like he never dared to before. She was pulling at him again. He looked deep into her glassy eyes. "Tonight sweetheart," he whispered, "I'm going to make you feel like no other man has. From this night forward, you belong to Reggie."

He caressed every part of her, stroking and kissing, and she clawed at his arms. Brea shook in anticipation of him and she pulled at him again. He looked into her eyes and waited for her. "*Reggie please,*" she whispered, and he made passionate love to her.

After they had returned from another place and time, Brea was now certain in her heart that she had just crossed the threshold into what she had looked for all of her life, and that she would always belong to him.

He was now certain he had just sealed a permanent bond for their lives together forever.

THIRTY-SEVEN
JADE

THE MONDAY AFTER the pajama party was not a good day for Jade. That evening after work she went home, called Terry and invited him over for a drink. She needed a friend and she missed Wendy. He came about seven and they started on a bottle of Chardonnay.

"Are you cooking a Turkey for Thanksgiving?" She asked him, pouring wine into their glasses.

"Not living. I'm going to North Carolina to see my grandparents. That's been a family tradition for the last um-teen years."

"When are you going?"

"Thursday morning, the highway will be almost empty and I can make better time." Jade told him about the party and the experience she had with Star, and that whole night of drama.

"Damn, home girl! You aw-ight?"

"Oddly, I'm fine, she was a nice girl. We both just happened to get screwed, but that's life." Jade felt better being able to talk about it.

"Y'all set his ass up, huh? I tell you, you women are cruel!" He was laughing. "Seriously though Jazz, you okay?"

"I really am Terry. I'm going down to the country for the holidays, take care of my house and my business, and enjoy myself."

"You're not having dinner with your folks?"

"They my dear, are on a cruise.

"That's wonderful, and that's how I hope I'll be able to spend my retirement. Have you talked to Wendy lately, what's she up to?"

"No, I haven't and I don't know."

"I hope you enjoy your holiday, you deserve one after that calamity. You're a good person Jazz, I'm kind of glad you're out of that situation with Mitch. He seemed to be constantly causing you grief. Like I said before, you could be with anybody you wanted to be with."

"Could I be with you?" Jazz asked him, teasing.

"Circumstances being a little different, you probably could." He looked uncomfortable with her question.

"What circumstances?" She pursued the question out of curiosity because he looked so uneasy.

"Jade, you've just been hurt. I don't know what you're getting at, but if you're reaching out, I'm here for you. Trust me when I tell you, the pain *will* go away."

Jade and Terry talked for hours. They ran through the bottle of Chardonnay and opened another one. They were sitting on the floor by the fireplace and Jade reached over and gave Terry a kiss of friendship. He was so sweet and he kissed her back.

"Okay, that's enough." Terry said.

"It's okay Terry," Jade told him. "I'm not trying to get revenge or use you to rebound Mitch. I just felt I wanted to kiss you, that's all." Jade said. They were both buzzed.

"We're both high Jazz and anyway, I'm seeing someone and I think it's getting serious."

"I didn't know, but don't misunderstand my kiss. I'm not trying to steal you away from her. Is it someone from school? Do I know her?"

"Now you're being nosey, but yes it's someone from school and yes, you know him." Terry said.

"Excuse me? Did you say him?"

"I did. I'm thinking about "giving it a try with a guy"! I'm bisexual."

"**Terry**! Are you sure about that, you're not gay."

"I didn't say I was gay Jazz, I said I'm bisexual."

"Bullshit!"

"We've been friends for a long time. He says he's fallen in love with me. He's convinced me that the fact I'm even considering our relationship, and that I'm also attracted to women, means I'm bisexual." Terry said.

"Bullshit Terry! Are you sure he's not someone taking advantage of your naivete."

"I don't think that, he's a pretty level headed guy."

"So are you saying you wouldn't date me if you had the opportunity?" She asked.

"If this had been a few years ago, I would have *killed* for the opportunity." He was laughing. "I can't tell you how many times I fantasized about being with you and Wendy at the same time, Umh!"

"You mean a manage de trios? You're just a closet freak Terry Brooks." They laughed for fifteen minutes not because it was funny, but because they were toasted!

"But Terry, I do love you, and you know how I mean that."

"I love you too, Jazz," he looked sad. "I'm going the hell home now, I'm drunk."

"Can you make it two blocks without getting stopped by the police?" Jade asked giggling. She was walking him to the door.

"Yep-yep." He said, stumbling.

"You're fine Terry." Jade wrapped her arms around

Terry, opened her mouth and gave him a long, deep, slow kiss and he kissed her back. "I seriously think you need to reconsider your decision Terry. Goodnight boy."

The Thanksgiving pot luck dinner at the station was a big success, everyone enjoyed it. Anthony baked two "Better than Sex" cakes, the station manager supplied the turkeys, and each department prepared dishes that made up the rest of the meal. The audio crew made spiked punch and from what Jade heard, it carried quite a *punch*, she wasn't touching it. "This was fabulous Traci and Michelle. Enjoy the holiday. You know I'm out the rest of the week." She reminded them. Jade drove out of the station garage and headed up North Capitol. Traffic was outrageous! She went into the house and checked her messages—

"Jazz, Terry. Let's go for a drink at Colonel Brooks or Ellis Island for happy hour. Call me."—**Beep**

"Hey girl, I'm okay and I miss you. I'll try you back later. If I miss you, have a good holiday." **Beep**!

Damn, I missed Wendy again. She called Terry and got his machine. *"Guess we're playing phone tag—you're it!"*

Jade went upstairs and started pulling things out of the closet to take to Westbury. Anthony had taken her car to Fuller's for service and gassed up for her earlier that day. She was undecided whether to leave that night or the next morning. She answered her phone.

"Hey, Black woman, did you get my message?"

"Yes, I did Terry, you driving?"

"I'll pick you up in twenty."

Colonel Brooks was crowded, so Terry nudged Jade toward the steps leading upstairs where there were fewer people. A three-piece jazz combo was playing, when she looked harder, she saw Brea. The combo playing was Brea's backup group "Ice", she waved and went upstairs. Terry ordered their best champagne and appetizers.

"Are we celebrating something Terry?"

"I'm celebrating your release from the devil, and I'm celebrating something you helped me realize the other night."

"Would you expound upon that please?" Jade asked, in a mock British accent, holding her champagne glass up.

"No, I will not."

"Now wait a damn minute, why would you spark my curiosity and leave me hangin'? He held his glass up.

"To releases!" They toasted.

"So, when are you leaving Jazz?"

"Now that we're here drinking, I guess tomorrow."

"Good, I wouldn't want to see you drive down there tonight."

Terry and Jazz stayed about two hours. When "Ice" took a break, Brea and Reggie went upstairs and sat with Terry and Jazz for a while. Jazz doesn't ever remember seeing Brea so happy in all the years she had known her, she and Reggie looked joined at the hip. Terry dropped Jade off at home and gave her a big hug. "Have a safe trip and a good holiday Jazz."

"You too Terry, drive safely." She reached over and kissed him a little kiss of goodbye.

THIRTY-EIGHT
NOEL

"**WENDY, I'M TELLING** you and I can't explain it, there's something about Lila's ramblings that feel real. You have to pick through her wild claims and you faintly hear the smack of validity." Noel told Wendy.

"Nothing surprises me anymore Noel. Maybe I'm being cynical, but do your homework girl." Wendy was biting into a sandwich in the courthouse cafeteria.

"She said her lawn person was James Wright and he could verify what she claims."

"James Wright? He does the lawns on my block," Wendy said, surprised. "You know D.C. is really a small town. James has done my lawn for years."

"Would you see if you can find anything out from him Wendy?" Noel asked excited.

"I don't see him as a rule. I just send him a check

every month. For you though, I'll try to catch him but I can't tell you when that might be."

"I understand. I'm going to take your advice and do a little homework on my own". Noel said.

"Have you talked with Marcus about this?"

"No! I want to have all of my information right before I approach him. I pray every morning and every night, that Lila's accusations are imagined. I love Marcus Wendy. I can't fathom him being that evil. I just don't see that in him."

"Don't put anything past anyone." Wendy said, looking at Noel. She hoped this would simply turn out to be the gibbering of a crazy woman, for Noel's sake. She would hate to see Noel hurt.

"I told Marcus I needed to have my ring size adjusted and he told me to give it to him, he'd do it.

I explained to him they needed to fit it to my finger. I asked him where he had purchased the ring. He said it didn't matter, any reputable jeweler could size it, but he never answered my question."

"That's interesting." Wendy said, chewing.

"I think I might have a way of finding out where he bought it." Noel said. Noel and Wendy finished their lunches and went back upstairs. Noel reported to the courtroom for her next case and it didn't take long, it was only a formality so they ran right through it. She was itching to get back to the plaza to see if

HILL FOXES

she could find Lila. She stood and watched people come and go and there she was. Lila was wrapped up in Noel's jacket begging for money.

"Hi," Noel yelled. "How are you today?"

"Ma'am, could you help me out?" Lila asked her.

Noel looked into Lila's eyes and it was painfully clear, the Lila she had spoken with before, was not there that day. She didn't remember Noel, and it made Noel want to cry. She watched her walk away and approach a man in a suit.

Noel slowly walked back around to Indiana Avenue, she was getting depressed. She wished she could talk to Wendy, but she was so busy Noel didn't want to bother her again. She had wanted to ask Lila if she knew a good jeweler, thinking she might find out where Lila's ring was bought and to confirm her own suspicions.

Marcus was coming for dinner that night. She had invited Brent and Bryan too, but Marcus said, "Not during the week."

After Noel's Lasagna dinner, Marcus pushed away from the table. "Uh, that was excellent Noel." He said. "You know how much I love your Lasagna."

"I'm so happy you enjoyed it, have some more."

"Ohh, no I'll pass, I can't move now." He said laughing.

"Are you staying tonight?

"I need to get home, I have a very heavy day tomorrow but we'll see," he said, rubbing her butt when she brought his Sherry to him. They went to sit in the living room to watch the news.

"I see you're still wearing your ring, did you have it sized yet?"

"Not yet." Playing dumb, she asked, "where did you say you bought it again, maybe I'll take it there."

Marcus started laughing. "Look at that fool, he knows better than that." He was laughing at some man on TV and completely ignored her question—*again*.

THIRTY-NINE
JADE

JADE AWOKE AT five o'clock, left D.C. and arrived at Westbury around nine. When she got to the farmhouse, the first thing she did was to start a fire with the wood that was stacked on the back porch. She wasn't experienced doing it, but she managed to get the fire going before she burned the whole house down. She put on a CD, cut the thermostat up and got a book from the shelf. Jade got to page three and she was asleep. She didn't know if she was more angry than scared when she awoke to Keith and Buddy standing over her. Buddy jumped on the sofa nearly crushing her to death. Keith probably didn't know she was there because she had parked in the garage.

"I'm sorry Jazz. I didn't mean to startle you. I came by to see if everything was all right before you got here, and I see you're okay. Who made the fire?"

"My fairy god-father," she said, still shaking.

"Are you sure you're okay?"

"I'm fine Keith." *It was so good to see him.*

"Is there anything you need?" He sat down across from her in the chair.

"I plan to run out to the grocery store before it gets too late for what I need."

"I take it you haven't looked in the kitchen yet. I put some things I thought you'd need there, but if you want something else, I'll get Ben to run out for you. Just make a list and I'll check back with you." Keith stayed for few minutes before leaving.

Jade went to the kitchen to make a sandwich and check the refrigerator as Keith had suggested. She was making a list of things she wanted when the phone rang.

"Jade, this is Jeff, I see you made it. We're supposed to meet at two, is that alright?"

"That's fine Jeff."

"I'll pick you up at one-thirty." Jeff came for Jade and they drove into town to City Hall. She felt she should have asked Keith to come because he knew all the ends and outs, but she was a big girl now, she needed to do this for herself.

Brathwell County City Hall was a festive place that afternoon, the office workers were having parties and serving punch. Jeff said the building was closing early so they needed to get started with the necessary paperwork. When they finished, Jade felt like she had just fought in World War I. Jeff walked her to the accounting office to pick up her check, and she thought she was going to faint! She had just been PAID! No wonder Wendy told her she didn't have to work unless she wanted to, and to think, that represented only a small portion of her land, she had plenty left.

On their way back to Westbury, she mentioned to Jeff she would have been a little more comfortable if Keith had been there. He smiled. Sarcastically, he said, "Don't let his absence fool you." He let her out at the house and she thanked him again. When Jade got inside she could tell someone had been there, grocery bags were on the butcher block island and perishables in the refrigerator, the items were from her list. There was a note from Keith to call him, so she did. She was so excited she could hardly wait to tell him about her transaction. "Hello Miss Jazz, I've missed seeing you." Ben said, when he answered.

"I've missed you too, Ben." *She started to say—that's your boss's fault.* "Keith asked me to give him a call."

"Just a moment."

"Jazz, how did everything go?"

"I'M RICH....I'M RICH!! She said grinning and jumping.

"I'm glad you're happy." He was laughing.

"I'm ready to celebrate!" She said.

"How do you want to celebrate?"

"I don't know. *I-I-I—just want to cele-brate!* She sang.

"I'll see if I can come up with something and call you later." Keith told her, laughing.

Jade went upstairs and pulled out a dress from the bag in case he wanted to take her to Antonio's. She went back downstairs and opened some champagne for her private celebration. She got comfortable in front of her fire. Obviously Keith had added more logs while she was out.

She started to think about all of the things that had happened to her that year. She thought how disappointing Mitch had turned out to be—just like Wendy had said. She thought about her renewed friendship with Terry and wondered what their "release" celebration toast had been about. Did that mean he was coming out of the closet or did that mean he realized he wasn't gay? She wondered who this magnificent lover was, he would never tell her although he said she knew him. Ohhh—Raymond Perry? There was more than one picture of him in Terry's house, and Raymond wasn't married either. Come to think of it, his stats were questionable. A young, good-looking, financially stable judge who wasn't nor had ever been married living in Washington, D.C.? *Impossible* unless…you're gay! It had to be him.

Jade thought about Star and for some reason she felt sorry for her. She liked Star, and wondered how she was recovering from Mitch's betrayal?

She thought about Wendy and how much she missed being around her. She prayed God would see Wendy through her predicament. She was pulled away from her thoughts by the phone.

"Hello?"

"Still want to celebrate?" Keith asked.

"I would like to."

"You did bring warm clothes here didn't you?"

"You mean heavy outdoor clothes?"

"Yes, you need to put on your warmest clothes and maybe you should even layer them, I'll pick you up at eight."

Just before eight, Jade put on heavy slacks, a flannel shirt, socks and boots. Keith knocked on the door at eight. He had come to pick her up in a horse-drawn buggy. He helped her in, covered her with a blanket, and they were off into the chilly winter night. She snuggled up close to him relishing his closeness. She was reminded how comfortable she felt with him. The horse trotted down the dark winding roads and ended up at their secret place by the lake. Keith must have been there earlier because there was a small fire going. He brought a thermos of hot chocolate, and a thermos of warm brandy. It was a clear, crisp night and they wrapped up in the blankets, and sipped their drinks. They talked about the sale of the property and how she should invest her money. Keith roasted marshmallows and hot dogs. It was fun, a good old fashioned winter picnic, and she loved being with him. They didn't stay too long because of the cold, and soon headed back to Westbury Farm. They sat in front of the house for a little while watching the stars while they talked.

"This was very different Keith. I enjoyed it."

"I thought you might like a quiet celebration. Not much to do around here, anyway."

"Are you coming in?" She hoped he had mellowed in his decision to be with her again.

"I've got to get Apple back to the staples and wiped down, I'll call you tomorrow. By the way, what are you doing for Thanksgiving dinner?"

"I think I'm going to make a huge Hoagie Sandwich and watch the Macy's Day parade and the football games."

"You're going to have a sandwich for Thanksgiving?" Keith looked at her like she was crazy.

"What's wrong with that?"

"Ben's cooking, why don't you come over?"

"Ben's cooking?

HILL FOXES

"He's doing his traditional Thanksgiving dinner, would you like to come?"

"Oink-oink!" She said, and Keith fell out laughing. "You're a mess. We'll expect you at three."

"Tomorrow." She said, and went inside.

Sleep didn't come easy. Keith occupied all the corners of her mind. She had just fallen off to sleep when she heard something at the front door. There were all sorts of wildlife around there in the woods, she was scared. Jade tip-toed downstairs and cut the porch light on to scare whatever animal it was away. She didn't see anything at first, and then she saw Buddy. "Get in here boy, you scared me to death." Jade called Keith to let him know where Buddy was, hearing his voice just added to her loneliness. He said Buddy often did that when he let him out at night. He usually had to ride over and get him. Buddy slept at the foot of her bed and sleep finally came.

On Thanksgiving morning, Jade was up early and made breakfast for herself. She decided to stay in her P.J.'s and relax in front of the TV and the fire. She went through the mail, made out some bills, and watched the Macy's Day Parade. Keith called her at ten.

"You okay this morning?"

"I'm great this beautiful, country Thanksgiving morning," she said, jubilantly.

"What are you doing today?"

"Just bumming around the house and watching the parade.

"Ben says dinner will be at three, so why don't you come a little earlier for drinks. The Dallas game starts at one."

"Okay, so I'll see you later." Jade watched the rest of the parade and got ready to go to Keith's. She started to throw on some jeans, but decided to dress instead, it was Thanksgiving Day. She wore black suede pants and a pearled sweater, black heels, her mink coat and black leather gloves. She grabbed a bottle of Merietta Cellars wine from Aunt Judith's stash to take as a gesture of appreciation, jumped in the car and headed to Keith's. She and Buddy drove the winding roads listening to Teddy Pendergrass. Ben greeted her at the door and they hugged like long lost friends. She handed him the wine.

"Jazz, I'm here in the game room." The game had started, and when she walked around the couches, she saw that he had guest. Keith introduced his friend Jim.

"It's nice to meet you Jim." Jade said, shaking his hand.

"Wooow! Look how dazzling you grew up to be.

HILL FOXES

You probably don't remember me from our school dances we used to have. We all miss your aunt and uncle here in Brathwell County. They were good people." Jim said.

"Yes, they were." Jade agreed.

"Have you moved here or are you visiting?"

"I come down as often as I can, but I don't live here."

"We're waiting for Brenda, Jim's friend and another couple." Keith said to Jade.

That was interesting. She wondered if he already had couples coming for dinner, who was he supposed to be with. She was glad she'd decided against her jeans, everyone was dressed for a formal dinner. Keith handed her a glass of wine. "Thanks Keith." The doorbell rang and he excused himself to answer it. "I've got it Ben. She heard voices laughing and coming toward the game room. "This is Dave and Margo Lynch," Keith said. "Dave and Margo, this is Jazz. We all have wine, but if you want something stronger, just let me know." He bent down and whispered in Jade's ear, "Do me a favor sweetheart, get the horsd'eorves from Ben, please."

Jade went out to the kitchen and returned with a tray, like the perfect little hostess. "Thanks sweetheart," Keith said, taking the tray from her. *What the hell?* Everybody started concentrating on the game and helping themselves to the appetizers. Keith took a seat next to Jade and put his arm around her. So why did Mitchell Dawson have the best game he had all season? All you could hear the announcer saying was Mitchell Dawson—Mitchell Dawson—Mitchell Dawson.

"I tell you," Jim said, "that Mitch Dawson is baaad! He's had a hell of a season, knee and all." Jim started reciting Mitch's stats like he was reciting the Preamble to the Constitution. Jade cringed every time they called his name. Keith never reacted or looked at her. He sat there with no expression, whatsoever.

"Jazz, do you get out to any Buckskin's games?" Dave asked her.

"A few." For some reason Jade felt the need to hold Keith's hand as if to reassure him that it was okay.

At halftime, dinner was served in the dining room where Ben had prepared a beautiful traditional Thanksgiving dinner. He joined the group at the table, only getting up to serve the next course, and Buddy was in "bone heaven". After the feast, they all returned to the game room for coffee, cappuccino and the end of the game. Mitch was named MVP and the Skins actually won.

Keith put soft jazz on the system while they talked. He had been overly attentive to Jade, anyone would have thought she was living there, and she felt that was the impression he was trying to give for whatever reason. Jade also thought perhaps Jim and Brenda would have been more comfortable had they opted for a motel room for the evening, they were sickening. At one point Keith finally said, "Damn man, let the woman up for air," and everybody laughed. Jade figured they weren't married, at least not to each other.

It had been a wonderful Thanksgiving evening and his guests started leaving around eleven. They said polite goodbyes, and nice-to-meet you's, with promises to get together again soon and they were gone.

"I really enjoyed my day Keith, I like your friends." Jazz said, walking away from the door where she stood with Keith waving goodbye as his guests left.

"Old high school buddies, we get together now and then." He said. "Let me get you another wine Jazz."

"I've had enough," she said, yawning. "I'm getting ready to hit the road myself if you'll get my coat, please."

"Your friend had a good night tonight," he said.

"Whatever." Jade said, starting for the door and not wanting to open up that subject. "Have a good night Jazz."

Jade got into her *warm* car thanks to Ben. She drove down the winding dark roads with Buddy riding shotgun. Once she got inside the house, she poured a glass of champagne and sat in front of the fire place hoping it would make her sleepy. Since that wasn't working she continued drinking. She wondered why Keith was pretending they were together for his friends. Keith hadn't done a damn thing to move their relationship forward, but that's right, he'd left the next move up to her. He left it up to her to decide when she was ready to be with only him, and she could only come to him after she had discarded her *baggage*. She had finally discarded that baggage and got screwed in the process. She wasn't in a particular hurry! She loved Keith, always had.

Jade was hitting Aunt Judith's stash pretty good and by her fourth drink, the wine told her to go upstairs and have a long hot bath in scented oils. Enjoying the warmth and fragrance of the oils, she closed her eyes, sat back and sipped her champagne. After a while she toweled off, put on her lavender silk gown, lavender evening heels and freshened-up her make up. Following her heart and not her head, she grabbed her mink, whistled for Buddy and they were on their way back down the dark winding road. She rang Keith's doorbell, she rang it again

HILL FOXES

and after a short while, he opened it standing in his pajamas.

"Buddy's ready to come home." Jade whispered.

"What took him so long?" Keith whispered, picking Jade up and closing the door with his foot.

FORTY
LAUREN

LAUREN HAD BEEN crazy busy. With the holidays approaching, the Post's traditional holiday sales advertisements kept her working overtime. She had thrown herself into work to avoid facing the realization of her decision about Mustafa.

She had given into Mustafa's wishes yet again. The doorbell rang at seven-thirty while she was preparing dinner in the kitchen. She wiped her hands on the kitchen towel and opened the door.

"Good evening, please come in." She said.

"You have a lovely home." Haaydia said, looking around. "Thank you for inviting me." Haaydia handed Lauren a bottle of chilled Sparkling Apple Cider.

"May I pour a glass for you?" Lauren asked her.

"Please."

"Mustafa, could I offer you a glass or would you prefer Chablis?"

HILL FOXES

"I'll take Chablis my Sister." *Surprise.* They took a seat on her plush sofa.

Lauren, Haaydia and Mustafa sat in the living room with their drinks. Haaydia complimented Lauren on her display of photographs around the room, and her collection of African artwork. Lauren was uneasy, she allowed Mustafa to bring Haaydia into her home against her better judgment. He felt it was absolutely essential that they got to know each other and to bond. He had already planned several activities to accomplish that. It was disgusting enough that she had let him involve her in the Trios', but did she also need to be directly involved with his woman? There, she had said it—his woman. Those words caught in the back of her throat like a rock.

Lauren excused herself and went into the kitchen to check the oven. She had prepared a baked Spinach casserole with Ziti, tomatoes, Parmesan cheese, and she baked Dilly casserole bread. Haaydia was a Vegetarian. Mustafa would eat Zebra's knees if you put them on his plate.

"Please, come take a seat, dinner is ready." Lauren said, inviting them to her dining room table. During dinner, Haaydia dominated the conversation with how she felt Lauren needed to make use of her talents and open her own studio instead of working for other people. She thought it was imperative that she become self-sufficient for her gender as well as her race.

After dinner, Haaydia busied herself helping Lauren clear the dinner table. "Oh, Haaydia, you don't have to do that, I'll put these things away later."

"If we work as a team, it'll be done and out of your way." Haaydia said, smiling. "We are a team."

"How about another glass of Cider?" Lauren asked her.

"I'd love some Sister." Lauren poured a wine glass of Cider for Haaydia and a glass of Chablis for Mustafa and herself. They went back into the living room. Haaydia and Mustafa sat on the sofa. Lauren took a seat across from them in her lounge chair.

"I think we should go together to hear Abdullah Malik speak next week. I've heard him before and he's very inspirational." Mustafa was saying as he unconscientiously twisted a loc of Haaydia's hair. A cold chill ran down Lauren's arms as she watched his display of affection for her. Then her emotions changed to a slow sensation of anger rising from the pit of her stomach. How dare he—how dare he make her witness the very hands that stroke and touch her body, touch Haaydia's. Haaydia must have said something funny because when Lauren's head returned to the conversation, they were laughing and Mustafa took Haaydia's hand and kissed it.

"Please excuse me for a moment," Lauren said, getting up from her chair. She walked toward her bedroom to keep from screaming. She went into the bathroom and wiped her face with a cool towel. She looked up from the sink and in the mirror she saw Haaydia standing behind her.

"My sister, are you alright?" She asked Lauren.

"I'm okay."

"You know Lauren it seems to me you're still uncomfortable with our arrangement."

"I can't do this," Lauren said, walking into the bedroom. Tears began forming in her amber eyes. Haaydia embraced Lauren as Lauren's shoulders shook.

"Shhh, you're going to be fine." Haaydia whispered. She wiped the tears from Lauren's tear-stained cheek. Haaydia had such a gentle touch—the healing touch she possessed, soothed Lauren's anxiety. Lauren had experienced that very same sensation each time in the past when Haaydia had done her hair. Her touch was almost mystical, spiritual.

"I'd like to teach you something my sister. If you meet with me, we can begin to meditate together. It will free your mind and make you more receptive to receive the love that's around you." Haaydia told her.

"I'm not so sure about that."

"I'll show you how." They walked back into the living room.

"Are you two alright?" Mustafa asked Lauren and Haaydia. He was finishing the bottle of Chablis.

"She's not comfortable yet Mustafa."

"How could you not be comfortable Lauren?" Mustafa sympathetically wrapped his arms around her. "I love you Lauren, we love you." He whispered. He nibbled at her lip then kissed her deeply. Lauren tried to pull away, she felt awkward, Haaydia was standing right there with them!

"I'm tired," Lauren said. "I need to go to bed." She needed them out of her house. Her head was running the gamut of emotions.

"We'll let you get your rest." Haaydia said. "Thank you for a wonderful meal, and remember my offer still stands for meditating together. You still have some issues you need to work out." Mustafa helped Haaydia into her wrap. He put his arm around Lauren's waist as she walked them to the door. He took Lauren in his arms and kissed her a long, deep loving kiss. Haaydia leaned over and kissed Lauren too.

Lauren stared at the place where they had stood long after they were gone. "Oh, hell no! It's *not* going to be this kind of party!"

FORTY-ONE
JADE

DRIVING BACK INTO D.C. after Thanksgiving was a freakin' nightmare. Holiday travelers were returning to the city in mass. Jade finally made it to her house, unpacked the car and checked her messages before doing anything else.

"Hey girl it's show time. Be on your Pees and Ques. I'll call you when I can."—Beep!

Something new must have happened with Wendy.

"Hey Princess I miss… **Slam***!*

Jade called to let Keith know she was back safely and what a wonderful time she had. She was so happy they were back together, she knew for sure this time it was going to stick!

She called Terry to see if he was back from North Carolina but she didn't get an answer. *"Black man,*

I'm home." Click. She was hungry and since her food *wasn't* going to be prepared for her, she ran out to Horace and Dickey's for a sandwich. When she returned she called Terry again, *"Black man, where are you?"* Jade finally gave up and went to bed.

Mondays were always horrible at the studio. The weekend crew left everything out of place and you couldn't find shit. Michelle called on the intercom to let Jade know that Bob wanted to see her in his office—pronto.

"Good morning Bob, I trust you enjoyed your holiday?"

"Very nice," he said. "We have a hot one brewing today. I'm not sure if you've been following the Richard Sweet case or not, but it goes to court today. I've been informed that it should be very newsworthy and to expect breaking news."

"I've followed it but what makes it so hot today?" Jade asked him, fishing for information.

"I'm not sure myself, something to do with misconduct or blunders made within the system. I was promised it was going to be hot. Just get the story Jade."

"Who are you sending with me, I don't think Jason is back from vacation?"

"You can take Anthony if he's free." Bob said.

"Cool, I'm right on it." *It's happening. Something's finally happening."*

Jade met Anthony in the parking lot. They jumped into Truck One with Colin. When they arrived at the courthouse, all of the news teams were setting up. The court official was at the top of the marble steps giving the usual instructions.

"Listen up people," he said, trying to get order. "The drawing today will be done by Eleanor Johnson from DMV." Eleanor stuck her hand into the box and pulled out a slip of paper, and the court official read it. "For national—CBS." The CBS team gathered their equipment and went inside the security gate. Eleanor pulled out another slip. "For local—Fox affiliate Channel 5. Anthony looked like he was going to faint. "Oooh, that's us." Jade and Anthony rushed inside to set up. Colin moved the truck into the reserved spot next to the CBS truck. The courtroom was off limits to the rest of the press. They had allowed one national and local team inside.

Anthony and Colin tested for sound then tested with Jade. "Jade," Colin said over the walkie-talkie, "blot your lipstick, everything else is fine."

The courtroom was packed! The first person Jade saw was Wendy, she was poised and beautiful. She wore a Black suit that *screamed* money, dark hose and six-inch Black heels. Her blouse was crisp White and was adorned with a single strand of pearls, *real ones*. She was going through papers in her Coach satchel.

Jade settled down in her seat and flipped open her notepad. As she looked around the courtroom, she noticed that *everyone* who was *anyone* from downtown was there, all of the DCPD brass. *What the hell?* Then Jade noticed the courtroom was crowded with neighborhood people, dressed to kill. It was no secret that D.C. loved "Sweet Dick." If Jade were to wake up from a dream and saw all of those people, she would swear she was either at a class reunion or a church revival.

Jade looked toward the prosecutor's table and her head started to spin. **Oh my God, Terry.** He gave her the quickest glance in history.

That M***F! He had been trying to pump her for information about Wendy all along. Jade was remembering how many times Terry had asked her if she knew what Wendy was working on—*Bitch*! She was glad Wendy had insisted on cutting their communications off. She just may have confided in Terry, especially when they were drinking. Jade had broken into a cold sweat. *That two-faced dirty dog!* He was going to try to destroy Wendy!

"What's wrong Miss thang?" Anthony asked Jade.

"Nothing."

"I didn't know Wendy was defending him." Anthony whispered to Jade.

"I didn't either," Jade said, confused as to why she was in first chair? *What had happened?*

Wendy and "Sweet Dick" were going over papers, she knew Wendy well enough to know she was extremely tense. Jade's mind was whirling thinking about how Terry was going to go after Wendy, and tried to use her to do it. *Bastard*!

"All rise for the Honorable Judge Raymond Perry." Anthony had to grab Jade's arm to keep her from falling. *Oh-my-God, what was going on?* Both Terry and Raymond were going to end her career. Was that what the inside indiscretions were about? Was Wendy going to make her own charges of prosecutorial misconduct?

"Attorney Haines. How does your client plea?"

"Not guilty, your honor." "Sweet Dick" answered, standing tall and proud and still as fine as he *ever* was.

"Judge Perry, I would like to request a motion for mistrial." Wendy said.

"Mistrial?" Raymond asked surprised.

"Your honor, my client has been charged with the sale of contraband to an undercover agent when in fact, we can prove he was out of the country at the time. In addition, no one has produced the alleged contraband, the alleged marked money confiscated, the alleged tapes of the transaction, and I could go on and on your honor." Wendy said, with her palms open.

"Attorney Brooks?"

"Your Honor, DCPD's evidence holding room for whatever reason, has not been able to produce said evidence." Terry stated.

"What about a statement from the undercover agent?"

"Disappeared your honor, he's nowhere to be found."

"Attorney Brooks?" Raymond said. "Why are we here, please?"

"I certainly don't know your honor," Wendy interjected. "There are more ways I'm sure, to spend these good taxpayer's dollars other than inconveniencing the court and my client. Raymond hit his gavel twice. "I will declare a mistrial with prejudice," he said, and he walked out of the courtroom. The courtroom went wild! It was like a New Year's Celebration complete with confetti.

Jade was stunned. *What just happened?* Terry's words echoed …. When they were at Phillips he told her…. *"I've never changed. I'm still in the hood by choice and I'll do what I can to help my friends."*

"Jade, we're ready. In three, in two, in one…."

"This is Jade Zellmer, live from the D.C. Courthouse. The case against Richard P. Sweet was declared a mistrial today ……"

The rest of that day was off the hook. Jade got a statement from Wendy, one from Terry and it aired at the six o'clock. Jade went home and made herself a triple drink of Vodka and grapefruit and was gulping it down like water when her phone rang.

"Black woman, how was your holiday?"

"Terry ,what the hell…."

"**Hey**," he said, interrupting her, "why don't I just come by for a drink?" Jade guessed he didn't want to talk over the phone. She was dying to find out what was going on as she sat finishing her drink. It was so hard imagining the hatred she felt for Terry earlier that day. The doorbell rang and she let Terry in.

"Come in Black man, give me your jacket. "I just finished a Vodka, what's your poison?" He looked tired and strained.

"Anything that has alcohol in it," he said laughing, "how was your trip?"

"Damn a trip Terry! What was that today?"

"Jazz, it *was* what it *was*. You know I love you and we can talk about anything, but we won't be talking about that." He told her.

"What do you mean we won't be talking…"

He looked Jade in her eyes and said quietly,"again we can't talk about this, Jazz. How was Virginia?"

She took a long, deep breath. "It was great on several fronts." She said, giving up her pursuit of the story. She could tell he wasn't going to budge, at least not yet. She told him all about her land sale and how much she'd made on the deal, but she was still preoccupied with questions about the trial.

"Oh, so now I'm hanging with the rich and famous," Terry said, laughing. He took a long drink from his Hennessey.

"Everything's happened so fast, I haven't digested it."

"And as fast as it came, it can go just as fast. Get a financial planner." He told her.

"Terry, I know what you said about discussing the case, but I want to say this. You are one of the kindest, sweetest people I know. I'm trying to put together in my head what happened and if I'm right, I want to thank you for looking out." Jade kissed him a kiss of gratitude.

"I want to thank you for something too Jazz. All of those sweet little kisses you've been giving me? They helped me realize that I *am* gay."

"Damn, did I turn you off that much?" She asked him. "Say what you want Terry, you respond to my kisses." Just then the phone rang. "Excuse me a minute, hello?"

"Hey Princess I"…..***SLAM!*** "As I was saying

you're no more gay than I am, but tell me this, is it Raymond?"

"I'll just say if you lose your job at the station, I'll hire you as a detective," he said, laughing. "Let me get my tired, drunk ass out of here and go home."

"You don't have to go yet Black man, stay and talk." She wasn't satisfied she hadn't gotten him to talk yet.

"Nope, get my jacket, I'm out'a here girl." Jade walked Terry to the porch. "Thank you again for what you did," she said. She put her arms around him and worked her tongue between his lips until she found the warmth of his mouth. She pressed her body against him, leaning him on the pillow of the porch. "Terry," she whispered.

He opened his closed eyes, "Yes?" he whispered back.

"You're not gay fool!" And she pushed him off her porch.

The rest of the week went smoothly and was uneventful. Jade and Wendy were talking, and needless to say, she was ecstatic over the outcome of the case. She still wanted to keep a distance for just a little while longer until things quieted down. People in Washington were easy to forget. It only took the next scandal to avert their attention, and it looked like it was going to be the City Councilman who got busted with an under-aged young lady in Rock Creek Park. Wendy did make a secret "night visit" one night and they had a drink of wine together. Another night, she sneaked to Jade's and borrowed her car to meet "Sweet Dick".

During Wendy's "night visit", Jade told her all about Mitch's pajama party and what happened, how she had been spending time with Terry and that he had admitted he was seeing Raymond Perry, her property sale and her brief breakup with Keith.

"Daaamn! I missed everything." Wendy said. "Are you sure about Raymond and Terry?"

"He admitted it."

"That clarifies some things that were going on in my case then." She said. "I hope for Terry's sake, he's not serious about Raymond, Raymond Perry is a snake! He's also very vindictive and now that I think about it, oh hell!"

"What's wrong Wendy?" Jade asked, because she looked like she had just seen a ghost.

"Please tell me Lord Jesus, Terry didn't make a deal with Raymond on my behalf," she said, with her eyes closed. "Jazz, I don't have time right now to get into the whole thing but if he did, Raymond will have Terry beholding to him until he takes his last breath of air! Raymond's in a position to make or break Terry's career."

"What?" Jade whispered.

"Please try to talk to Terry Jazz, help him. I can't go near him right now. All I can say for the moment is that favors were done, what a mess. Sooo, you're in love with Mr. Keith now?" She said, trying to lighten the mood.

"I think I always have been. It just wasn't in the cards to be with him until now. I think it's our time. Tell me about "Sweet Dick"?"

"It's sweet!" Wendy said, laughing.

"Girl, you're still crazy. So what are the two of you going to do now that the trial is over?"

"For one thing, I'm giving up my job at the firm. We were lucky that this whole mess didn't blow up in my face. I'm not going to press my luck. It's just a matter of time before somebody links "Sweet Dick" and me together. I don't want to place my firm in that position, they've been too good to me. The main reason is that when the time comes—and it's coming, when Raymond Perry asks me to return a favor, he can kiss my wrinkled ass! That's why I concerned for Terry."

"Are you sure about giving your career up Wendy?"

"I want to do whatever it takes to be with Richard and not involve other people. I know what kind of life he leads and I've decided to be with him regardless."

"Damn, you really love that Black man, huh?"

"I do, I do!" Wendy said. "Speaking of I do," she flashed the ring on her finger at Jade."

"Damn! Does that come with an armored truck?" Jade asked her laughing. "When's the big day?" She asked, hugging Wendy.

"No day, until I get my business straight."

Jade and Wendy had the best "secret" meeting that night. They enjoyed being back together, if just for a little while. Before Wendy left, she made Jade promise to try to talk some sense into Terry. "I'll try Wendy, I'll try."

FORTY-TWO
NOEL

WENDY'S TRIAL HAD her all over the place, and not until she was writing checks for her bills, did she remember Noel had asked her to speak to James Wright, her lawn man. She called to ask him if it was possible for him to pick up his check at her office. She wanted to talk with him about something. He agreed, thinking there might be the possibility Wendy was letting him go or on the other hand, maybe she wanted to increase her services.

"Yes, ma'am, I can be there before you go to court at eleven." He told Wendy.

"Park in the lot across from the office, we'll validate your parking ticket." Wendy said. She asked her secretary to leave a message for Noel Ross that she had contacted James Wright, she'd know what that meant."

Noel spent all of her free time trying to find Lila

again. She started bringing sandwiches with her to work so she could eat them at the plaza while she looked. Her luck changed, she spotted the jacket she had given Lila. Lila was asking a woman for money. Noel rushed over to where she was. "Hi, how are you today?" Noel asked.

"Okay," Lila said. She seemed more focused than the last time Noel saw her. "Could you help me out ma'am?" Lila asked Noel, holding out her frail hand.

"Sure I can. Why don't you sit with me on the bench?" Noel asked her. They sat down.

"I need to get my ring sized to fit. Do you know a good jeweler I could use?" She asked Lila.

"I use Fink's Jewelers on K Street." She said. "I used them all the time before I got sick."

"You were sick?" Noel asked her.

"Yes, I'll probably always be sick because they tried to kill me." Lila said.

"Who tried to kill you?"

"My husband". "Tell me all about it," Noel asked, her hoping for a disparity of events, however, Lila proceeded to tell Noel the exact story as she told it before—verbatim!

Noel asked about the jeweler again. Lila told Noel she liked Fink's Jewelers. They took care of all her jewelry. Noel asked if that's where her wedding ring came from. Lila told her that her husband purchased it from Keisler's, a well-known exclusive jewelry store in New York City.

"That's a famous store," Noel said. "Where is your wedding ring?"

"I don't know. Are you married?" Lila asked.

"No, but I'm engaged and I need to get my ring sized."

"Why don't you ask Mr. Taylor at Fink's, he's nice."

"Thank you, I will." Noel gave Lila a $20 bill.

The next day on her break, Noel went to K Street. She entered Fink's Jewelers and asked to see Mr. Taylor. She was bringing in a ring to be cleaned for Attorney Holbrook, and he said to ask for Mr. Taylor.

"I'm Mr. Taylor, and of course we can take care of that. Where is Mrs. Holbrook, I haven't seen her in quite a while." He asked.

"I think she's been ill," Noel said, pretending to just be a courier. "I guess this is her ring, I'm not sure."

"Indeed it is." Mr. Taylor said. "I've been their jeweler for years, nice couple."

"I'll wait for it so I can return it to him this evening," Noel said taking a seat.

"Are you family? He asked her.

"No, I'm one of the secretaries at his law firm." She quickly flashed her court ID badge that was around her neck under her coat, just enough for him to see the emblem and her picture. When he was done, he handed Noel the box. "Give Mrs. Holbrook my best regards."

"I will." Noel said, and left the store.

Noel's world was turning upside down. Marcus would give her Lila's ring? Really? She felt sick to her stomach on her way back to work. *"Marcus Holbrook, what have you done?" She whispered.*

"Attorney Haines there's a James Wright to see you." The front office buzzed Wendy on the intercom.

"Please show him in Anna." Wendy met him at her door. "James, it's good to see you again.

"It's good to see you too, Miss Haines."

"I've asked you here James, because I need your help. I'm researching some information from an incident a while ago, and wondered if you remembered it. One of your customers, a Mrs. Lila Holbrook, has claimed that you witnessed a situation in which she walked in on Mr. Holbrook and a woman at their residence. Do you recall that event?"

"Yes ma'am, I sure do and it was a mess. I felt so sorry for her."

"James, I don't think this is going anywhere, but because Mrs. Holbrook is ill, I wanted to first confirm her claim before I made any decision to represent her if indeed it ever gets to that, there may be a divorce at some point. Is Mr. Holbrook aware that you witnessed this?"

"I doubt it. He was so busy getting the woman out of his house I don' think he even noticed me.

"Would you know her if you saw her again James?"

"The woman?"

"Yes, the woman that was in their house."

"No question, I know who she is."

"Is there anything else you can remember that would be helpful?"

"Not really, it was a while ago, but I know that woman had been in the house more than once. I'd seen her several times, and it was always when I was there cutting in the middle of the day. I'm not saying I know what went on in that house, but it looked funny to me. Mrs. Holbrook came outside screaming and crying after them and I tried to console her. Miss Haines it was sad." He said shaking his head.

"James, thank you for helping me with this decision. Like I said, this probably won't develop into anything, but in case it does and you had to swear to this under oath, would you?

"Yes ma'am. It wouldn't affect me one way or the other. They don't even live there anymore."

"Thanks James, here's your check and don't forget to stop at the desk so Anna can stamp you parking ticket."

When Wendy got to the courthouse she went to the lounge looking for Noel.

"I'm billing your ass for my services," Wendy said, smiling at Noel. They walked out into the hallway and found a quiet spot.

"Look Noel, when you open Pandora's Box, you find all kinds of stuff in it. You've opened the box, are you prepared to deal with what's inside?" She asked Noel.

"I am." Noel said softly, looking into Wendy's eyes.

"I spoke to James Wright. He has confirmed everything Lila told you. The woman *was* in her house that day and he'd seen her there before." Wendy told Noel. Noel was staring down an empty hallway into space. "How can you get that low?" Noel whispered. "What am I going to do Wendy?"

"Let's think about this for a while Noel, I'll tell you what you can do."

FORTY-THREE
JADE

THE SETS AT Fox 5 studios were decorated with live Poinsettias, the foyers and offices with beautiful ornaments. Lord and Taylor provided the anchors with Red and Green blazers to wear in turn for thousands of dollars' worth of free advertising. As the song says, it was beginning to look a lot like Christmas!

Jade picked up her schedule for the upcoming week and held her breath. She was praying she'd be off when her intercom buzzed, "Your daily flowers have arrived," Michelle said. "I hope you're going down to Virginia this weekend. That little butt-ugly flower delivery man and I see so much of each other, we're about to have a relationship."

"Michelle you are stupid!" Jade said, laughing. Jade and Anthony decided to walk over to Union Station that day to have lunch and to marvel at the breathtaking decorations. Union Station was extra elaborate that year, they even had the security people dressed as Elves. Jade and Anthony were all over the place and got so excited by the decorations, they never did eat lunch.

After Jade got off from work, she gassed up on New York Avenue, and hit the highway arriving at Brathwell County around seven-thirtyish. Driving up the winding road to Keith's was a spectacular sight. Better Homes and Gardens obviously didn't know about his place or it would have been the cover page for December. The trees along the road were simply magnificent as they twinkled with tiny white sparkling lights. The closer she got to the house, the two huge pine trees on either side of Keith's house were lighted and the lights magnified their gargantuan size glowing against the night sky.

Jade tooted her horn and Ben, Keith and Buddy were at the door that was decorated like a big gold package, with a huge bow. Keith put his arms around Jade and they hugged for a while before going inside. "Everything is absolutely beautiful Keith. I shudder to think how many lights you had to buy."

"Come on sweetheart, you know I didn't do this. I hired a company and let them figure it out." He laughed.

They spent an intimate weekend riding in to town for dinner, and window shopping at the stores.

HILL FOXES

For the first time, Keith went back with Jade to D.C. to do his Christmas shopping there. She had to work, so she showed him how to get around on Metro from Brooklyn station. He met her downtown after work and they went window shopping. Woodies and Hecht's were having their traditional fierce competition of window displays.

Keith met her at the station the next day and he was introduced to everyone. He seemed to enjoy the attention they were giving him, especially the women "ooing and awing" over him. She bought Anthony a red Ralph Lauren wool scarf to go with a coat he was getting. She sent diamond studs to Wendy's office, they were still not being public yet, she planned to finish the rest of her shopping the following week.

Jade and Keith had dinner at her parent's house and that was fun. They had known him since he was a teenager and they liked him, they were happy to see him and Jade together. Before they knew it, his visit was over. "I wish I didn't have to go either," Keith said hugging Jade. "I can't wait for you to come home next weekend." He kissed her a long kiss of goodbye and drove back to Virginia.

Jade told Terry she would meet him at Chanel Inn for dinner. She was happy to get out of the house and shake off her blues after Keith left. Terry gave her the most beautiful pearl earrings and she was embarrassed, she hadn't bought him a gift.

"Terry, this is so nice, but I didn't get you anything."

"I'm not looking for anything in return Jazz, I just appreciate your friendship and I'm glad we're in each other's lives again. Merry Christmas, Black woman."

They probably should have been arrested for public drunkenness that night, but somehow they got home. When Terry walked Jade to her door she was scrambling around in her pocketbook looking for her keys. "Give me that purse Black woman, you're taking too long, I have to pee." They both started giggling. "Please-please don't make me laugh or I'll be scrubbing your porch," he said, "hurry up now." They were making so much noise in the name of whispering, that porch lights on the block turned on, then they really started laughing. Jade finally got the door open and Terry ran straight for her powder room.

"Whew, what a relief that is." He said. "I'm going to miss your silly-butt next week girl."

"I hope you enjoy your holidays, Terry."

"And you enjoy yours," he said, and missed two of her porch steps leaving.

"Be careful Black man," she said, watching him drive off in his Jag.

Friday came like molasses rolling out of an ice-cold jar. Finally, she got on the crowded highway by six and headed in the direction of Brathwell County and when she arrived, everybody was waiting for her. Ben had his usual dinner surprise and after dinner, Jade and Keith sat by the fire and talked until they went to bed.

The week was full of rushing and doing last minute shopping. Jade bought Keith a pair of designer gloves from Georgetown Leather Designs. The inside tag was personalized with his name in gold. Set her back $150 but what the hell, she could afford it. He'd seen them while he was shopping in D.C. and almost bought them. She got Ben a gift certificate to an exclusive men's boutique.

Christmas Eve, Keith had a few friends over and they exchanged gifts, mostly wines, Brandy and Cognac. She gathered they did that every year. She met a few people she hadn't met before. Dave and Margo kept telling Keith they had to go play Santa to their kids, they couldn't stay long. They had mentioned that a couple of times.

"Come on man, we got to go," Dave said to Keith.

"Oh guys, it's not midnight yet," Keith said, grinning. "Keep cool, Santa's coming." A *rare* sight, Keith Lassiter high!

Ben came in with a tray of exquisitely etched crystal

cocktail glasses, and a bottle of Dom Perion. He gave each person a glass. Keith popped the cork and walked around pouring some in everybody's glass. He seemed to be having trouble steadying himself. "I want to make a toast." He said. "A looonng time ago, there was a young man who made a promise to a young lady at a place now called Lassiter Lake. Fate got in the way, and regretfully that promise was broken. I'd like to make good on that promise tonight. *Jade started getting nervous.* Keith looked at Jade. "Jazz, I promised you that one day I'd replace the friendship ring I gave you with a diamond. *What is he doing?* Keith got down on his knee and in front of all of his guests, opened a box and Lord above! The diamond he took out made everybody gasp. "Jazz will you marry me?" Jade couldn't move. She couldn't talk. She honestly and truthfully had been caught by surprise.

"Come on baby," Dave said, laughing. "You know the man got bad knees and we got to go play Santa Claus."

Jade took Keith's hands and pulled him back up and threw her arms around him. "I'll take that as a yes." Keith whispered. The women clapped and the men were giving "hoots". Ben was the first to hug her and give her best wishes, the others followed. Jade found out later that everybody knew about the proposal except her.

The rest of the holiday was as if it were written for a movie. She was going to be Mrs. Keith Lassiter.

After the holidays, Jade caught up on her mail back at home. She read through the cards and there was a beautiful one from Star. Her note said she was fine, and was spending Christmas in Jamaica with friends and her new man. Jade smiled.

Jade and Keith were responsible for those potholes in the roads between D.C. and Brathwell County. Jade's folks were tickled to death about her and Keith's engagement, so was Wendy. "We should have a double wedding," Wendy joked with Jade. Wendy was deliriously happy too, the heat was finally off of "Sweet Dick" and street gossip was just beginning to link them together.

Jade met Wendy for lunch downtown at Blackie's House of Beef. They hugged and went inside.

"I wanted to run something past you," Wendy told her. I've finally decided to turn in my resignation at the firm, and leave downtown all together. I'm opening my private practice in the hood. I had always promised myself if I ever hit the lottery, I'd work for those who needed legal help but couldn't afford it. Jazz, you have no idea how many people get screwed simply because they can't afford *good* representation." Wendy told her.

Jade sat looking at Wendy. "You're willing to do pro bono work for the majority of your clients?"

"Of course, I'm willing to do that. Richard has bought me a vacant building on Bladensburg Road, I'm going to set up there plus, I'll have access to 5D Precinct too. I'm excited about it."

"What can I say Wendy, if that's what'll make you happy, more power to you."

"My objective is to do my work without being beholding to anybody, and whatever decisions I make, will be *my* decisions.

"I wish you nothing but luck." Jade told her. "Have you guys set a date yet?"

"We're thinking springtime. We're still debating the whole thing because Richard wants to get married in Aruba and fly everybody down there to party."

"What about you two?"

"We're leaning toward late summer, early fall. It's so pretty there that time of year, and we're thinking an outside ceremony."

"Tell the truth Jazz, are you as excited as I am?"

"I am, but we still have a lot to work out, like where do we live? Do I quit my job or do I commute or what?"

"Jazz, seriously, I hope you don't think that man's going to leave his estate."

"I know." Jade said, softly. "You have to keep me updated now. You know you're my maid of honor or maybe by then, matron of honor." They laughed.

"Same here. There won't *be* a wedding without you sugar!" Wendy said, laughing. Jade and Wendy quickly finished their lunches to free up the seats for some fussy waiting customers. They did cheek kisses and waved goodbye.

You could tell the Christmas holidays were over. People were back to their grumpy, rude selves.

When Jade got home that evening, she had a message from Terry to come for dinner. They hadn't seen each other since before Christmas and they had a lot to catch up on. She changed, grabbed a bottle of Chardonnay and drove to Terry's. While she was parking, she saw the Jag in front of his house, but a tag that said *JUDGE ONE. Umph, so Raymond was there.* She rang the doorbell.

"Black woman, come on in." Terry said opening the screen door. He took her coat. "Of course you remember Raymond from school."

"Raymond Perry," she said, "how nice to see you."

"Where *have* you been hiding your fine self?" He asked her, grinning. They hugged and Jade asked God to forgive her for what she was about to do, she was about to become a devil-woman.

"I haven't been hiding, just working hard." She said.

"It's just so good to see you and you're as beautiful as ever," he said, grinning.

"Thank you, Raymond."

"Let me get you a glass of wine." Terry said.

"Sure baby," Jade gave Terry a peck on his lips.

"So how's TV land Jazz?" Raymond asked, with that shit-eating grin on his face that she always hated.

"Its TV land what can I say." As they drank, they went through a litany of *have you seen's*. Raymond sat in the lounge chair and Jade sat next to Terry on the sofa, practically in his lap.

After thirty minutes, Terry served dinner in the dining room. He had a seafood Gumbo to die for, rice and cornbread with Jalapeno peppers, an appropriate meal for a cold winter's night. Jade ate most of her meal from Terry's bowl, which was meant to suggest intimacy to Raymond. After dinner, they were back in the living room to finish the bottle of wine Terry served, and open the one Jade brought. Jade was about to get her buzz on and she thought from the looks of Terry, his was already there.

Excuse me Lord! "Terry, I'm going to look upstairs and see if my earring is on your bedroom floor somewhere. Have you seen it yet? She was walking up the stairs. When she came back downstairs, she sat next

HILL FOXES

to Terry. "I didn't see it honey, but keep looking for me." Poor Terry was speechless and she felt guilty, kind of.

"Jazz," Raymond said with that shit-eating grin plastered across his face, "that's undoubtedly the biggest diamond I think I've seen in a while. Aren't you afraid to walk around with that on? Who's the lucky man?"

Terry's head snapped around like the little girl in the Exorcist, she guessed he hadn't noticed it before. His eyes were glued to her hand but he didn't say anything.

"Oh, this is a piece my Auntie left me, she passed recently," she said, messaging Terry's neck. "I'm not afraid to wear it. I figure most people will think its fake."

"Look at the time." Raymond said. He got up and pulled his coat from the closet.

"*We* really enjoyed your company Raymond." Jade said, standing up. "It was great seeing you again."

"The older I get, the more I realize how strange life is." Raymond said, walking to the door laughing. Terry jumped up and opened the door. "Terry man, thanks for inviting me, I enjoyed dinner. Jazz, it's been a pleasure, let me kiss the ring." He said, kissing Jade's hand. Jade and Terry stood on the porch until he drove off. Terry went back inside and Jade followed him. He started removing the glasses from the coffee table and taking them into the kitchen.

"Terry?" Jade said. He placed the glasses and the dinner dishes into the dishwasher.

"Terry?" He began pouring the leftover Gumbo into a bowl. "What's wrong Terry are you angry with me?"

"Nope." He put the bowl in the refrigerator.

"This is me Black man, what's wrong?"

"You couldn't tell me you were engaged? And that earring shit in my bedroom, what was that Jazz?"

"First of all, I haven't seen you to tell you anything, and I couldn't tell you during dinner."

"Oh, you could have, but you were too busy leading Ray down another path. Why would you do that Jazz, I thought you were my friend?"

"Terry, I'm sorry, then again I'm not sorry. This is probably none of my business, but I want you to be careful of Raymond. I don't think he's good for you and I know it's not my place to say that, but I have my reasons." Terry was wiping off the table. "Terry, sit down please." He kept wiping the table.

"You like them football players, huh?" He said, sarcastically. "You haven't learned your lesson yet, huh?"

"Keith hasn't played football in years if that's what you're referring to. He coaches and teaches."

HILL FOXES

"Best wishes." He said.

"Terry, are you upset with me for not telling you about my engagement or because of Raymond?"

"I'm cool, have another drink."

"I'll have one if you have one with me." Terry poured them Chardonnay and sat down on the sofa.

"So Black man, how was your holiday?" She said, trying to make him comfortable enough to talk.

"Obviously, not as exciting as yours."

"Okay, you're going to have to talk to me." He seemed to be mellowing out some.

"I surprised myself tonight. When Ray pointed out your ring, my heart dropped out of my body and I can't explain why Jazz, I don't know why." He looked beaten. "Maybe it's just the *way* I found out." Jade moved closer to him and placed her hand on his. "Why don't you think about that, think about what's really bothering you."

"I just spent the last three months *thinking* about my feelings and here I go again. I'm just F'd up." He said.

"You know Terry, I already know the answer to your questions, and I also know it's something you're going to have to work out for yourself. I love you baby, but I can't help you." He took her face in his hands and kissed her a kiss that was about to start a whole bunch of ****! "Terry, chill. We've been drinking and you're depressed, I've got to go anyway." She stood up to get her coat.

"Jazz, you've been playing with me. If you weren't prepared to serve the meal, you shouldn't have handed out the menu." Terry grabbed her and was all over her. She literally had to fight him off. "Terry, stop!"

"Just let me love you Jazz," he whispered, his grip was too strong for her to get away.

"I thought you loved Raymond?" He let her go and sat down on the floor by the fireplace.

"I'm sure this is not the time, but I think Raymond is taking advantage of you and I don't think he's someone you want, or need. You can be as pissed with me as you need be, but I believe that Terry. I'm only sorry if you're upset with me for giving him the impression we're together, but I'm *not* sorry if I messed with his head.

You need to get a good night's sleep and think about who and what you are, Terry."

By the weekend, Jade was trying her best to get to Brathwell County before the predicted snowstorm. She thought about Terry while she drove. She felt so sorry for him, and she honestly thought she was helping by showing him he wasn't gay. He told her, and she guessed he was telling the truth, that he and Raymond hadn't slept together yet, so he didn't know what "gay" meant. Her other thought was that he felt beholding enough to Raymond to allow him to lead him down that path, but Terry was sharp and intelligent, that was hard for her to accept. Whatever, he needed to work all of that out.

When Jade arrived, Keith, Ben and Buddy were there waiting dinner as usual. She got comfortable and had a wonderful meal. They sat by the fireplace after dinner and watched a football game and naturally, she fell asleep. He woke her up and whispered in her ear. "Look at the snow falling sweetheart." It had already covered everything and when they went to bed, it was still coming down.

The next morning when she looked out, she panicked. "I'm never going to get out of here," she said.

"Get comfortable sweetheart, you're stuck like Chuck."

"How am I going to get back home? This isn't going to disappear by Sunday. I'm going to have to call the station so they can get someone in my place."

"I'm sure they're having their own problems," Keith said. "This storm is as far up as New Jersey, and as far south as South Carolina."

"So what am I going to do Keith?"

"Let me say this while we're on the subject, we keep talking around it. I expect you to leave Washington and be here in Brathwell County as my full-time wife. You don't have to work, and I don't need your income to supplement mine. I can support you in the manner you're accustomed on my own." They debated that for a while, since it had been the elephant in the soup. It needed to be ironed out for once and all because it directly affected their marriage. She told him although her job got on her nerves sometime, she wasn't sure if she was ready to give up her career yet, nor was she ready to give up D.C.

"I told you a while ago I plan to die here. I have too much invested in Brathwell County. One of us is going to have to make a sacrifice." That was Keith's final stance.

Keith and Ben dressed in heavy clothing and went out to clear some of the roads. It was customary for a group of the guys to take heavy snow equipment and snowmobiles to clear each other's areas, an all-day thing. Keith and Ben left early in the truck.

Jade called in to work, she told them she was stuck. Bob wasn't a bit happy. She watched television all day. When Keith got back that night, she had a big pot of fresh homemade soup waiting, one of the two things she knew how to cook. While Ben and Keith ate, Keith couldn't stop grinning he was so surprised. Ben complimented her on dinner, although she knew he was being nice, at least it was something hot and he didn't have to cook it.

"Thanks, Jazz." That's just what we needed."

"I hope you enjoyed it, now follow me please." She took his hand and led him into the Jacuzzi that was already bubbling and ready for Keith to get in.

"Here's your glass of wine sir, if you need anything, just push that little button there. He smiled and laid back and closed his eyes, she knew he had to be tired. He came upstairs to bed when he finished and they talked about their plans some more. They settled on Labor Day weekend as their date. They agreed to have the ceremony at Lassiter Lake, and the reception in the Wandering Garden. They decided on the number of guests, and she found out that the honeymoon was to be a surprise to her. She would start shopping in D.C. for her dress. Her mother was going to love that.

By Monday morning, typical of the south, the sun was out, the weather was mild, and the snow was melting. The highways had been cleared so Jade started on her way back to D.C. Since she got there around the time her show was ending, she decided to go straight home. She checked her messages and there was one from Mitch. Now she had decided he was just plain stupid, there was no other explanation for him. She called Terry but didn't get an answer, so she left a message for him to come over for dinner.

A couple of days had passed and she still hadn't heard from Terry. *Is he that angry with me?* After work she drove pass his house before going home. Call it intuition, mother-wit or whatever. She felt in her soul that something was wrong. There were three Washington Post papers on the porch, and the mailbox was full. Jade peeked in the front window and it looked like his house was in disarray. *Had a burglar broken in and hurt him?* Jade's stomach felt queasy. She started knocking on the door, but he never came to open it so she began beating on the door. She walked to the side of the house and peered through the little window of the garage and Terry's car was inside. *Oh my God, something's wrong!*

"Terry!" She started to knock again. Had that been her street, everybody would have been out front peeping and being nosey by then.

"Terry! Terry! Open the door ,it's Jazz." Finally Terry came to the door and threw it open. **"WHAT!"**

"Black man, are you okay?" He looked terrible! He hadn't shaved, his hair hadn't been brushed and he smelled like he looked.

"What do you want, Jazz?"

"What do I want my hind parts," she said, pushing him out of the way and walking into the house. What she had seen from the front window, was just a preview of the chaos inside. "Black man, what the hell?" Terry looked like a lost soul on a ship to nowhere. Jade took him by his hand, and led him upstairs to his bedroom which looked like a tornado had gone through it. She went to the bathroom and started to run a tub of warm water. While it ran, she led Terry into the bathroom. "Take your clothes off Black man." She went back into the bedroom and searched his dresser for fresh pajamas and underwear. She thought about calling Raymond, but she wasn't too sure he would appreciate her knowing about him. She went back to the bathroom and Terry had gotten into the tub. She gently sponged his back and told him she didn't know what had happened, but she promised him she would be there for him.

She got Terry to sit on the chaise while she changed the sheets then got him into bed. Jade climbed over the pieces of furniture downstairs and found canned soup in the pantry. She took a big bowl of it upstairs and fed him.

It had gotten dark outside. She cut the lamp off by Terry's bed, lay beside him and gently rubbed Black man's shoulders until he fell asleep. When she awoke six hours later, it was twelve forty-five. She got up to go downstairs but as soon as she moved, he awoke. "Terry, do you want anything?" She asked him, but he didn't respond. He went to the bathroom and got back into bed.

"Something happened here, do you want to talk about it?" Jade whispered to him.

"There's nothing to talk about."

"Did something happen with you and Raymond?"

It took a long time for him to answer, but he finally said, "Yeah."

"Did you two fight in here?"

"Yeah, it's over."

"I'm sorry." He closed his eyes and Jade held him until they fell asleep again.

FORTY-FOUR
JILL

JILL WAS SCHEDULED to work a round-trip flight to Miami. She would do the morning roundtrip, and deadhead back to Miami from D.C. by nightfall to stay at the Sunset Beach Cottages for a few days. Bryce made reservations for her since she would no longer be staying at Cheyenne's, sneaky whore! Cheyenne made sure Julius knew about Bryce, so it was just a matter of time with them anyway. She was curious to know however, just how long Julius had known about Bryce. When Jill told Brea what had happened, Brea was surprised by Jill's hostile attitude toward Julius.

"Jill, how on earth could you possibly be upset with Julius when you have a man in every port? Hell, you should have been a sailor."

"I know what you're saying, but *my affairs* are with men unknown to anyone. It's not like I slept with one of his co-workers. If I had, I could agree with your analogy, but I didn't do that and as God is my witness, I see a difference Brea."

Jill was seriously considering changing her home base, but she wasn't ready to leave her precious D.C. She packed a few extra beach pieces for her stay. She expected this visit with Bryce to be drama free, he had taken vacation leave. She wasn't sure what he told Saundra he was doing, and it really didn't matter. She figured he could handle his business and so far, he had never put a ring on Saundra's finger, so he was available as far as she was concerned.

Jill worked the roundtrip and once they made their hair-raising landing back at National, she finished her paperwork, had a seafood salad at one of the airport restaurants, and hopped the last flight back to Miami.

Bryce was waiting for her in the passenger pickup lane. "Hey baby," he said, smiling and grabbed her bag. He handed her a single red rose bud, and they hugged. Bryce helped her into his Wrangler. She freed her mop of curly hair from the tight clamp, and let it blow in the humid breeze as they exited onto the interstate. Jill closed her eyes, and inhaled the salty ocean air, she loved that smell.

They arrived at the Sunset Cottages. Bryce opened the door and took her bag in. He had been there earlier, and had stocked the cottage with wine and food. There were several cottages along the beach. They each had private decks and private beach areas. Each cottage was a different color and name. They were staying in The Peach Dolphin, two bedrooms with all the amenities imaginable. Jill loved the peaceful, intimate atmosphere of the Peach Dolphin. Bryce had made a good choice.

Bryce wanted to cook a meal for her. Jill took a long shower while he cooked. She discarded her uniform that seemed to be glued to her after a day of back-to-back flights. The warm water trickled over her shoulders, relaxing the built up tension in her muscles. She stood with her eyes closed under the spray of water, her mind cluttered with thoughts of her recent drama. She wanted to quiet her busy mind long enough to summon her feelings—she had shut them off and buried them deep within. She'd been too busy to deal with problems.

Had Julius carried out the ultimate betrayal? Jill had loved Julius, and though she walked a little on the wild side herself, he was the one she had given her heart to, the man she'd chosen to be her number one.

Jill searched her feelings for Michael, Clark and Bryce. Michael was just plain fun and she always enjoyed being with him whenever she was in West

Palm Beach. The fact that he was married just helped keep their arrangement intact, with no hassles. He would always find time to spend with her when she was there and he left no stone unturned. She was lucky—maybe it was even a gift, but she was always able to keep her feelings separated. There was fun, and then there was love. She permitted her *playmates,* as she referred to them, to play just outside the gate of her Secret Garden, but she never let them in.

There was something different about each of them. Clark in Atlanta was a strong yet sensitive man, who showered her with love and affection, not to mention extravagant goodies, and the sex was amazing!

Bryce was her favorite though. He was aggressively tugging at the gate to her Garden, but she had managed to keep him out. He had his own drama with Saundra who was insanely jealous, and wanted to know his every move. Saundra wanted Bryce to put a ring on her finger.

Knock-knock! "Did you drown?" Bryce asked, pushing open the bathroom door.

"I just might be sleep standing up." Jill said, laughing. "I'm coming, sugar." She toweled off and rubbed down in Jean Nate', her smooth chocolate skin glistening from its wetness. She wrapped in the lime-colored beach wrap, pulled her bushy hair into a bunch and tied it with a lime scrunchie. Bryce had placed a glass of wine on the bedroom nightstand for her.

He was busy in the kitchen fixing Coriander Crusted Swordfish, and a Chickpea Artichoke Salad for their meal. "Can I refill that for you Jill?" He took the bottle from the refrigerator. "We can eat in about twenty minutes."

"I'll take another one."

"It's good being with you again. This time, I promise we're not going to be disturbed." He was chopping up Artichokes and onions. "What happened at Cheyenne's? You said you would tell me about it."

Jill gave him a blow by blow, starting with finding the tennis bracelet in Julius' bathroom months earlier. She told him how the portrait kept registering in her mind's eye, but not in her conscious mind.

"How are you feeling about it Jill?" Bryce asked her, softly.

"I'm a little hurt, I'll admit that." She said, and he took her in his arms and rocked her. "Enough of that," she said, pulling away.

Bryce lit candles and lowered the lights for their romantic dinner, he refilled their glasses. After their meal, they strolled down to the private beach just outside their cottage. Bryce brought a beach blanket, red wine and glasses. They lay on the blanket in each other's arms enjoying the twinkling wonders of the sky. They talked until the wee hours of the morning. Close to sunrise, Bryce kissed her, she tasted like a rare sweet passion fruit, and she was delicious. A warm breeze caressed them. He loosened the scrunchie from her thick hair, and slid the wrap from around her. She moved closer to him and tightly held on. She listened intently while he shook at the gate of her secret garden.

FORTY-FIVE
JADE

WASHINGTON HAD ONE of its worst winters on record. Jade and Keith continued running up and down I-64, taking turns at each other's places.

Terry snapped out of his depression and seemed back to his old self. Jade was with him every day and night when she could be, until he came out of his slump. It seems like the breakup had been because of her. She felt bad about that, but she also felt it was the best thing that could have happened to Terry.

Raymond Perry was bad news! Raymond got pissed off with Terry's reaction to Jade's ring that night, before she told them it had been her Aunties, and one thing led to another. Terry figured out he was neither bisexual nor gay but hell, Jade already knew that. Raymond had moved on to another bright, ambitious young lawyer in Georgetown, just like that! *Somebody* sent an anonymous letter to the

Honorable Judge Raymond Perry, suggesting there may be information linking him to preferential treatment in exchange for sexual favors from young men. "*Hum.*" Terry buried himself in work and started coaching tennis to the neighborhood kids.

Wendy resigned from her firm and was in her newly renovated building on Bladensburg Road. Jade and Wendy had lunch together at least twice a week, and shopped for their weddings together. Wendy and Keith finally got to meet and just like Jade knew, they were crazy about each other. For whatever reason, only God knew, Mitch was having an affair with her answering machine.

Jade and Keith took a trip to New York, took in all of the sights, shopped and ate in the finest restaurants and had a wonderful time. New York was his old stomping ground, so he was in his element. They watched the ball drop in Times Square as they began a new year together.

Keith insisted that Jade spend her birthday with him in Virginia in March. She drove down the dark road toward Brathwell that Friday after work. She stopped on the highway, went through the drive-thru at Golden Chicken, and bought a chicken and biscuit combo, then continued down I-64, she was starving. When she arrived at Keith's, it didn't seem like anyone was home so she took her key out and went inside. That was the first time she could remember Keith, Ben and Buddy not meeting her at the door, but what the hell, she was no longer a guest.

She headed up the stairs with her bag. The lights in the game room popped on and everybody yelled— **SURPRISE!** *Everybody* was there, Wendy and "Sweet Dick", the *Hill Foxes*, Dave and Margo, *Hot* Brenda and Jim, and other people she hadn't met before. When the doorbell rang and Anthony and Dave walked in, Jade was just too through!

"Jade, you beat us here. We passed you a couple of times on the highway praying you didn't see us." Anthony said laughing.

Jade looked at Keith. "Thank you sweetheart," she whispered to him. "This is wonderful."

"You're quite welcome, now enjoy your party." He said, handing her a glass of Dom Perion.

It was the party to beat all parties. Their guests were treated to the best cuisine and drinks on the east coast, and they partied until the wee hours of the morning. Ben had done his magic, and everything was fabulous. Jade was refilling her glass again, she'd lost count.

"Let's go feed this alcohol girl," Wendy said, walking toward the buffet table. "Honey, does the man cook like this all of the time?"

"He sure does, and I'm going to resemble a Hippo if I *keep –eating—this*—Wendy grabbed Jade's arm. Jade's words sounded like they were far—far—far away to her.

"Hey, that's the end of your champagne, honey," Wendy told Jade.

"Wendy, I'm going to be sick," Jade whispered and held her stomach. Wendy beckoned for Keith. He came running over and put his arm around Jade, and led her up the stairs.

"We'll be right back," Keith said, smiling, "First victim." Everybody laughed and kept partying. Jade got to the top of the stairs and made a mad dash for the bathroom. She threw up everything she'd had all day—or maybe all week! She was drunk!

Keith wet a towel and placed it around her neck. "Why don't you lie down for a while, sweetheart?" He pulled back the covers from their bed and helped her in. "I'll check on you again in a few minutes. The room was spinning around so fast and oh Lord, she was *never* drinking again. Wendy and Keith took turns checking on her, she was in and out. "Just let me sleep." She had asked them.

Keith had arranged for everyone to stay in his house as well as at Westbury. Brenda and Jim led the way for the ones staying at Westbury, and Keith finally came to bed at four-thirty.

HILL FOXES

"Thank you so much honey, this was really special and I'm so embarrassed. My friends understand, but your friends probably think I'm a lush," and with that said, Jade was back in the bathroom. Keith rubbed her with the cool towel and brought her some black coffee.

"Honey, I don't drink coffee…Ugh!" The smell of the coffee sent her racing back. She finally got to sleep, and when she woke the next morning, all she needed was a leash –she felt just like a dog! Keith had already dressed and was downstairs hosting the buffet breakfast. She managed to get showered, dressed, go down and join everybody. Wendy and "Sweet Dick" had gone out somewhere, and the *Foxes* had come in from Westbury. They were leaving after breakfast.

"What can I help you with Ben?" Jade asked, coming into the dining room *like she could actually do something*.

"I think everything's under control Miss Jazz," Ben said. Jade looked at the scrambled eggs, did an about face for the stairs, and was draped over the toilet when Wendy came up.

"Here," Wendy said, handing her the pregnancy test she and "Sweet Dick" had gone after.

"What the hell is this for?" She asked Wendy, as if she had lost her mind.

"Just do it, make *me* feel better," Wendy told her,

and the damn thing turned blue. She was as pregnant as hell! Jade started crying and couldn't stop.

"What am I going to do? What am I going to tell Keith?"

"The first thing you need to tell him is that he got you knocked-up." She said, laughing.

"Wendy, this isn't funny. What about my wedding? We have deposits down and reservations made and oh…"

Jade was over the toilet again.

"Come on, wipe your face and get yourself together, you have guests." They went downstairs and chit-chatted with the girls. Anthony and David were leaving. She gave them hugs and thanked them for coming. "Be safe."

"This was the bomb girlfriend." Anthony said. "You got that nasty bug and you can keep it right down here."

Jade went to the game room to talk to the *Foxes*, anything to get away from the smell of food. The girls had gathered their things to leave. "Sweet Dick" brought their things down too. "I thought you were staying the whole weekend," Keith said.

"We were, but Richard got a call and needs to get back to town." Wendy said, so that he and Jade could have some private time. Jade and Keith walked them to the car, Ben had brought it around to the circle for them. "See, I'm getting me one of him," Wendy whispered in Jade's ear and they laughed. Wendy hugged Jade and she started crying again.

"Call me if you need me," Wendy said. It's going to be fine, the man loves you."

"Thanks for inviting me man, this was nice." "Sweet Dick" shook Keith's hand. After the last car drove off Jade started crying and couldn't stop.

"Baby, baby what's wrong? Calm down and take deep breaths, you're about to hyperventilate." She scared him.

"Were you surprised last night?" He asked, trying to calm her. Let me get you some ginger ale or juice. I think you have a bug, I'm putting you to bed." She went back to bed and the flood gates opened again. What was she going to do about all of the wedding plans?

"Sweetheart, if you feel this bad, I'm going to call Dr. Winters and ask him to come over."

"No, Keith, I'm pregnant," and she was on her way back to the bathroom. She lay on the cool tile and he picked her up, held her face in his hands and asked her how she knew that.

"Wendy gave me a pregnancy test this morning." Keith grabbed Jade so tight she thought she was going to throw up again.

"I thought something was wrong. It's just that my

son does *not* like Dom Perion." He was smiling that Kill-a-woman-smile, showing all of his teeth.

"What about all of our wedding plans Keith?"

"Damn a wedding plans. We're getting married right now! You're having my baby woman." He said, grinning.

FORTY-SIX
NOEL

NOEL'S SOMBER MOOD was a reflection the day, cold and miserable. She had spent the past two months trying to convince her self she was wrong in her suspicions of Marcus, but she was developing a healthy case of skepticism. On top of that, she was no closer to bonding with Brent and Bryan than she had been six months earlier. She began to wonder now, if he ever intended her to. How could they become a family when he shut her out of their lives? She didn't get it.

Noel's daily trips to the plaza had been in vain, Lila had simply disappeared. Noel thought about looking for her at the women's shelter, but Wendy had warned her to stay away from there. They were able to briefly talk away from Marcus at Jazz's birthday party in Virginia.

"Noel, I'm working on it, I just ask you to be

patient and stop trying to take matters into your own hands. I promised I'd let you know what to do, and I'm going to keep that promise." Wendy told her.

Noel overheard a conversation the guys were having by the fireplace in Keith's game room. Keith, "Sweet Dick" and Marcus were comparing wedding plans.

"Sweet Dick" said he wanted to fly everybody down to Aruba for their wedding in the spring. Keith said they expected everybody to return there for his and Jade's wedding Labor Day weekend. Keith asked Marcus when he and Noel were getting married, and Marcus said, "Noel hasn't set the date yet." ***What ? What had been the purpose of that lie?***

Noel had an appointment after work to meet Wendy in her new office on Bladensburg Road. She parked and went inside the building.

"Your office is very impressive Attorney Haines," Noel said smiling. "I'm proud of you, girl."

"Why, thank you Madame Ross, we try."

"How is everything working out for you down here?"

"I'm loving it, Noel. I feel so free and relaxed."

"So have you heard anything new about Lila?"

"Let me ask you this first, how is Marcus acting, and what does he say about the status of his divorce?"

"He hasn't said much, but that's how he is. I'm

under the impression that the required time period of separation hasn't ended yet?"

"Huh." Wendy grunted. "I asked you when we started this journey, if you were prepared for what you'd find inside Pandora's Box. I'm asking you again Noel. This is some very serious stuff." Wendy got up and locked the front door of her office, and pulled down the "*closed*" shade. She poured both of them a drink.

"Go ahead, Wendy." Noel said softly.

"I had Lila taken to a hospital in Delaware, that's why you can't find her. The hospital has told me that apparently Lila's been misdiagnosed. She is *not* schizophrenic." Wendy took a drink from her glass. "The first thing the hospital did was to detoxify her of all medications she'd been given, before they began therapy. I—we have found out that she was diagnosed with schizophrenia because of her hallucinations. Everything she was doing seemed to add up to that. Easy medical error, I'm sure it happens every day. Anyway, Lila was hallucinating because she was being fed an herb called Salvia Divinorum in her salads, at least twice a day. The seeds from that plant were also put in her food."

"**WENDY**! Where are you getting this from?"

"You've opened the box Noel." Wendy reminded her.

Noel began to cry, Wendy poured her another drink.

"Salvia Divinorum is a green leafy plant that's grown in Mexico, and perfectly legal to buy here in the states. Marcus won't be getting that divorce right now, because he can't find Lila. *I* want to be able to control what goes on with Lila right now. *You* need to decide what you want to do."

"Are you saying he did that to her? Marcus didn't fix Lila's meals, Wendy." Noel said, defending Marcus.

"Do you know Mrs. Prince?" Wendy asked her.

"I've never actually met her, but I know her."

"She's an older Mexican woman who is retired from nursing." Noel sat silently taking in the heartbreaking information. "Think about what you want to do, you have options." Wendy said.

"Options? What options?"

"Your options need to be carefully weighed. I can bring Lila back to D.C. and Marcus can complete the divorce process so you two can be married *or*," Wendy took another drink from her glass, "on Lila's behalf, I can represent her and charge Marcus with First Degree Aggravated Assault, he can go to prison." Noel's mouth dropped open. "Marcus would be investigated, charged, disbarred, whatever. That depends on what you want Noel." Wendy explained.

HILL FOXES

"What's going to happen to Lila?"

"Either way, I'm going to help her. No one should have to live the hell she's lived, just because she was set up and she was *definitely* set up. See how easy it is to do that to somebody? That scares me." Wendy said. "Regardless of which option you choose, I'm going to see that Lila is put into a rehab program, one that will also help get her employment. Lila is a very smart woman. I plan to see that custody of the two boys is given to her parents in Virginia. Lila might even want to move back there to work. Search your soul Noel. Do what your heart tells you and I promise I won't judge your decision, either way."

"I'm becoming afraid of Marcus. He's going to be furious with me, Wendy."

"Why? *Lila* will be charging him with what he did to *her*. You have nothing to do with that, nor do you know anything about it. That's why I've asked you to leave it alone."

Wendy and Noel finished the bottle of Merlot. Wendy consoled Noel while she cried her eyes out and questioned how the man she loved and planned to marry, was a total stranger to her.

When Noel got home that night, she was so stressed she couldn't sleep. Her head was spinning with thoughts of what Marcus had done to Lila. He'd left a message on her machine, but she didn't want to talk to him. The sound of his voice on the machine made her tremble. She thought of how easy it was to wreck someone's life, and it made her angry! What a dangerous game Marcus was playing.

Two days later, Noel stood in the hallway of the District Courthouse waiting for Wendy to come out of the courtroom. Wendy pushed the door open and looked into Noel's eyes and smiled before Noel uttered a word.

"Let's do him!" Noel said.

FORTY-SEVEN
JILL

THE LANDING GEAR thumped as the plane began its approach to PBI. After landing, Jill stood at the cabin door thanking passengers for flying Eastern. She finished her inventory report, said goodbye to the co-pilot in the cockpit, and took the elevator upstairs. She hailed a cab outside of the terminal and rode to Gina's where she stayed when she was in West Palm Beach.

Jill had called Michael the night before and told him she would be in town, and wanted to see him. She took a quick shower, splashed on some Bejan', threw on shorts, a halter top and sandals. Jill took out the wine she had chilled in the refrigerator and poured herself a drink. She walked out on the deck to watch the golden Florida sunset. She was listening to the Four Tops sing McArthur Park....

...Someone left the cake out in the rain,

I don't know if I can take it,
'Cause it took so long to bake it,
And I'll never have that recipe again,
Oh Nooooo….."

The doorbell rang.

"Michael!" Jill was smiling.

"Hey baby, you look good." He said, and kissed her.

"Let me get you a glass of champagne."

"Sure. Did I miss you when you were here the last time?" He asked her.

"No, actually I haven't been on this run for a while. Follow me. I'm out by the pool." They exchanged small talk and watched the sun disappear while they drank the expensive champagne.

"Michael, the main reason I wanted to see you, although I *always* enjoy seeing you, is that my schedule is changing soon and I won't be coming to West Palm anymore. I wanted to say how much I've enjoyed you each time we're together, and to thank you for the good memories." Jill said.

"What? You're not coming back at all?"

"No, I'm going to be working the Gulf side, Tampa I think, but we'll keep in touch."

"I'm going to miss you Jill," Michael whispered. He grabbed her hand and kissed it. "I guess I never thought about the possibility that one day you'd be gone."

"I'm going to miss you too Michael, but things change." They talked until midnight finishing off the bottle of champagne. Michael never stayed out too late, one of the things she respected him for. He valued his wife and his home, and so did she. She walked Michael to the door and they had a long goodbye kiss.

"Be good Jill. Let me hear from you sometimes."

"I promise I will." She said, and he was gone.

She propped her feet up in the chair in front of her back on the deck, she wasn't sleepy yet. She was going to miss Michael. He had been so cool, and so much fun. Gina was cool too. That sister and brother act was a hoot when they got together. She'd still see Gina occasionally in D.C.

Jill dialed Bryce's cell. He was on duty, so they talked for a while before he had to go. She called Clark in Atlanta, put on her pajamas, stuck a movie in and fell asleep.

The next morning Jill dressed and got a cab to PBI. She worked the run to ATL and got off. She'd made reservations for a room at the Marriott in Buckhead. The night before, she had asked Clark if he would meet her there after he got off work. He wanted to make arrangements for a suite at the Westin for them, but she told him she was fine in Buckhead. There was a tap at the door and she welcomed Clark inside the room.

"Hello Clark," she said hugging him. "Come in and have a seat." She said

"Jill you look wonderful," he grabbed her hand. "I've missed you."

"Would you like a drink?"

"I'll have a Baileys if there's some." She opened the refrigerator-bar and took out the bottle of Baileys Irish Crème. "It's cold but would you like ice?"

"This is fine." He said. "How've you been Jill?"

"I've been very busy working hard, you know Eastern."

"Tell me about it." They talked about the company, and he told her things going on at his job at Eastern, general chit-chat. "Have you eaten Jill? Would you like to go to a restaurant or we could call room service."

"I had a really big meal before I left and I'm not very hungry," she lied. "Clark, I asked you to meet me this evening because I have a bit of bad news. My schedule will be changing soon. I won't be laying-over here in Atlanta anymore."

"What?" He looked like he'd been hit by a bus.

"It looks like I'm either going to be on the west coast Florida run, or I'll be non-stop to Miami." She lied again.

"I don't know which one it will be, but I won't be stopping here anymore."

"But, this is our hub! I don't understand." He was distraught.

"I'm disappointed too, but I've already been notified." Clark's attitude was pissy, like Eastern was doing something to him personally.

"That makes no sense." He said. "You have seniority, they can't do that."

"Actually Clark, I don't mind. Keeping up this pace is wearing me down. I'm always tired, the up and down, on and off, is getting the best of me. Half of the time I don't even know where the hell I am." Clark got quiet. He went to the refrigerator and opened another bottle.

"What am I supposed to do?" He asked her angrily.

"What do you mean, Clark?"

"I mean, am I supposed to just never see you again?"

"I suppose you will continue your life as you live it when I'm not here." He was silent and sat in the chair like a wounded child. "You do remember our original agreement? She reminded him. "When I'm here I'm with you, but it goes no further. I care for you Clark, but life moves on." His look was so intense it scared her. He got up walked to the door and slammed it behind him.

Jill was satisfied she had closed the chapters and tied up the loose ends of her life. She had decided she would make Miami her home base—yes she was leaving her beloved D.C. Bryce was providing her with a happiness she'd never dreamed of before. He managed to break through the door of her secret garden, and she had decided to let him stay.

FORTY-EIGHT
JADE

AT THE END of March, Wendy and "Sweet Dick", David and Margo, Ben, Jade's parents and Buddy, attended Jade and Keith's private wedding ceremony held in Brathwell County. It was a beautiful service, with the Right Reverend R.L. Brooks officiating—Amen.

Jade wore a silk off-white suit, a small hat with a vale and white gloves. Quite different from the $2000 dress she had ordered, but it worked. Keith was handsome in a black shark-skin suit and boutonniere. Jade's father gave her away, Wendy was her maid of honor, Dave stood with Keith as his best man, and Jade's mother cried during the whole service—loud!

"We're still having a large reception here in the fall," Keith announced, "so we expect you all back for the bash. We're taking our honeymoon at a place unknown to Jade at this time, and when we go, Mom and Dad will be here taking care of my son." Everybody laughed. Jade *handed* Wended her bouquet of white gardenias.

With the constant urging of Keith, Jade gave a month's notice to Channel 5. Anthony was spastic, she was leaving him. Since she wasn't showing yet, she didn't share her news with anyone except Anthony. When she told Terry, he hugged her and wished her well, he looked sad though. "You know I'm always here for you Jazz, I love you Black woman," and it finally dawned on her—he really did.

Jade was busy with announcements and arranging for her house to be leased. She would never sell her house; people in D. C. didn't sell their property.

Brathwell County was starting to come alive in April with tulips and spring flowers. The trees had small buds and the air was a little warmer. It was rainy season. The rain started, and did not stop.

"I made reservations at Antonio's yesterday for dinner. Do you want to go out in that mess or should I cancel?" Keith asked Jade.

"Maybe it'll slack up later." She said. They decided to take a nap before they went out, and they slept for two hours. Keith and Ben had surprised her earlier that day. They took her to the bedroom next door. They had been busy right under her nose, converting it into a nursery.

It was already filled with stuffed animals. Ben had made a wooden rocking horse from one of the gigantic trees on the property, and painted it. She smiled. "Wake up sleepy head." She said. I guess we need to get ready for dinner. Do you still want to go, it's nasty out there?"

"I don't want Ben to have to cook. I already told him we were going out."

Keith was happy to have his Jazz with him finally, and a baby coming, just completed his life! He took her out to the truck under an umbrella. The rain came down in sheets. The windshield wipers were totally useless against the strong down pour. Trees along the winding roads leaned and blew in the forceful winds, it was just plain nasty. They were rounding a curve and right in front of them without warning, was the blare of truck headlights. The truck hit them head on and they rolled down an embankment.

Jade hadn't remembered much, images of flares and lights, an ambulance, and being placed on a helicopter. She was medivaced to Richmond. She had been sedated for days and the first voice she recognized was her mother's. "Shh, don't try to move around Jade."

Every bone in her body ached. It hurt to breathe and Jade recovered, painfully slow. During the horror of that evening, Jade lost the most important things in her life, her baby and her husband. She'd never be the same again.

FORTY-NINE

KEITH LASSITER HAD been a well-respected citizen of Brathwell County, a hero of sorts. His funeral was another large gathering of family, friends and associates. People from all walks of life came to bid him farewell. All of the *Foxes* had come down from D. C. to pay their respects, and to give their support to Jazz.

Keith's body was laid to rest beneath the beautiful, peaceful trees overlooking Lassiter Lake, where the ducks flew in and out of the water and gathered at the banks.

Keith left a will that had recently been revised since their marriage. He had taken good care of his daughter Kalia, as well as his best friend Ben, the rest was Jade's. Jade's decision to have Ben remain in the house was final. She would never go there again anyway.

HILL FOXES

Wendy stayed behind at Westbury after the funeral to oversee Jade's business, and to help her parents with her recovery. Wendy and Jade's parents were worried, Jade was despondent and no one could seem to reach her.

Jade returned to D.C. once she was well enough to travel. She cancelled the lease on her house and gave the people their deposit back, plus a rather sizable bonus for being understanding—whatever, she didn't care.

She had been in bed since her return home. She wasn't interested in seeing or talking to anyone. She had asked her family and friends to respect her wishes to be left alone. Wendy was devastated, she wouldn't see her either. Her parents were upset, but she didn't care.

"Jazz won't see anyone Terry." Wendy told him.

"I didn't know what was happening," Terry said. "I've been calling and leaving messages with no response."

"I'm really worried. I don't like the fact that she's locked up in that house by herself, but that's what she wants." Wendy told Terry.

"No, that's not good. I'm going to try something." Terry said.

Somebody kept knocking at Jade's door. They knocked and knocked and the knocking got on her damn nerves! She went downstairs and opened it, it was Terry. She must have looked a mess. She hadn't combed her hair or bathed in days. Terry called his office, took leave from work, and stayed with her at her house until he thought she was strong enough to stay alone. He was the only one who had been able to get through to her.

By summers end, Jade went to spend some time at Westbury. It was the first time she'd been there since she returned to D.C. That was the time of year her baby would have been born, and the time she— they would be taking their honeymoon, she learned to Paris. Ben came by twice a day to check on her and bring her food. He'd brought Buddy to stay with her while she was there.

Jade found out a little more about Ben. Ben and Keith had been inseparable in high school. He was Keith's receiver on their team, and they were both accepted to the University with the help of her Aunt Judith. Ben excelled on the football field, but he couldn't keep up academically, so he didn't return after his first year. Ben considered himself a failure to Keith's success, and he began drinking. On one of Keith's trips home from New York, he ran into Ben staggering down Main Street in town. Keith was so distraught seeing Ben like that, he starting sending

Uncle Ron money to get Ben help. Ben joined a program that helped turn his life around. He entered culinary arts school in Richmond and became a Chef. When Keith moved back to Brathwell, he eventually hired Ben. He told Jade that, he'd just left out the other parts. Their bond had been deeper than she'd known.

Keith's death had devastated Ben, but he was determined to move ahead with his life. With the money Keith left him, he opened a small Gourmet Shop and Restaurant—*Lassiter's Lament,* on downtown's Main Street. The restaurant allowed him to pay homage to Keith's memory, and it would allow him to support the upkeep of the estate he now occupied.

FIFTY

THE SWEET SMELL of honey suckles danced on the soft summer breeze, as Jade slowly glided on the porch swing. Only the hypnotic hum of crickets invaded the quietness of the night. Her eyes were closed. She felt Buddy move from her feet and stand at the edge of the porch steps. He could hear someone coming in the distance well before it was audible to her. A few minutes later, she saw headlights from an approaching car, but she couldn't tell who it was. The car pulled up and parked, a black Jag. It was Terry—Black man.

He got out and slowly walked toward the porch and planted his foot on the step. He put both his hands in his pockets and looked at her. They stared at each other for a while, his big sparkling eyes were fixed on hers.

"Hey Black woman," he whispered. "It's time for us to go home now."

The Hill Foxes

***Jill**—Flight Attendant* Sassy—Promiscuous—Guarded

***Noel**—Court Reporter* Trusting—Honest—Faithful

***Lauren**—Photographer* Hopeful—Naive'—Needy

***Brea**—Model/Singer* Sensitive—Sweet—Troubled

***Wendy**—Attorney* Ambitious—Skillful—Cautious

***Jade (Jazz)**—TV Anchor* Bold—Fun-loving—Mischievous

About the Author

B. J. Mayo is retired from the Washington, D.C. Public School System, and writes for her enjoyment. B.J. has shared her writings through the years with family and friends who in turn, encouraged her to publish.

Along with writing, she loves traveling. She divides her residencies between Washington, D. C., South Florida and the Atlanta areas.

Also read B.J. Mayo's, **All Prayed Up.**